# The Curse of Selwood
*A West of the Warlock novel*

# Written by
# Martin T. Ingham

Published by

www.martinus.us

*To my eldest children, Sylvia & Wyatt. Your innate talents will give you the option to do just about anything in this life, but be sure to make up your minds, and choose wisely.*

# The Curse of Selwood

## Episode 1:
# Blood on the Tracks

The dry wind of the arid expanse blew up tufts of dust against the stony hillsides. At a glance, most people would see a lifeless frontier, but scratching the surface, a larger ecosystem would be exposed. Tiny life scurried around amongst the underbrush—lizards and snakes that had adapted to survive in the harsh landscape; insects and worms that lurked in plain sight, too small to be easily spotted. All the while, old horse tracks revealed the presence of man. The desert is never as dead as one would assume.

A faint whistle blew in the distance, a sound of civilization. The train was several miles off, hauling passengers and cargo across southern Nevada to the various trading centers of the burgeoning west.

The creature crawled out of his cave, the thin, emaciated being in the rough form of a humanoid. While proportioned much like a human being, he was certainly not a man. Bony protrusions jutted out of every joint, forming a crusty exoskeleton over his slim body. The face was parched and flaking, akin to white sandstone, and the skin was sucked so tightly against the skull to appear ghastly. No hair could be found upon his scalp, but a few black tufts sat along his jaw line.

One might assume the creature to be native to the desert, and in recent years he had been, though that had not always been the case.

Hearing the train, the bony being moved to action, rushing across the dusty landscape like a jackrabbit. Speed increased with every lurching leap until the creature came to the top of a ridge and saw his quarry, the metal machine of man spewing black smoke from its stack, towing a dozen boxcars along the steel rails.

The train was picking up speed, going faster than any horse could run, though that did not deter the creature from continuing the pursuit. Racing down the hillside, the being rushed faster, darting along at remarkable velocity—soon matching, and then surpassing the rolling wheels of the locomotive. He was within striking distance of the caboose before long, and made his move onto the back deck, reaching it in one leap.

The moment was approaching at last; the time of retribution!

Smashing through the back door, the creature found himself in the luggage compartment. Boxes and bags littered the walls as he trudged down the central hallway, snorting and growling all the while. He'd need all the rage he could muster if he wished to succeed. Strength was at his command, but only so long as he willed it.

There was nothing he wanted with the luggage, so the creature rushed through to the next compartment. It was a mail car, something totally unexpected. The three postal employees were busy sorting stacks of letters when the horrific being burst in through the rear door. They froze in place, envelopes in hand.

The creature hadn't anticipated this. He was planning to find sleeping compartments, not these paper pushers! The surprise added to his rage, and gave him further strength to continue. But these little men had to be dealt with. No one must have forewarning of his presence, not until he'd found what he was looking for. Jumping into action, he was upon the startled men in seconds, knocking them to the ground and crushing their bones one by one. They could hardly make a sound before their throats were flattened, and light faded from their eyes.

Three down, dozens more to go.

The next car was the sleeping compartment, though nobody was lying down at midday. That worked in the creature's favor. The more concentrated the people, the less chance of detection before he found his true quarry... and the easier it would be to kill everyone all at once!

Exiting the sleeping area, the creature stopped at the door to the next car, glancing into the small window. This next one was a dining car, and lunch was being served. The well-dressed passengers sat with their coffee and biscuits and other assorted dishes, being waited on hand and foot by red-suited porters. How civilized, yet it was revolting to this inhuman creature. It was something he could never enjoy—not since *they* had taken it all away from him!

Thoughts and memories collided within the wiry beast, rekindling his rage into an inferno of hatred. The passion pulsing through his veins overwhelmed any conscious morality as he continued on his mission. There was no stopping, no mercy to be shown to these pampered people. It didn't matter what they deserved, the creature could only act on what he desired. Such was his curse.

Crashing into the dining car, the creature went to his bloody work. Leaping from one table to the next, he put an end to every life he found, with fist and foot, arm and leg, crushing bones and pulverizing muscles. Death was swift but painful for those people who hardly had time to realize what was going on.

In the midst of the murdering, a crack of thunder sounded, and a stinging pain erupted in the creature's left shoulder. The beast glanced at his shoulder, and saw one of his bony protrusions had cracked, and a hunk of gray metal sat lodged there. The soft lead had been unable to penetrate his exoskeleton, though it still hurt.

The shooter wasn't a remarkable man, nor did he have any badge of authority. He was a plain businessman with a two-shot derringer and the fortitude to fight for his life. Too bad he was up against a force more overwhelming than his mini arsenal could overcome.

The wiry creature jumped at the assailant, and slammed a fist against the man's chest, crushing the collar bone. Two more hits sent the man to his death.

The carnage continued for another minute, as people screamed and ran, seeking to flee from the hideous creature. A few managed to race into the next car, but that only delayed the inevitable, for the marauding beast came charging after them.

The next car was full of seats, a standard passenger car for daytime travel. The place was packed, and everyone was on alert, having heard the murderous rampage in the dining car and received advance warning from the few refugees who escaped the initial assault. Several passengers had rifles and pistols ready, and they didn't hesitate to use them. A slew of lead smacked against the creature's hide, causing a new surge of pain for the being. A few of the small caliber rounds managed to break his skin, but most just cracked exterior bones or bruised the leathery hide. In all, it accomplished nothing.

The creature repaid the bold passengers with killing blows as he cut through this new car like a scythe. He swept his arms around the room, slicing the panicked people with his hard extrusions. Blood sprayed as his fingernails and forearms cut their throats. Once he'd dealt with the armed men, the creature turned on those who cowered in their seats. He glanced at the fearful people, identifying each of their faces before killing them without remorse. One by one, they all fell until he reached the front of the car, where the final victim sat. It was a young woman, cowering against the wall, gripping a suitcase like a life preserver. The panic on her face could not diminish her beauty. Perhaps it was the lavish makeup that prevented fear wrinkles, or just good breeding. Either way, she was recognized.

"You," the creature said with a raspy whisper, like a rattlesnake choking on its own tail.

The terrified woman continued to shiver and cry, glancing at the horrible creature briefly, but unable to lock eyes with it.

"You... are Bettina Carter," the creature hissed.

The young woman squeezed her eyes closed, and nodded her head, too afraid to wonder why the creature would know her name. It was going to kill her anyway, so what was the point?

Though, a few seconds later, the creature proved her thoughts wrong. It grabbed her with one arm, even as she screamed in protest and struggled against the grip to no avail. Her squirming merely tore her blouse against the bony protrusions, and bruised her arms. There was no escape.

With Bettina in his grasp, the creature had what he'd come

for and made a grand exit, punching out a window, and enlarging it with several swift punches. The hard steel of the railcar peeled back like foil to the creature's blows, and once the hole was of sufficient size, the being leapt out with his female cargo. Leaping from a moving train would stun the strongest human, but the bony creature took the fall gracefully, bounding off into the dusty hills as quickly as he had arrived.

Ten minutes later, the train crossed into Nye County, though nobody discovered the massacre until the scheduled stop at Yucca Junction.

* * *

The streets of Selwood were usually bustling on a Tuesday afternoon, but people are bound to run for cover when they hear gunshots. Six loud blasts at uneven intervals cleared Main Street, as an inebriated elf came staggering through town. He was enraged, yet in his drunken state it was doubtful he could explain why. His motivations were not the law's concern. The fact that he was threatening public safety warranted his arrest, though it was a job easier said than done.

Joella Grimes-Talus ducked behind a hay cart as a bullet came her way. The deputy badge pinned to her chest assigned her the responsibility to deal with this sort of unruly citizen, but it didn't mean she was prepared to die. The cemetery was full of bold fools who took their jobs too seriously. The survivors knew when to hide.

Another bullet sank into the cart's side with a disconcerting thump.

"I see you hiding there," the drunk said with slurred speech. "Come on out and face me like a man, human scum!"

"I'm neither human nor a man," Joella replied from behind the cart.

Truly, anyone with a clear view couldn't help but spot her feminine features and the pointed ears exposing her elvish heritage.

The drunken elf put a bullet into the ground beside the hay cart. "You sound girly enough, but ain't no woman gonna wear them britches I seen."

"Why don't you come over here and find out," Joella challenged.

"You think I'm stupid?" the drunk asked, letting off another shot down Main Street.  "Expect me to walk into your range, coward?"

Joella peeked over the hay cart to spot her opponent, and ducked as he took aim.  "No, I'm keeping you distracted until my husband can sneak up from behind."

As the words registered with the drunk, he turned around, only to get a rifle stock to the head.  The hard walnut dazed the unsteady elf, and a second blow knocked him out cold.  The public nuisance was subdued.

Boron Grimes adjusted his grip on the hefty 1873 Winchester musket and set the stock on the ground as he glared at the drunk.  The weapon was almost as long as the dwarf was tall, which had aided him in his latest endeavor.  Without the longer reach of the rifle, he wouldn't have been able to buffalo this vagabond.  Shooting him dead was the alternative, but it was nicer to save killing for more deserving opponents.

"You okay, Joella?" Ron asked after kicking the drunk for good measure.

"Just fine, dear husband," Joella answered flamboyantly, rising from her hiding spot with vigor.

Ron still wanted to cringe every time she called him that. Their marriage was nothing more than a sham, designed to keep Joella from becoming an unwilling bride to her late-husband's cousin.  Ron had been dragged to the altar at gunpoint, though since then he'd gained a certain level of respect for this unconventional lady.  Still, the bias of his upbringing precluded them from being anything more than friends.

With the drunken shootist subdued, life returned to normal, and the residents of Selwood began roaming the streets again.  By the time Ron and Joella had their prisoner to the Sheriff's Office, you could hardly tell there'd been a disturbance.

Ron opened the door as Joella dragged the unconscious body of the drunkard into the office.  It was a small area without decoration; just a desk with a few chairs and a gun rack behind it. An open archway led to the jail cells in back, and a narrow staircase on the left wall led up to the living quarters on the second floor.

"Well, that was enough excitement for one day," Joella said, dropping the drunk in the cell. "Any idea when the sheriff will be back?"

"Doliber said he had some personal stuff to handle, that he'd be back when he was done," Ron replied, locking the cell door. "That was three days ago."

"It's nice to see he trusts us to handle things," Joella replied.

"Me. He trusts *me* to handle things," Ron corrected. "I'm the senior deputy around here."

"Of course you are, little man," Joella said, mildly amused. "Just don't let that ego outgrow your britches." Kneeling down, she gave him a peck on his bearded cheek.

Ron turned to the sheriff's desk and tossed himself into the padded chair behind it. "Not possible," he replied.

With a little effort, he set his feet on the desk and leaned back to get comfortable. Joella shook her head and walked out the door.

* * *

The tall grass swayed as a stiff wind came in off the ocean. The small patch of lawn hadn't been cut all spring, and the rugged Maine climate didn't stunt its progress in the least. Hay was one of the few things that truly flourished down east.

James Doliber turned his coat up as the first drops of rain came flying his way. The storm was blowing in off the bay, and it was chilly for late June, even in northern New England. The miserable weather reminded the warlock sheriff of his days at the Guild Academy in San Francisco. It seemed fitting, considering his current objective.

Doliber walked up to the weathered farm house up on the hill. As he approached, he noticed there wasn't a spot of paint on the old building; just the natural gray of age. The walls were sided with cedar shingles, so rot hadn't set in, and a wisp of smoke trickled out of the brick chimney top, revealing the place to be inhabited.

Stepping up to the door, Doliber rapped his knuckles against the boards, hoping his leads were correct. The last few days had given him a headache as he sought to find the one man who might be both capable and willing to give him some answers.

A minute passed, and Doliber knocked again. Nothing. He feared the occupant was giving him the cold shoulder, and was about to walk off when the door finally opened.

Doliber turned around to greet the home-owner, only to see a double-barreled shotgun stuck in his face.

"Is that the stench of a Guild Warden I smell on you, or are you just a federal thug?" the old man holding the shotgun asked. His white hair and stubble revealed his years, but his voice was as smooth as his peachy skin.

"I'm not here to cause trouble," Doliber replied, keeping his hands up and carefully eyeing the shotgun. Both hammers were cocked and waiting for an itchy finger to pull one of the double triggers. The right spell could deflect a load of the heaviest shot, but that was assuming the shells weren't enchanted, themselves. Doliber wasn't in a hurry to find out the hard way.

"Well, you can go back to whatever taskmaster sent you," the old man grumbled. "I've paid my penance, and have kept true to my word. No magic, no meddling. Not that I care for either, anymore."

"Sir, I didn't come as anyone's agent, though my visit does concern the Guild. If you'd allow me to explain... without a gun stuffed in my face."

The old man studied Doliber's face, and eventually decided to lower his aim. He uncocked the hammers and set the shotgun at his side, but he still looked annoyed.

"Based on your words and demeanor, I guess it's safe to assume you're Harold Paxton," Doliber said.

"Never assume anything," the old man warned, "but, yes, I'm Paxton. Now, who are you and why are you here?"

"My name's James Doliber. Could we continue this inside?" he asked, feeling his hair getting damp. "The rain's picking up."

"The rain won't dampen your voice," Paxton said, leaning against his front door. The roof's slight overhang was keeping him dry.

"I'm a Journeyman Warlock, Delta Grade. I came for your counsel on a personal matter."

"What, you don't have a lady friend to tell your troubles to?" Paxton mocked

"The Guild has offered me the Master's Exams," Doliber snapped abruptly. "I need to know more about them; what they entail, how they affect the mind. I can only get that information from someone who's been through the process."

Paxton made an indignant snort. "It's forbidden for anyone other than a Master to know what the trials entail. Wash-outs have their memories purged, and no active member would ever betray their oath."

"Which is why I've sought you out," Doliber admitted. "You're one of the few Guild Masters who has ever been excommunicated, and the only one currently alive."

"So, you figure I'd be willing to betray the promise I gave to never reveal the secrets of the Guild?"

"They betrayed you first, and we both know it," Doliber said, keeping his cool. "You were the only Master of the Guild who dared to actually fight in the War Between the States, and they nailed you for it."

"The Guild had its reasons," Paxton replied solemnly, lowering his gaze.

"So did you. So did the dozens of Med-locks who challenged the Guild's non-interference edict and chose to heal the wounded soldiers on both sides. But you were the only one with the wherewithal to enter combat. The way I see it, the Guild disowned your for doing the right thing."

"It's more complicated than that." Without taking his eyes off of Doliber, Paxton opened his front door. The older gentleman was finally warming up to his uninvited guest. "Come in, if you want to hear the truth."

Doliber accepted the late invitation and stepped inside, trying not to trip over the wide assortment of tools and junk cluttering up the entryway. It seemed to be booby trapped with all the farm implements stuffed into such a tight space, but a narrow path wove through it all, leading to the kitchen door.

"So, you want to know what really happened in Atlanta?" Paxton asked as he stepped into the sweltering kitchen. The cook stove was putting off a lot of heat, far too much for Doliber's comfort.

"I'm certainly curious," Doliber replied, anxious to get to the more pertinent subject of the Master Examinations, though he knew it would take time to coax those answers from the old man. Best to have a few mild curiosities revealed, and hopefully gain his trust during the exchange.

"I drew the short stick," Paxton said.

Doliber waited patiently for him to elaborate.

"I'm sure you've read about the siege of Atlanta and that final day; how my paralytic spell put down the defenders in mere moments without bloodshed. It would have taken the Union forces weeks to kill their way to victory, assuming they broke through at all. Tell me, Journeyman Doliber, do you think our boys in blue would have succeeded without mystical intervention?"

"I believe it's as you said. There'd have been more bloodshed, but we'd have won out in the end."

"We?" Paxton asked, seeming offended by the terminology, and then began to pace a little as he continued. "Well, why do you think *we* would have won the siege?"

Doliber sensed a trick question, but had no choice other than to play along.

"I'm not a military expert, but the Union troops held most of the advantage. More men, more supplies..."

"Ah, but there's the key. What if I told you we didn't have more men? At least, not on that last day."

"You say the news reports were inaccurate?"

"Not inaccurate, but incomplete," Paxton corrected. "They don't account for the rebel sorceress who was turning the tide for the Confederacy."

Doliber's attention picked up at the mention of a "sorceress." While ignorant laymen might use such a word as a synonym for a lady warlock, no Guild member would ever make such a mistake. The two were completely incongruous, and held far different meanings. A sorceress was a practitioner of demonic magic, something strictly forbidden by the Guild.

"So you see, the secessionists weren't playing by the rules— not that there really are any in war—but they crossed the line, recruiting the aid of a demonic congruent. Somebody had to stop them—stop her—before it was too late."

"What was she doing, exactly?" Doliber asked.

"She was turning our best men against us, using a frightening form of enchantment to rewrite our soldiers' thoughts and memories, making them believe they were fighting for the Confederacy!"

The very concept was frightening. The power to manipulate minds was a difficult and limited ability by Guild standards. Not even Guildmaster Silvestri had the power to create false memories—at least, not to the best of Doliber's knowledge.

Paxton continued.

"The sorceress had been picking our boys off for weeks, slowly swelling the Confederate ranks and depleting ours. A few of us med-locks figured out what was going on and resolved to stop it. Only, to do that, one of us would have to defy the Guild, knowing full well what that would mean. There were six volunteers for the job, and I won the draw.

"The rest, you know. I used my spell-casting abilities to paralyze the Confederate troops, and allowed the Union forces to capture Atlanta. When the dust settled, there was no sign of the sorceress, and I was held accountable by the Guild for violating their edicts."

"I see," Doliber said, finally understanding the particulars.

"Indeed," Paxton said. "The Guild's punishment was twofold. To spare my life, I was commanded to never use my mystical abilities in any way, and I was further condemned to never have any significant impact on human events. I was assigned this homestead in this small farming community, and here I'm forced to remain for the rest of my life, never to leave town. On occasion, I get a visitor from the Guild who wants to check up on me, and sometimes they pose as a government representative, who tries to convince me to work for the greater good again. It's all a game to entrap me, just to make sure I'm still committed to our 'bargain,' such as it is."

It was a sad affair, for certain. This man who had done what he knew to be right was being punished for it, but the Guild had reason to be so critical. The lessons of the past echoed in Doliber's head as he recalled the many abuses of power that had shaped the world at large. From ancient Rome to Medieval Europe, the bane of magical meddling had cost many lives and hindered man's progress more than it helped it.

Prominent among Doliber's memories was the tale of Edward the Longshanks using mystic knights to subjugate Scotland. The Guild had been perfectly fine with such action, considering it a warlock's duty to serve his king and country. That was all well and good until different Guild Chapters found their kingdoms in conflict, and it all came to a head in the fourteenth century, as war erupted between England and France. Both sides used warlocks as cannon fodder, and the most proficient spellcasters of the day slaughtered one another by the score. When it was all over, there were only a handful of Guild members left on either side.

Following the magical bloodbath of the Hundred Years War, the Guild imposed strict limits on their worldly influence. They denied their members from ever utilizing their talents to alter the natural course of human events. Thus, they prevented future abuses of power, but also tied the hands of well-intentioned warlocks.

"You know this is fair," Paxton said, as if he were reading Doliber's mind.

"No, it's not," Doliber said, "but I understand that it's necessary."

"Then you also understand why I can't tell you about the Master's Examinations. To violate my oath to the Guild, I would be signing my own death warrant, and I am not prepared to die yet."

Disappointed, Doliber stood up and headed for the door, feeling he had all the answers he could hope to receive. The visit hadn't clarified his options, as he would have hoped. Instead, the path ahead seemed more uncertain than ever before.

As he reached the cluttered entryway, Doliber heard Paxton's voice echoing from the kitchen. "I believe you should accept the Master's training."

"How so?" Doliber asked, turning his head, but keeping one hand on the door latch.

"Your concerns are understandable, but you have nothing to fear. The Master exams will merely focus your mind, and allow you the opportunity to perceive reality in ways you cannot fathom as a mere Journeyman."

"And what of my job? Would the Guild ever allow a full-fledged Master to serve as a sheriff?"

Silence lingered in the air, and Doliber clicked the door latch to make his exit. It was high time he got back to doing his job, even as he considered a path that might force him out of it. In the meantime, he would continue to serve to the best of his abilities. It was the least he could do.

* * *

The train rolled into Yucca Junction at a quarter past two. A small crowd had gathered around the platform to meet and greet the passengers, and it was more than your average reception party. A brass band was standing up against the ticket booth, playing a cheery march as the steam locomotive chugged to a stop. It was all the fanfare you'd expect for an arriving dignitary, or someone very special.

Fletcher Atwood was rubbing his palms together with nervous distraction. His heart was racing and the sweat was rolling down his cheeks in the mid-afternoon sun. This was a moment he'd been waiting for his whole life, the moment his bride-to-be would step off her train and into his arms. It had been several months since he'd last seen her, but it felt like only yesterday they had parted. He'd gone ahead, back to their hometown of Selwood, to prepare for their big day. Now, she was arriving, and they'd never be alone again.

A bald gentleman in a gray suit slapped Fletcher on the shoulder and grinned. "Never thought I'd see you shiver in the heat, son," the man said.

"Thank you, Father, that's such a compliment," Fletcher said sardonically.

"Oh, I didn't mean it like that, Fletcher," his father replied. "I know what you're feeling. I've been there, you know."

Fletcher couldn't imagine his father being young and fidgety. The old man was as tough as nails, the unmovable pillar of the community. The Mayor of Selwood, a town that partially bore his name.

As the train came to a complete stop, the crowd inched forward to greet the disembarking passengers. Yet, nobody emerged, not even a porter. It caused a slight stir, and a few bold souls ventured aboard to investigate. They didn't get far, and stopped as soon as they could peer thorough a window.

"Mayor Atwood!" one of the men shouted. He tried to say more, but only stuttered incomprehensibly.

Fletcher felt his heart sink, as his mind grew suspicious and worried. Imagination could sometimes be a dangerous thing, and as he stepped forward his mind was running through all the things that could be wrong. Whatever sad truth lay aboard the train, he knew it would change his life forever, and not for the better.

The mayor grew impatient with his son's sluggish movements and took the lead. He pushed his way up onto the train, and nudged past the two men who stood staring into the dining car. "Out of the way, man," he snapped, trying to get inside. He forced his aging form through to the car's door and had a look at the bloody devastation inside.

Fletcher came up beside his father, even as the old man waved for him to stay back. There was no avoiding the truth as he looked at the overturned tables and broken bodies strewn in plain sight. Dozens dead, and in such an inhuman manner. Their corpses were so tattered and broken, like a landslide had crushed them. What manner of assassin could wreak such havoc?

Fletcher had to find her; his bride to be. If she were among the dead, he needed to know. He ignored his father's protest, and ran deeper into the dining car, feeling his shoes squishing against the blood-soaked carpet. The stench of blood, bile, and excrement stung at his nostrils as he made his way through the entire length of the car, examining the broken faces of the dead. None looked familiar, and he continued to the passenger car, daring to hope he would find his fiancée alive.

He continued the search, looking upon every face he came across, feeling more and more detached with each dead person he saw. By the time he passed through all the cars, he no longer cared about the many bodies he encountered. All that mattered was the one that was missing.

Coming back to the dining car, he saw his father holding a sheaf of papers. "Bettina's not here," Fletcher said.

"I know," his father replied, handing over a crumpled hunk

of yellow paper. "She's been kidnapped."

Fletcher looked at the paper, but failed to understand it. "What is this?" he asked.

"The mark of a man who ought to be dead," was all his father said as he walked out of the railcar.

Fletcher studied the strange symbol, and realized it was painted in blood. A figure eight with three horns sprouting out of each oval—not much to look at. Whatever it was, it had his father spooked, and nothing struck fear into the heart of Mayor Charles Atwood. Nothing, until today.

Fletcher tossed the note aside and ran after his father. The truth, he feared, would be worse than his imagination.

## Episode 2:
## A Few Good Men

The sheriff's office in Selwood wasn't the largest place, and when the dozen riders from Yucca station came charging in, the place felt packed. Ron Grimes was alone at dusk, as Joella had retired to her room at the boarding house for the night. That left one dwarf to stand before an armed and angry mob who demanded action.

"Where's Doliber?" Mayor Atwood asked, slamming his fists onto the desk.

Ron Grimes looked up at the bald man with disapproval. He'd never been the servile type, and he wasn't about to bend over backwards to please the local elites, no matter the circumstances.

"I don't know," he finally replied, setting his feet on the desk—quite a feat for someone of his stature.

"Don't take that tone with me, Deputy," Atwood snapped, narrowing his gaze in an attempt to look menacing. "Dozens have been murdered, my son's fiancée has been kidnapped, and all you can do is sit there doing nothing?"

Ron grumbled under his breath and bit his tongue. There was no sense provoking the mayor further, and the man was partially in the right. It was the deputy's job to investigate this crime, but with his boss on vacation it left him with little in the way of support. He wanted to explain the situation, but knew it would accomplish nothing. The mayor wanted action, not excuses.

"Look, it's getting late, and there's not a whole lot to be done at the moment," Ron said, hoping to get the man off his back.

"Come morning, I'll round up a posse, and we'll go down the train tracks, see if we can't find this runaway bride of yours."

"Runaway? She's been abducted!" Fletcher protested from across the room. "And you want to wait until morning? That might be too late!"

Most of the crowd shouted affirmation, all sounding eager to get on with things.

"Look, Grimes, these men are fine, upstanding citizens of our fair town," Atwood continued, suddenly sounding more politician than angry bureaucrat. "They're prepared to ride out now, and track down Bettina's kidnapper; the same savage that likely killed that trainload of innocent people. All they need is legal sanction. Deputize them, so they can get the job done."

"I'm afraid I can't do that," Ron said, remaining calmly detached.

"Can't? You're the law, aren't you? Sheriff Doliber left you in charge during his absence. That makes you interim sheriff."

Ron hadn't thought of it that way, and wondered about the full ramifications. "I wasn't aware that gave me the right to deputize anyone," Ron mentioned.

"I say it does, and that's good enough," Mayor Atwood said. "Now, break out the badges, and let's get going! We've got a murderer to catch!"

"I think I'd better see the judge first," Ron said, disliking the sort of shady maneuvering the mayor had up his sleeve. He wasn't sure if he was within his rights to deputize anyone, and he didn't want to find himself indicted for empowering a lynch mob. At the very least, legal posturing could buy him time.

"Willis, go get Judge Raymond!" Atwood shouted, and one of his angry minions rushed to the door.

As Willis reached for the knob, the door opened, and a thin man in a rawhide trench coat clomped inside. "What's the rush there, kid?" the older gentleman asked.

All eyes followed the stranger as he sauntered up to the desk, sliding up beside Atwood. The gray-haired man with a weathered Stetson stood in front of the desk and stared down at the dwarf sitting there. "Well, you're not Doliber. Where's that shady spell-spinner, anyway?"

"He's not here," Ron said, putting his feet down. "What can I do for you?"

"Ned Rodgers, U.S. Marshal," the man said, tossing his badge on the table for the dwarf to see. "I hear you had a train robbed up by Yucca Junction today."

"Not quite," Atwood interrupted. "Nothing was stolen except my son's fiancée."

"Mayor Chuck, I wasn't aware you'd been elected sheriff as well," Marshal Rodgers said with mocking disdain. Turning back to Ron, he said, "I assume Doliber left you in charge, or you wouldn't be sitting there all cocky and full of yourself."

"That's right. Deputy Boron Grimes, at your service."

"Good, because that's what you'll be, *at my service*," Rodgers said authoritatively. "This is a case for the Marshal's Service, not some local good-old-boys network. While this case is being investigated, you, and any other deputy of Nye County, will be answering to me and my men. Understood?"

The crowd erupted in protest, angered by the sudden usurpation. Ron sat back and watched as the angry mob drowned out the Marshal's calls for order, looking almost ready to lynch the federal agent. It got heated enough that Rodgers felt the need to push his coat back to expose his Peacemaker. The great equalizer silenced the room quickly enough.

"Now, all of you men can go home, before I have Deputy Grimes lock you up for disturbing the peace," Rodgers said.

Most of the men followed the order, knowing when to call it quits. Atwood and his son weren't so easily persuaded, and remained.

"Damn you, Rodgers," Atwood cursed, clenching a fist under the Marshal's chin. "You think that badge gives you the right to come here and push my people around? You have no right!"

"I have every right when it comes to upholding the law," Rodgers rebutted. "Trust me, Charles, it'll be better for everyone if you don't send a bunch of undisciplined yahoos out into the desert to hunt whatever it is that killed those people. This is a job for the professionals."

Atwood stomped his foot and headed for the door, looking thoroughly flustered. "Just remember, this is my town. The voters didn't elect you to anything, not even to shovel horse crap."

"Then you'd best get back to it," Rodgers retorted.

Atwood stormed out the door with his son in tow.  The windows rattled as the door slammed shut behind them.

Relieved to have the angry mob dispersed, Ron set his feet back up on the desk.  "Thanks for the backup, Marshal," Ron said.

"Don't be thanking me just yet, Deputy," Marshal Rodgers replied, looking smug.  "You might find that I'm a harder boss to deal with than your warlock compadre."

"You ain't my boss," Ron said, setting his feet down, sensing the other shoe was about to fall.

"Don't be so sure about that," Rodgers said, giving him a peculiar wink.  The gray-haired lawman turned to leave, but kept talking as he headed for the door.  "A massacre of this magnitude on the rails is Federal business.  Don't expect they'll leave this in the hands of some backwater Sheriff's Department."

The Marshal disappeared out the door, and Ron gave his absent backside a rude gesture.

* * *

The Lucca Saloon was packed to the brim with angry citizens eager to drink out of frustration.  A good manhunt was what they were after, but in lieu of that a stiff shot of whiskey could soothe their rage, or inflame it.  Either way, the would-be posse members were drowning their disappointment.

Fletcher Atwood didn't drink, but sat at the table as his father downed shots.  It wasn't the most uplifting environment for the lovelorn groom.  "Damn it, Father, what are we going to do about that no good Rodgers?"

"We wait," the mayor replied, downing a third shot.  "You know Rodgers.  He likes to flex his muscles, but when it comes down to it, he'll need our help if he wants to get his man."

"How do we even know it's a man?" Fletcher asked with a harsh whisper.  "You saw the people on that train.  What man is capable of that?"

Mayor Charles Atwood didn't reply, but stopped drinking.  It could have been he'd had enough, but Fletcher doubted it.

A clean figure in colorful apparel slid up to the Atwoods' table, and the men instantly recognized the establishment's elven owner, Solen Lucca. "Mister Mayor, what a rare honor. To what do we owe the privilege of your presence?"

"Like you haven't heard," Mayor Atwood said, irritation flowing out with each word.

Solen brushed his long, blond hair back and sat down. "Well, I suppose it was bound to happen eventually," the elf said.

"What do you mean?" Fletcher asked.

"I take it your father hasn't told you about the curse of Selwood," Solen said knowingly.

"Hold your tongue, pointy," the mayor snapped. "Those old superstitions are nobody's business."

"What are you afraid of, Charles? That they might be true?"

"They'll do nothing but add fear to a bunch of already scared people."

"Seems to me that's what you're after," Solen said, standing up. Locking eyes with the mayor, he added, "Would you like anything else to eat or drink? Perhaps a date with one of the ladies upstairs?"

"Enough!" the mayor growled, slamming his fist against the table. "I'll tell you when I want something out of you, elf."

Solen shivered and headed back to the bar.

"What was he talking about?" Fletcher asked. "What curse?"

"It's nothing; just an old bandit's musings," Atwood said dismissively.

"Father, if this has anything to do with what happened—if it could in any way help us get Bettina back—you have to tell me!" Fletcher said, urgently grasping onto any inkling of hope.

"I suppose you won't stop bugging me until you hear it," Atwood said, shaking his head, "though I'm afraid it won't help much.

"You know the history of Selwood, how we started out as a way station for prospectors heading to California during the gold rush. You know how some of us stayed after the fact, fought roaming bandits and wild Indians to make our homes here. But there are certain things that aren't widely discussed, things only the earliest residents remember. One is the origin of the curse, as Solen calls it."

Atwood reached for the bottle to pour himself another drink, but Fletcher pulled it away. If the old man got too intoxicated, he wouldn't be telling much of anything.

"You want to know about the curse or not?" Atwood grumbled.

"Say it sober, or not at all," Fletcher ordered, keeping the bottle.

"Damn temperance movement. You and that preacher always deriding a man for an honest drink." Atwood shook his head.

"You were saying, about the curse?" Fletcher prompted.

"Oh, fine," Atwood said. "You remember what I told you growing up, about the bandit wars of fifty-three? How the town was beset upon by wave after wave of outlaws seeking to turn Selwood into their own little hideout? Well, there was this one group of banditos who almost did us in. Their leader was a mean old half-breed called Raethanon, learned the ways of the Shaman from his Paiute grandfather. They killed near half the town before we turned them back, but we managed it. Too bad for us, we ended up killing Raethanon's son in the melee. Afterwards, the grizzled half-breed laid a curse on *'the heartless leaders of the town,'* swearing that someday he'd get his revenge and we'd all pay in blood for our crimes. I never gave it much mind, until I saw that note."

Fletcher recalled the yellow hunk of paper drawn in blood. "The horned eight?"

"It was his mark, the only scratch he ever made. Seems pretty clear who killed those people, but it was no curse. It's just the actions of an evil man who needs to be hunted down once and for all."

Fletcher filtered through the telling with careful concern. A native shaman's powers were not to be trifled with, and the old man knew it. The only reason he'd make light of it would be to cover his own apprehensions.

Knowing the culprit and his motivation, Fletcher knew why Bettina had been kidnapped. To steal the bride of an Atwood, surely it was the theft of a birthright. Taking her was like abducting all the generations to follow and holding them hostage! Raethanon was sending a message, and it was only the beginning.

Sliding the bottle back over to his father, Fletcher stood up and turned to leave.

"Where are you going?" Mayor Atwood asked.

"To pray," Fletcher replied with all sincerity.

\* \* \*

Joella Grimes-Talus couldn't sleep.  The sheets at the Bormans' boarding house were scratchy wool, not the ideal substance to rub up against bare skin.  Of course, a good set of pajamas might detract from the discomfort, though Joella preferred to be bare at night.  Other alternatives existed, such as buying her own bedding, or finding other accommodations altogether.  Either would serve, and she swore to look into the matter first thing in the morning, just as she'd told herself every other night for the past month.

As Joella tossed and turned on the edge of sleep, a knock came to rouse her.  She sat up suddenly, instantly alert and irritated by the disturbance.  It was too late for anyone civilized to come calling, and she had her suspicions about who might be interested in disturbing her sleep.  Still, best to make certain.

"Who is it?" she asked, grabbing her blouse off the floor.

"Ned Rodgers, U.S. Marshal," an unfamiliar voice replied.

Joella gathered up her clothing and got dressed in a hurry.  This was wholly unexpected.  What would a Marshal want with her at this hour?  The possibility of a ruse did not escape her, and she made sure to attach her gun belt before answering the door.

"What can I do for you?" Joella asked, cracking the door open just a hair and shining lamp light onto the stranger's face.

"I need to speak to you.  It's about your husband," Marshal Rodgers said.

Joella opened the door a little more.  "Is Ron all right?" she asked, feeling genuine concern.

"For now," Rodgers said, setting his hand on the door and pushing it.

Joella resisted his attempt to force entry, and kept the slot narrow enough for comfort.  "Then why do we need to talk about him?"

"It's for his own good, and yours," Rodgers said, removing his hand from the door.  "May I come in?"

"Where's your badge, Marshal?" Joella asked, growing suspicious about this midnight caller.

Rodgers removed his hands from the door and slid his jacket away from his chest, exposing the silver badge for her to see. "Satisfied?" he asked.

It looked real enough, so Joella decided to let him enter. Rejecting his request seemed pointless, and she felt comfortable enough with the revolver strapped to her hip. Stepping back, she allowed the door to swing wide, and studied the Marshal as he entered. Despite his obvious age, he looked as rugged as an ox, and he held a glint in his eye that said you'd better not mess with him.

There wasn't much space in the room, barely enough for the bed and a small reading table with two chairs. Joella slid alongside the bed to reach the far chair, and sat down before she said, "Now, what's so important you have to harangue me in the middle of the night?"

"Pardon me," Rodgers said, pulling the second seat out from the tiny table. He reached over and fiddled with the lamp, seeking to maximize the light output. "I would have waited until the morning, but it's important we talk now, beforehand."

"Before what?" Joella asked, readjusting the lamp. She had to pay for oil, and wasn't the most affluent person at the moment.

"You've heard about the train massacre?" Rodgers asked.

"Yes," Joella replied. It had been a hot topic of conversation at dinner, as she'd braved another night in the company of the boarding house's regulars.

"Then you know I'm forming a posse, to hunt down the man or creature responsible."

"You?" Joella asked.

"That's right. There were over a hundred people murdered on that train. United States citizens, all of them, and damn few of them from Nevada, let alone Nye County. This is a case for the Marshal's Service, not some elected sheriff, even if he does have a twist of magic up his sleeve."

"Then why are you talking to me?" Joella asked.

"Because I'd like to do my job without that warlock sheriff and his pint-size deputy getting in my way. I figure you can help arrange that for me."

Joella felt like laughing at the suggestion, but contained herself. Emotion was never something she let slip if she could help it, but the comment had caught her off guard.

"You'll do it," Rodgers replied simply. It wasn't angry or pleading, but a flat statement of fact.

"Oh, will I?" Joella asked.

"Unless you'd like Mactus Sellius to hear that you and your husband sleep in separate rooms."

"That's not uncommon," Joella replied nervously. "Many couples sleep apart."

"Regardless, I doubt you'd like to explain that to Mactus, or your clan's High Minister. They'd be happy to see your sham marriage annulled."

"It isn't a sham," Joella said, refusing to give an inch.

Rodgers shook his head and smiled. "I knew you'd be stubborn, but I never thought you'd be stupid. Would you really risk the hassle of having your marriage picked apart by elvish bureaucrats rather than cooperate with me?"

"You manipulative scoundrel," Joella cursed bitterly, knowing she'd been made. He had her over a barrel, and they both knew it.

"What I propose is simple. You're going to make Doliber and that husband of yours work for me, whether they know it or not."

"How am I supposed to do that?" Joella asked.

"I'm sure you'll find a way. Elves always do," Rodgers said, standing up. "We'll talk again later. Good night, Missus Grimes."

As Rodgers stepped out of the room, Joella got to her feet and shouted at his back. "That's Grimes-Talus!" she boasted her proper, elvish married name, then slammed the door.

The strain of the short meeting made Joella eager for bed, even as adrenaline pulsed through her veins. She needed time to think, and the comfort of darkness was her ally in that respect. Blowing out the lamp and climbing out of her clothes, she slipped back under the uncomfortable covers, wondering what she would do to protect the life she was building.

Who would she have to betray to save herself?

* * *

The cast iron skillet smoked atop the small cook stove. The melted lard was hot and ready, and a drop of spit crackled, announcing the temperature like a signal flare. A large, flat hunk of beef slid into the cooking implement, and a thin lid clanked down over it to keep the juices from splattering.

Ron hopped down off the little stool in front of the stove and took a seat by the window. It was still dark outside, and the handful of street lights were down to coals. In another hour, the sun would come cresting over the dusty hills to the east, and then life would get interesting again.

The pre-dawn had always appealed to Ron; a great calm before the daily storm.

There would be a storm, Ron knew, as the memory of last night lingered in his thoughts. The people of Selwood weren't the sort to take things lying down, no matter who told them to back off. That posse would still be itching for a fight, never mind orders from any law official. He couldn't blame them. The citizens were angry and afraid, so they wanted blood to soothe their frayed emotions.

Ron went back to the stove and turned his steak over with a heavy, two-pronged fork. Spots of grease spit out at him as the moist side of the meat hit the heat. The hot liquid spattered against his shirt sleeve, but didn't burn his hand. A grease burn would've been the last thing he wanted, so he thanked God for small favors as he reset the lid.

"I hope you've got enough for both of us," a familiar voice sounded.

Ron jumped a little at the unexpected presence, and turned to see Sheriff Doliber looming in the archway leading to the sitting room. The warlock had a pesky habit of sneaking up on people, and his magic made him far too proficient in it.

"I reckon I can split the steak," Ron answered, returning to his seat by the window.

"Much obliged," Doliber replied. He walked over to the stove and kicked the small stool aside, then checked the vents and dampers. It was *his* stove, after all, and he had to make sure it was being used properly. "So, what's new?"

"Oh, you're gonna love this," Ron said sarcastically. "Some nut massacred a train load of passengers coming into Yucca Junction and made off with the mayor's daughter-in-law to be. I got half the town looking to form a lynch mob for whoever or whatever did it, and I've got some Marshal breathing down my neck, looking to flex his muscles."

"Rodgers, right?" Doliber remarked, lifting the skillet lid to examine the browning meat.

"You heard of him?" Ron asked.

"Yes, we've had dealings in the past," Doliber said. "I've never much cared for the old buzzard, but he's competent enough."

"Competent enough to head up this investigation?" Ron wondered.

"It depends. What really happened?" Doliber asked as he slid the skillet off to the cooler side of the stove. He grabbed the fork and placed the meat on a waiting plate, then headed for the small eating table in the corner.

After grabbing a plate to share the steak, Ron provided a thorough retelling of events. Over breakfast, he went over everything he'd personally witnessed and everything he'd heard, hoping his words would suffice. He'd rather not have the sheriff prying into his thoughts again, as the warlock was apt to do. A quick telepathic scan could show Doliber everything he needed to know, with all the accuracy of a firsthand memory, though Ron preferred to keep his private thoughts private.

As the explanation came to a conclusion, Doliber mentioned, "I can see why the townsfolk are in an uproar, and why Rodgers is eager to maintain order. I doubt this is the work of an ordinary man, though. Seems we'll have a busy morning ahead of us."

* * *

Bettina Carter awoke to complete darkness. Not the faintest glimmer of light shone where she found herself, leaving her completely blind. Her mind was still lethargic from whatever supernatural force that creature had used to incapacitate her during the kidnapping. She tried to remember what had happened on the train, but much of it was a blur. She recalled a lot of screaming, and falling into the arms of the bony beast, but little else.

Now, she was here, in the dark.

The ground was soft and moist, and the air was clammy. This had to be underground somewhere, deep in a cave or mineshaft, Bettina surmised. She had to learn more about her surroundings. Perhaps there was a way to escape?

Getting to her feet, she staggered forward on rubbery legs, stretching her arms out in front of her, seeking anything solid. After a few steps, she felt a hard, uneven surface. It felt like rock, all right, sandy with bits of smooth lumps stuck in it here and there. Composite stone of your typical cavern, nothing to get excited about. She followed her hands along the wall, finding it went on in a circular direction. After going around for a few minutes, she was certain she'd lapped the same spot at least twice, and to be certain she knelt down to the floor, feeling her repeated footsteps in the soft soil. She'd been pacing, and from the curvature of the wall she'd guessed her pit prison wasn't more than ten feet around.

Reaching her arms up, she began feeling for a handhold. Up had to be the only way in or out of this trap, though try as she might, there was nothing to grip. She was stuck in this infernal place.

Falling to her knees, Bettina began to cry. It seemed the appropriate thing to do under the circumstances. To be kidnapped by a monster on the eve of her wedding was a fate worse than anything she could have imagined, and being stuck in the dark—alone—why, it only compounded her emotions. The waiting and wondering made her tense, as imagination began to work on her psyche.

What would become of her here? Would she die a slow death, forgotten in the pit, or would that creature come back? What would the creature do to her if it did return? She shuddered to think, and cried some more.

As her whimpering abated, an echoed voice caught her attention. It was too distant and distorted to be recognized, but it was the first external sound she'd received since awaking. Someone was coming, and she stood up straight, desperate to understand a single word. Try as she might, the voice remained identifiable, as the echo of the cave continued to slur it.

What if that voice belonged to a search party? She had to let them know she was here!  Screaming at the top of her lungs, she cried for help, letting anyone up above know she was alive and well.

In response to her cries, the talking stopped, leaving Bettina worried that she might have frightened away the only assistance she could receive.  If those had been bandits or Indians, they might flee at the sound of a stranger, leaving her to die alone and forgotten.  How could fate be so cruel?

As her hopes began to fade again, visual stimuli appeared. High above her, Bettina saw the faint flickering of torch light, giving her a slight view of the upper cave walls.  There was a large room above her, but this deep pit was at least twenty feet below it. Whatever lay above was mostly concealed by the walls of her prison, but the light continued to dance around up there, letting her know there was someone there.

"Hello?" Bettina cried.  "I know someone's up there.  I can see the light.  Please, help me!"

Just as Bettina's optimism was growing, the bony head of the creature peeked over the edge of the pit, sending her heart dropping back into despair.  The horrifying being glared at her with that almost skeletal face, before its spindly arms reached out to grip the side of the enclosure.  With slow and steady movements, it crept down into the pit, joining the terrified woman in her cramped prison.

The light up above was barely enough to provide illumination at the bottom of the pit, but it was enough to show the creature plainly as it crept forward.  Bettina had nowhere to run, but tried to keep her distance, sliding along the wall of the cave, begging to be left alone.  "Please, stay back!"

"Need," the creature grumbled with its deep guttural voice. It repeated the word several times, as it reached out its bony arms toward Bettina.  Grabbing her by the shoulders, the creature opened its mouth and licked the side of her face with a fat, cylindrical tongue.

Bettina screamed.

**Episode 3:**
# Runaway Train

Ron and Doliber showed up at the Yucca Junction train station at the crack of dawn. The sun was barely cresting over the dusty hills as the two men materialized on the platform, teleported by the sheriff's mystical abilities. At once, they noticed something was amiss at the station, and it didn't take long for them to realize what.

"Where the hell is the train?" Doliber asked.

"It goed on down the tracks," the station man replied with his folksy accent. The middle-aged man with broken teeth swaggered out of the wooden ticket booth as he continued. "Them cars is money, soes the comp'ny done ordered her on down the line."

"That train was a crime scene," Doliber said. "They had no business tampering with it."

"Tain't what the Marshal done said," the station man mentioned. "He done give the go ahead for them to clean 'er up and head 'er out."

"Clean it?" Doliber said, exasperated. "You're telling me they're already removed the evidence?"

"Don't rightly knows what yer gettin' at," the station man said. "Them men been dead closer'n a full day. Ain't no sense leavin' all uh that blood around."

"I needed to inspect those rail cars, unaltered!" Doliber shouted. "The clues I might have uncovered. Were there any magic traces? What type of magic? What sort of foot tracks? Was there any subtle pattern to the killer's methods? All little things you clearly couldn't see!"

The station man blinked a bit, then gave Doliber a blank stare.

Doliber knew it was useless talking to the slack-jawed attendant. The guy wasn't in charge of anything, and was just saying what he knew. The real culprits were the meddling money men at of the rail company, and the arrogant Marshal Rodgers. Even they were merely pushing the status quo.

Doliber was the only man interested in doing more, it seemed.

"So, what's our next step?" Ron asked, looking down at the empty tracks.

To any other sheriff, the options would be nil. The train was gone, racing fifty miles an hour off into the countryside. No horse could outrace it, yet one thing about a warlock was, you didn't always need a horse.

"When did the train leave?" Doliber asked the attendant, "and which spur did they take?"

The attendant got all thoughtful, rubbing his cheek nervously. "Oh, seems they got out about an hour ago, maybe. She done flipped the nor'west switch, so they must be headin' to Tanner. That's the regular schedule, or thereabouts."

"Thank you. That's quite helpful," Doliber said. Turning from the attendant, he motioned Ron over to him. "Come on, Grimes. We have a train to catch."

In mid-step, Ron Grimes felt a cold tingle roll across him. One second, he was on the weathered platform, the next he was stumbling over a steel rail of a train track. The sudden dislocation left him disoriented enough to lose his balance, and he found himself planted face down in loose gravel and wooden ties of the rail bed. His diminutive height prevented the fall from hurting him all that much, and he hopped to his feet in short order, brushing the dust off as the ground rumbled beneath him.

"What the..." Ron asked, as his ears came back to life. A loud chugging of a steam locomotive caused him to turn around, and he saw what had to be his doom. Five feet away, the train was bearing down on top of him, racing along at full steam. There was no way he could get out of the way in time. In seconds, he'd be dead, a bloody speck on the front of the engine.

Yet, fate—and Sheriff Doliber—had other ides.

As Ron was certain the train would hit him, time froze all around him. For several seconds, the train's speed slowed to a crawl, and he felt someone grab him by the collar and yank him out of the path of the steel beast. As he was planted on the ground beside the track, time returned to normal, and the train sped on by with unabated velocity. A gust of wind created by the speeding locomotive almost knocked him over, but he was safe.

Shaking off the shock, feeling adrenaline course through his veins, Ron looked over to the man who'd pulled him out of the train's deadly path. "Blast you, Doliber. You sure know how to throw me into harm's way."

"Sorry about that," Doliber said nonchalantly. "I miscalculated the train's position a hair, and cut our approach a little close. At least we have a visual bearing now; shouldn't be hard to teleport aboard."

"Wait!" Ron shouted, as he felt the familiar tinge of static coating him again. It was too late, and a second later he blinked his eyes to see the inside of a vacant dining car.

As Ron shook off the shock of a latest teleport, Doliber paced around the room, looking for whatever clues he could find. His eyes were wild as he studied layers of reality unseen by normal man.

Ron didn't have any magic tricks up his sleeve, and was left with only his keen eyes to examine his environment. Even so, he could notice the rush job that had been done on the compartment. Several windows were still missing, and some of the tables had damaged tops, deep scratches like claw marks dug into the wood, mostly on the edges. The floor had been scrubbed recently, as evidenced by the damp spots on the wooden inlay beside the wall. The eight-inch hardwood planks were set from the wall, leading inward about two feet and disappeared under a newly laid strip of red carpeting.

The clues were minor, and nothing Ron could figure out. What was the point of this exercise? Would Doliber find something to lead him to the killer, a magical trace to reveal the villain's identity? Not every case was based in the mystical, and rarely was a skilled magic user unlawful. No harm in ruling things out, though.

"That was a nifty trick back there, slowing time and all," Ron mentioned, still riled by the incident. Talking about it made him feel better.

"I didn't slow time so much as I sped us up. Everything else looked slow, because we were moving so fast. It's not something I'd recommend on a regular basis. It can be pretty rough on the metabolism."

Ron nodded his head, and realized he was hungry all of a sudden. Was it a side effect of the magical manipulation, or simply his oversized stomach playing tricks on him? Then again, they were in a dining car, a place reserved for fine cuisine. That might make anyone ravenous.

As Ron contemplated the source of his hunger, Doliber continued to scan the dining car with mystically enhanced senses. Peering beyond the ordinary layer of reality, he studied the energy being emitted by different objects in the room. Mostly, it was ordinary, cold, bleak things that held little or no magical potential. However, a few spots showed promise, spots on the floor and grooves in the wall that radiated gold and red colors; hot spots of magic.

Doliber knelt down to get a closer look at a few sparkling dots.

"See anything?" Ron asked.

Doliber shook his head, realizing what he was seeing. "No. It's just the blood of some parlor magician," he said. The spray retained a weak signature of the spellcaster that had shed it. From the looks of it, the victim might have had a few nifty illusionist tricks up his sleeve, but nothing comparable to Guild-grade ability. Clearly, his amateurish tricks hadn't spared him from the deadly assault.

The car was pretty clean, otherwise. The clean-up job had been hasty, but thorough. Other than the few drops of blood, there wasn't much left to show anything untoward had happened.

Turning around, Doliber was blinded by a painful light. The unnatural brightness burned into his skull like a million needles. The staggering effect left him stumbling backwards.

He hadn't been expecting a mystical assault, and his attention had been too focused on the floor to perceive the threat. His attempt to dig a needle out of a haystack had left him at the mercy of some unknown foe.

"Ron, where are you?" Doliber asked, vainly seeking assistance.

No reply came, and a second flash of light silenced the sheriff's mind. The soothing darkness of sleep claimed him before he hit the floor.

* * *

Ron Grimes woke up to something hard jabbing his shoulder. Otherwise, he didn't feel all that bad. It was no worse than waking up after a dreamless night, only he wasn't lying down. He was sitting in a hard chair, and flexing his arm muscles he realized they were both tied down.

"Time to rise and shine, boyo," an accented voice said.

Ron's eyes felt heavy, though it wasn't impossible to lift them. Once the haze cleared, he found himself staring into the face of a short gentleman in a bowler hat and black spats. The diminutive fellow also carried a straight cane with ornately carved veins running down the wooden shaft.

"You... you're Irish," Ron said, swallowing profusely. His mouth was salivating in an inordinate fashion.

"Aye, but no' just any Irish. A Leprechaun, I be," the fellow said, sounding proud of himself.

"What?" Ron asked, caught off-guard by the man's admonition.

"How do ye think I wuz able ta get the drop on you an' yer warlock friend, eh? I used me own special talents, the kind only gained by the Guild itself!"

"Doliber? What did you do to him?" Ron asked, concerned for his boss.

"Nothing more than I did to ye," the Leprechaun replied. "Now, why'd you think I'd be offended by me rightful name? Have ye never met a Leprechaun before, lad?"

"Sure, I've met plenty of Irish dwarves. I just figured you'd want to be called something different," Ron admitted, "seeing how all of them I ever met took Leppercon to be some sort of insult."

"Bah, that's 'cause they're *Irish Dwarves*," the Leprechaun answered. "Not a spit o' magic in the lot of 'em. Those of us in tuh Guild, we be proud of our heritage, and take the name rightly."

Ron worked it all out in his head, and wondered why he'd been so ignorant. Leprechauns were dwarves capable of mastering magic? That was a new one on him. He'd never met a dwarf with any mystical skills, other than the occasional empathic talent. To think any of his people could wield the sorts of powers Doliber and his ilk displayed; it was something to be proud of.

Too bad the first magic dwarf he encountered had to take him prisoner.

"Why are you doing this?" Ron asked. "What are you after?"

"Don't worry, Grimey Boy," the Leprechaun said, keeping an amiable tone. "Ah've only been paid to keep ye tied as far as Tanner." He dug a large, gold watch out of his chest pocket and glanced at the dial. "That'll be within the hour."

The answer was wholly dissatisfying, the sort that merely incurred more questions. What was this all about? The Leprechaun was a paid henchman, obviously, but who was he working for? Marshal Rodgers, perhaps? No, the Marshal didn't seem the sort to play such an underhanded trick. Mayor Atwood? Possibly, though would he act before talking to Doliber, personally? Then again, there were any number of outlaws who might hold a grudge against the lawmen of Selwood.

Ron needed an answer. "Who's your boss?" he demanded.

"I'm me own boss!" the Leprechaun snapped. "If ye be meaning who it was that paid me to restrain ye, that you'll learn when we reach Tanner."

"You gonna deliver us into their waiting hands?" Ron asked.

"Somethin' of the sort," the Leprechaun assured him. "Like I said, I'm to hold ye only 'til then. Now, sit back and relax. We've not far to go."

\* \* \*

Tanner was a bustling mining town west of the Cactus Mountains, and right on the border between Nye and Esmerelda County. The desolate hills surrounding the settlement were bitter and foreboding, desirable only for the hoards of silver locked within their rocky faces. The massive quantities of ore had caused a population boom in recent years, enough to warrant a rail spur for the town. The line had caused quite a stir back in seventy-nine, as the county seat of Selwood remained without a connection, while this new town got preference thanks to corporate payoffs.

Spencer Davis was wearing out the platform at Tanner Station, but nobody noticed. There were dozens of other people standing around in differing states of excitement, as they waited for their train. Some of them had been waiting since last night for this ride, as the regular route had been interrupted by the unsightly slaughter. Word of the incident was spreading fast, but it didn't deter anyone from riding the rails. What alternative was there? The age of the stagecoach was fading fast, and nobody wanted to waste time and energy on that antiquated form of travel; not if the train could take them to their destination.

Spencer wasn't here for a ride. He was waiting for someone to arrive.

The telegram had been brief, but specific. Spencer was to wait at the station for the eight o'clock from Yucca Junction, where he would take possession of two "special prisoners." The handler would be a short Irishman, but nothing was said of the captives, or what was to be done with them. Spencer expected the delivery man would have further instructions.

Such was the life of a hired gun.

Spencer hadn't been looking for this sort of job, but when you work for Albert Silcox, you do what you're told. The cattle baron had enough money and clout to command obedience, and half the men in Nevada would kill to be on his payroll. He paid twice what anyone else offered, and treated his help fairly, for the most part. The only downside was the occasional "odd job" you were asked to perform.

It wasn't such a bad thing, Spencer thought. He only wished he knew what the heck was going on.

The crowd got noisy, as the distant whistle of the train called out from a distance. Spencer was on the east side of the platform, and could see the black dot on the horizon, with a tuft of smoke streaming above it. In minutes, the small speck became the obvious front of the train, a large 19 sitting in the center of the round nose plate.

Time for the trade off.

As the train came to a stop, porters emerged from different compartments and began taking tickets. There weren't any passengers coming off initially, but Spencer knew to stand and wait for it. After the crowd flowed into the passenger compartments and the platform got empty, three figures made themselves apparent. Two dwarves and a leather-clad man came clomping out of the dining car near the front of the train, and they wasted no time hurrying over to Spencer, who waited at the appointed location.

"You be Spencer Davis?" the finely-attired dwarf asked with an Irish accent.

"And you're a short Irishman," Spencer replied.

"You might say that. Name's Michael James Flaherty, at yer service."

"Who are the prisoners?" Spencer asked.

"Prisoners? No, they're not prisoners. They're me new friends I just met on the train. Now they're your friends."

Spencer wasn't sure what to make of the fellow, or the job. "What should I do with our *friends*?" he asked, concerned he might be asked to do something he hadn't the stomach for.

"Take 'em to Byron, and ride wit' 'em back to Selwood," Flaherty said. "Yer boss ought to be waitin' there by then, an' should be able to square things up."

"That's it?" Spencer asked, feeling he was getting off light.

"Yes, sir, tha's the lot of it. Now, if you'll excuse me, I've a train to catch," Flaherty said, turning back to the waiting locomotive. He hopped back aboard, tipping his hat to the porter on duty before ducking into a passenger car. No papers were exchanged, but it wasn't surprising. Mr. Silcox often liked his "guests" to ride in anonymity.

Spencer briefly examined his two captives, and felt a lump swell up in his throat. He was nervous. He'd never done anything like this before, and he didn't like the idea of riding over a hundred miles with these strange men. Even with Byron Burch at his side, it would be a long, uncomfortable trip.

"All right, let's move out," Spencer said, waving the two to follow him.

"I think that's far enough," one of the men said.

Spencer froze in mid-step and began to turn around. He knew it wasn't going to be that easy. Looking back, he saw both the man and the dwarf still had their hands tied behind their backs, and neither one appeared armed. That was a relief.

"Do you have any idea what you're doing?" the man challenged with a cold, commanding voice.

Spencer didn't, but did he dare to admit it? "Now, Sir, if you'll just come along nice like, we'll get you some grub, and then we can get you on down to Selwood. Might take a couple of days, depending on the trails and all. I'm sure Mr. Silcox will square things up when we get there."

Straightening up, the dwarf said, "Free food? Well, who could argue with that? Lead on."

Spencer's concerns faded only slightly as he led the way off the platform. Once on the ground, he had his *friends* take the lead, so he could keep a careful eye on them, as they walked down the deeply-rutted road ringing the edge of town. It wouldn't be so bad once they met up with Byron. That man could handle any rustler or hustler in the West. Old man Silcox would have his meet and greet, sure thing.

* * *

"Keep it up, Grimes," Doliber's voice echoed inside Ron's head.

"What?" Ron thought back, feeling creepy about the sheriff having a telepathic telegraph wire fixed to his mind. Privacy was a top concern for the dwarf, and he never appreciated telepathy's potential for voyeurism.

"Don't act too friendly in front of this thug," Doliber cautioned as they began walking down the street. They were steering clear of the bustling center of Tanner, following a lane on the outskirts of town.

"Maybe I wouldn't be so hungry if somebody hadn't eaten half my breakfast steak," Ron replied.

"It was for your own good," Doliber mentioned. "You could afford to skip a meal or two."

"Hey, I ain't fat. I'm just built stout!"

"I'm sure," Doliber said dubiously.

As they turned a corner, Ron asked, "So, how long are we gonna play along with this dude?"

"Until I've got enough information," Doliber answered.

Whatever that meant, Ron couldn't tell. It was anyone's guess what *enough* might be, though they were amassing quite a pile of answers. These kidnappers clearly worked for Silcox, so obviously he was behind their kidnapping, but a larger question remained. Why would one of the wealthiest man in Nye County want to kidnap the sheriff and his top deputy?

It was doubtful the two law men would uncover the whole truth before their ruse of submission was abandoned. Ron could tell Doliber was itching to break free and get down to business. A simple spell was all it would take, but every minute the sheriff held back was another minute their foes might reveal something of vital importance.

They stopped in front of a run down flop house with an open porch. The place might have been part of an older settlement from the looks of it, though once you got inside things appeared more civilized. The entryway had a strip of gold carpet running toward the staircase in the back, and a doorway to the right revealed a dining room with enough room for two dozen guests. Tucked in one corner, sitting in a pillowed rocker, was a man taking a nap. A floppy black hat was covering his face, but it couldn't conceal the hissing snore.

Spencer walked over and prodded the man's foot gently. "Say, Byron, our guests done arrived," he said.

The slumbering man flinched to awareness, and slowly sat up, sliding his hat back on top of his head. His dark brown eyes glared out at the captive law men with knowing conviction. "So, good old Flaherty got the drop on Sheriff Doliber, did he?" Byron mentioned.

Spencer almost leapt out of his skin at the comment. "This is the sheriff?" he asked, looking terrified. "Of Nye County?"

"Nah, of Nottingham," Byron quipped, rising from his chair. Seeing the blank look on Spencer's face, he added, "Of course of Nye County!"

As Spencer panicked and Byron stood up, Ron felt the ropes slip off his wrists, and knew that ruse time was over.

With lightning speed, Doliber's arms came out from behind his back, and he grabbed Byron by the collar. "You'd better start explaining yourself if you want to keep off the gallows."

Byron burst out laughing, but calmed down after the sheriff shook him. "Hey, nobody's gonna hang for grabbing you. Not with Silcox signing the governor's paycheck."

"Nobody's above the law," Doliber challenged, shoving Byron backwards. The cattleman staggered and fell back into his chair.

"Seems to me the law isn't so lawful," Byron challenged, still looking smug. "Not when it lets deputies run roughshod over honest drovers."

"Somebody has to," Ron added, feeling the need to inject himself into the verbal combat. He'd felt the sting of rowdy ranch hands in recent weeks, and wasn't about to give them a free pass.

"Pipe down, midge," Byron said, losing his calm arrogance. "If tinhorns like you'd learn to play nice, we wouldn't have to be teaching you a lesson."

Furious, Doliber activated his mystic abilities, lashing an invisible rope around Byron's waist. With a single yank of his right arm, he pulled the cattleman out of the chair to face him.

"What *are* you gonna to do?" Byron goaded.

Doliber reversed his spell and shoved Byron against the wall with a magic force. "I'm taking you in, both of you. Selwood's cells have been empty for too long."

Byron narrowed his gaze. "Good luck with that."

Answering the challenge, Doliber clenched his fist several times. He remained frozen in place for several seconds, after which a startled look flowed over his face.

"Satisfied?" Byron said, regaining his confidence.

"What's wrong?" Ron asked, feeling the other shoe was about to drop.

"I just tried to get a lock on Selwood, but nothing happened. I can't teleport," Doliber answered.

"Oh, we thought of that; needed to make sure you couldn't leave once you got here. That's why we hired Flaherty. The magic midges have a knack for neutralizing other mystics."

Doliber sent a magic lash around Byron's throat and began

choking him. "I still have command of other spells, so you'd better start talking!" He relaxed his stranglehold enough so the cattleman could breathe. "Now, why are we here? This is a mining town. What interest does Silcox have here?" Doliber demanded.

"Nothing, which is *why* you're here. It's out of the way, so it'll take time to get back. That's all that matters."

"Why? What's so important that you have to get us out of the way?" Doliber asked, even as suspicions dawned upon him. "It wouldn't have anything to do with the train murders, would it?"

"What?" Byron asked, showing a moment of bewilderment. "Nah, we've got nothing to do with that. This is about justice being served, justice you and your crooked court won't deliver."

The talk was familiar, and Ron's mind harkened back to a scene not so long ago, where Joella had been confronted by a drunk at the bar. The surly cowpuncher had dared to mock her virtue, and had paid for his insolence with an ounce of flesh. Threats had been made, ones neither Ron nor the sheriff had taken seriously at the time. Obviously, things were more serious than either man had thought.

"Lockward!" Ron exclaimed.

Byron nodded and smiled.

Ron stomped over and punched the cattleman in the gut. "You nabbed us just to get to Joella, you rat bastard!"

"A man's bound to be cranky after having half an ear lopped off by an elf whore!" Byron said, cringing in pain from the hard hit. "You and that crooked judge made him cut a deal to let the hussy off, but she'll get what's coming to her. Now there's nothing either of you can do to stop it!"

Ron was about to punch the man again, but Doliber held him back. The dwarf knew better than to argue with the sheriff, and decided to stand down. There was no sense bludgeoning this hired hand, though it might feel good to give him a walloping.

With a flick of his wrist, Doliber cast another spell, and Byron collapsed. A simple sleep spell had hit the large man like a gallon of whiskey, and would keep him sedated for hours.

While Doliber was distracted with the unconscious man, Ron turned to Spencer Davis. The young man had been quaking in his boots during the whole verbal exchange, and looked ready to make a run for it. Ron wasn't going to let him. Rushing forward, Ron slammed his shoulder into Spencer's gut and tackled him to the ground. Three firm blows to the face did the trick. It may not have been as elegant as Doliber's magic spell, but Ron put his foe to sleep, just the same.

"Good work, Grimes," Doliber said, setting Byron's unconscious body in the chair. "Now, go find us some rope. We'll be taking these two back to Selwood, only not how they envisioned it."

Ron looked around the house, but found it was devoid of life. There were beds made upstairs, and fresh vegetables in the kitchen, but whoever stayed here was out for the morning. Peculiar, but not unheard of. Perhaps Byron had sent them packing, or asked them nicely to vacate for a few hours.

There was some old twine in the bottom of a kitchen cupboard, and it seemed tough enough for a restraint. Ron hurried back with it and began tying the men up, as Doliber picked through the possessions of their would-be captors. Among the assorted trail gear were three pistols and two rifles that Doliber laid out on the dining room table. The rifles were a pair of beat up 1866 Winchesters, easily identified by their brass receivers, and the pistols consisted of a pair of nickel-plated Hopkins & Allen XL #8 Frontier revolvers, and a double-action Colt Lighting with factory fresh case-hardened finish. Several full bandoleers assured the guns all had sufficient ammunition.

"Think that Leprechaun has our guns?" Ron asked after firming up the line around Byron's wrists.

"Maybe," Doliber replied, sighting one of the H&A revolvers. "As things seem to stand, I suspect they'll be with Silcox by the time we hit Selwood. He'll want to return our hardware as part of smoothing things over."

"He'd better," Ron said. "I've had that Remington since the war, grown kinda partial to it."

"I'd never have guessed," Doliber replied, clicking the pilfered pistol's cylinder. Ron could see the case rims as they rolled into line with the opened loading gate.

There wasn't much advantage to sticking around, and as soon as Ron had both men restrained and Doliber had had a chance to pick through their gear, they headed out. The train would be leaving for Yucca Junction just as soon as the freight cars could be loaded with bullion. That was the driving force behind the speedy recommissioning of the locomotive; it had a fortune in silver to transport.

As Ron and Doliber stepped out on the front porch, they heard the chugging of the train, and saw the long line of cars rolling away from the nearby station. They were too late.

"Damn," Ron remarked, dropping Spencer's unconscious body on the porch steps. "How'd they load so fast?"

"They probably have a displacement charm," Doliber mentioned. "Expensive piece of equipment, but it saves on freight hands."

Displacement charms were a handy thing in society, specialized mystical devices that allowed non-magic-users to move freight short distances in an instant. Depending on the quality of the charm and the density of the material being moved, a person might load a stagecoach or an entire boxcar before draining the object's power. Generally, the expense of the charm would negate any cost savings incurred by reduction in time and manpower, so not everybody used them.

Clearly, the mining companies of Tanner favored efficiency.

"No sense running for it," Ron remarked, knowing how fast the train would be going. Even a dragon-like sandmare would be hard-pressed to catch up to the train, and an ordinary horse didn't stand a chance. There was no possible way they could reach it now.

"Looks like we'll be riding to Selwood, after all," Doliber said, sounding frustrated. He carried Byron's body along as he walked out into the street.

Ron followed the sheriff, doing his best to drag Spencer's body as he walked around the weathered boarding house. Around back, they found four horses hitched to a watering trough, saddled and ready to go. All they needed were the saddle bags that Doliber had picked through inside. Silcox's men had been well equipped for the ride back to Selwood, so everyone would have decent food and shelter during the trip.

It was a simple enough thing to retrieve the saddlebags and

tie the unconscious men to their horses. Once their prisoners were set, the lawmen mounted the remaining horses. Spurring the brown steeds to action, Ron and Doliber trotted out into the street, and followed it to the rail bed. A hard-packed trail followed beside the rails, all the way to Yucca Junction, over a hundred miles distant.

It was poor timing on the part of these cattlemen to pull a lousy stunt like this. If anyone else was hurt by the beast that had massacred the trainload of passengers, Doliber would be out for blood.

As urgent as the situation was, Ron's mind kept harping on Joella, wondering if she'd be safe. Men capable of getting the drop on a trained warlock like Doliber would most certainly pose a threat to an elvish woman with very limited magic at her disposal.

"There has to be something we can do," Ron mentioned as they rode along. "We can't leave Joella to fend for herself."

"Our options are limited," Doliber said, slowing his horse a little. He lowered his head in thought before adding, "There is one possibility. It's a long shot, but maybe he'll help us."

"Who?" Ron asked, eager to grab at any chance.

"A dead man," Doliber replied.

**Episode 4:**
# One of Those Days

Breakfast was served early at the Bormans' Boarding House. Most of the regulars were professionals of one sort or another, and kept tight hours. Sunrise meant the work day had begun, and sunset was time to sleep. While there were some exceptions to the rule, most people saw fit to schedule their lives accordingly.

Joella Grimes-Talus came downstairs at a quarter past five. The glow of the sun shone in through the large bay windows beside the front door at the foot of the stairs, and the smell of fresh coffee and baking biscuits greeted her from the adjoining kitchen. Old Mrs. Borman was busy as always, with the help of a cousin or two, preparing the food and serving it up to the dozen guests at the table in the dining room. The large ranch house was well suited to accommodate all comers.

Joella generally avoided breakfast in-house, but this morning she was feeling particularly famished. The walk across town to the sheriff's office seemed too long a distance to travel on an empty stomach, so a meal with the commoners was necessary. So what if they were lowly humans? They were decent, moral people, for the most part. Often she despised the elitist streak that had been bred into her, though avoiding situations that stirred it up seemed to be the only effective remedy.

Most of the guests were single men, though a few ladies and one peculiar foreign couple filled out the table. Joella found herself glancing over at the dark-haired foreigners as they rambled back and forth in their curious language. It sounded similar to

Elavic, the ancient legal language of the elvish clans, though dissimilar enough to prevent easy translation.

Some of the men were also staring at the strange couple, and Joella could only image what they were thinking, as she lacked her Cousin Doreen's mentalist skills. Even so, humans weren't that hard to read. A lift of the brow, or a twitch of a cheek muscle could tell you a lot.

The food arrived, and the Borman women sat down near the head of the large table, by the old man. He was relatively thin, but his fat face revealed the prosperity of his past. There was something wrong with him that was sapping his strength and withering his muscles, or so it seemed. Maybe he was just so old his body was tired of living.

Joella waited patiently for the trays of food to be passed so she could fill her plate. A good helping of eggs and biscuits were hers for the taking, even after six ravenous men picked at the platter before her. The Bormans knew the needs of their boarders, and made sure to prepare an adequate spread. There were hardly any leftovers, but never any complaints about empty stomachs.

Most of the men ate quickly and left before Joella had even gotten through her first biscuit. There was no rush for her, and mealtime was something to be savored in her opinion. Her fondest memories were those long, drawn out meals around the supper table, where father would prattle on about the day's activities. He'd been trained as a lawyer, though ended up with his own ranch outside of Ravenna West in eastern California. So many elvish professionals had taken to the plow in those early years, when taming the wild country to forge their own community had been top priority for the pioneers. Joella had never known the soft life, even though her upbringing had been less than harsh. It had been respectable and ordered.

Joella's daydreaming let her food get cold, and as she drifted back to present time she found herself alone at the table with the elder Bormans. They weren't harsh in their expressions, but she knew they considered her to be weird; not for being an elf, but for being an elf married to a dwarf who never spent the night with her. Everyone thought that was strange, even Joella, but she understood why. It was a sham marriage to spare her the disgrace of becoming the fourth wife in a polygamous relationship. It was worth being considered bizarre, so long as it bought her freedom.

Sitting at the table with her cold food, a faint voice echoed inside her head, a voice she hadn't heard in days.

"Sheriff, is that you?" she said, straining to make the words clear in her mind.

"Yes, I'm back," Doliber's voice said, the words barely perceivable to Joella. "I'm with Ron, on the train from Yucca Junction. The damn Marshal cleaned it up and sent it on its way already, but there may still be some evidence to be found. I shouldn't be long. Man the office until..."

His voice cut out, and Joella figured he must be out of range. Telepathy wasn't her forte, so she wasn't well versed in the intricate dynamics involved with mind-to-mind communication.

Eating the last of her eggs and downing a glass of cloudy water, Joella headed outside. The day was breaking, and she had a job to do.

Walking down the dusty street, smelling the scent of burning coal and aerosolized horse droppings, she wondered what the day would bring. People were walking to and fro in their ordinary daily routines. Shopkeepers, cattle drivers, denim-clad miners, and finely-dressed professionals could all be seen on a daily basis, and today seemed no different. But it was. The train massacre hadn't been forgotten, and somewhere there had to be a gathering posse eager to hit the trail and hunt down the culprit. Joella had missed last night's mob, and wondered how well Ron and that Marshal had done to dissuade them. It must've been a bold move.

Marshal Rodgers was bound to be trouble, as well. Joella couldn't forget the threats he'd made, and still worried about the decisions she'd soon have to make. Subterfuge was one thing, but outright betrayal was not in her repertoire. This Marshal wanted her to play some sort of game, to persuade Ron and Sheriff Doliber to bow to federal authority. Was that something she could do? Possibly, but only if she believed it to be the right thing to do at the time. Whether that would serve the Marshal, who knew?

The Sheriff's Office sat in the center of town, amidst the stores and professional offices. Most of the lawyers and businessmen lived above their workplaces, just as Doliber did, and it was a boon to security to have the county's chief law enforcement officer in close proximity. Other than the disreputable barber across the street, nobody had a bad word to say about the arrangement.

Joella found the front door unlocked, as usual. The Sheriff's Office was always open, and someone was usually in-residence. If Doliber wasn't around, and the regular deputies were off duty, a suitably reputable resident of Selwood would stand guard over the facilities.

Stepping into the office, Joella spotted a scruffy character sitting with his feet up on the desk. The ratty leather hat sitting low on his brow and the frayed cuffs of the rawhide jacket identified him as one of the local cattle punchers, not the sort of man Doliber would appoint to guard the office in his absence.

"Can I help you?" Joella asked, keeping her right hand in the vicinity of her holstered sidearm.

"You bet yer life," the character said with a whiny inflection.

As Joella stepped further into the office, the door slammed shut behind her, and she whipped around to see a pair of men there. How had they sneaked up on her like that? Glancing at them, she saw one was wearing an onyx pendant around his neck; a cloaking charm.

"Don't do nothing stupid now," the scruffy guy said, pulling his feet off the desk. Turning his face toward the open archway leading to the holding cells, he shouted, "Hey, Joey, got you a present here!"

The two men behind Joella grabbed her by the arms as a large man stepped out from the empty cell block. The bushy-haired man with gapped teeth and half an ear missing was instantly recognizable. "Lockward," she said, almost spitting the name in revulsion.

The large man didn't say anything, but continued to grin, and began slapping a pair of leather gloves against his right palm. His gait was slow and methodical, as he savored every moment of the approach to his intended victim.

"We told yud pay," one of the men holding Joella said. She recognized the grizzly, bearded fellow, and recalled the threats he'd made after Lockward's trial. She'd given his boasts little mind, nothing more than angry cowboys making noise for their friend. Now, she realized how petty these men truly were.

Whatever the thugs had planned, Joella wasn't about to stick around. Calling upon her limited command of magic, she sought to displace herself, instantly transport her body to another location; anywhere but here. It was the only spell she'd truly mastered, and it had been long enough since she'd utilized her gift. Her reserve of mystic energy should have allowed an instant leap, but instead she felt a stabbing headache which left her flinching.

"Heh, thought you'd get away, didja?" the scruffy man at the desk remarked, waving a shimmering ring at her. The glowing amber in the center of the gaudy piece of jewelry revealed its supernatural power. Like a lightning rod, it absorbed mystical energy in its vicinity. It might not pose any threat to a real warlock, but it totally neutralized Joella's limited abilities. She was utterly restrained!

Joella could smell the liquor on Lockward's breath as he stepped up to her. The man probably had to be drunk to have the courage to pull a stunt like this. Breaking into the sheriff's office and assaulting a deputy? That took real courage, the sort Lockward obviously found at the bottom of a bottle.

Lockward reached a hand out and gripped Joella's cheek. "Yer so darn pretty," he said, rubbing her skin. He moved to her pointed ear and fondled the cartilage. The grin left his face, and he stepped back, looking sad. "I can't do it!"

"Come on, Joey. We done planned this," the grizzly man complained.

Lockward stepped back and shook his head. "Naw, I change my mind. I can't go touching that."

"Why not?" the grizzled one asked.

"It's not right," Lockward said, turning his head away from Joella in shame. "I'm sorry."

The man behind the desk jumped to his feet and started to walk over. "Well, if you don't got the stomach for it, I guess it's up to me to defile this here filly." The scruffy man started to unbuckle his belt as he approached, and his intentions were made clear.

Joella squirmed and kicked to break free from the two men

holding her, but they were incredibly strong. They hooked their legs around hers to stop the kicks while their scruffy accomplice neared.

"You'll be a whore, whether you like it or not," the grizzly man whispered in Joella's ear.

*'How could this be happening?'* Joella asked herself. This was the Sheriff's Office, the last place crime could take place! Where was everyone? Ron, Doliber, Marshal Rodgers, anyone? Were they all out hunting whatever killed the passengers? They had to be, or they'd be here to save her!

For the first time in her life, Joella felt truly helpless. There was no one coming to the rescue.

As the scruffy man yanked off his belt and reached for the buttons on his fly, Lockward punched him in the side of the head. The hard blow sent the smaller man to the floor, where he struggled to get up and then collapsed.

"Nobody touches her," Lockward said, shaking his fist at his friends. They promptly let go of their captive, and ran out the door in a hurry. Things obviously hadn't gone as expected.

Joella stood frozen for a few moments, looking at the unconscious man at her feet and the half-eared cattleman who'd saved her. The sudden turnaround left her bewildered.

"I reckon you'll wanna put me in a cell now," Lockward mentioned calmly.

"Uh, yeah," Joella said in a daze.

Lockward walked back to the cell block to be locked up, and Joella remained sedentary, crying grateful tears for unbelievable miracles.

* * *

Mid-morning came, and Joella sat behind the sheriff's desk. After locking up the would-be rapist and his half-eared accomplice, she found herself manning the shop alone. There was no sign of Ron or Doliber, and she could only assume they were off with the Marshal's posse. It was disconcerting to be so out of the loop.

It had to be that dirty Marshal's fault. Doliber knew what he was planning, and was trying to keep Joella out of it. How noble, and irritating.

Yet again, Joella found herself caught in the crossfire of someone else's ambition. Not so long ago, it had been her dead husband's cousin, and if she didn't watch herself it would be again. Why couldn't men learn to leave her alone?

The quiet of the office broke, as her assailant awoke from his knuckle-induced coma. The annoying shouts for attention drew Joella to the cell block, where she was prepared to feed the scruffy fellow a fresh fist if he didn't pipe down, only there came an easier solution.

"Shut up, Ribsy, or I'll give you another," Lockward threatened from his cell across the hall.

The scruffy fellow listened, albeit begrudgingly.

"Thanks, again," Joella said. "But don't think playing nice will let you off the hook."

"I know," Lockward said meekly. "Really, it wasn't my idea."

"We'll leave that to a judge and jury to decide," Joella replied, turning to leave. The seat behind the desk was dull, but she'd had her nerves frayed enough for one day, so she was eager to get back to it.

"Like the last time? Your sheriff and his judge buddy strong-armed me and you know it. Don't see it turning out any different now."

The accusation hooked Joella's interest. So much for sitting down and taking it easy.

Storming over to the cell, Joella pointed an accusing finger at Lockward. "Last time, you were mocking my husband and called me a whore. We both made mistakes, so Judge Raymond called it even. Seems you agreed."

"I did, and I know how I can get when I'm drunk, but the boys don't understand. Maybe they think they got a right to act that way. Either way, they wouldn't let me drop it, said I had to get some kind of payback or everyone would think less of me."

"What changed your mind?" Joella asked.

"You did," Lockward said, looking at his scuffed boots. "I look at you... you're so beautiful. Perfect. I just couldn't bring myself to do... that thing."

"Thanks," Joella replied, not knowing what else to say.

"It's why I was harassing you at the bar.  I saw you sitting there with that hairy midge, and it bothered me.  I knew I couldn't be with you, but neither should that runt.  You deserve better than either of us."

Joella frowned at the pathetic man in front of her.  She hated feeling sorry for people, and there was nothing else she could feel for such a sad sack of human flesh.  "Don't think you know enough to judge Ron, or me," she said, turning back toward the desk.

* * *

Around lunchtime, Joella finally got some relief.  The surly barber from across the way stopped by to file a complaint about the cattle brokerage down the street making too much noise, and it seemed only fitting the uptight fellow should serve a spell as a prison guard.  Joella slapped a badge in his hand, and threatened to scalp him if he didn't stay put until she sent a replacement.  It was obviously an empty threat, considering the man was as bald as an egg.

Joella wasted no time getting out of there, and ran over to the cattle brokerage, where she found someone more willing and reliable to serve as a sentry of the Sheriff's Office.  Peter Brink was a trusted dealer, and someone Doliber had put on temporary duty before.  Joella knew the barber would appreciate that one of his rivals was relieving him.

Feeling things at the office/jail were secure, she headed over to the Lucca Saloon for lunch.

There wasn't a huge crowd at midday—most of the Lucca's regulars were hard drinking gamblers who showed up later in the afternoon—so Joella was able to pick out a nice corner table that gave her a decent view of the street.

After a few minutes of staring out the windows, Joella was approached by the saloon's owner and chief barkeeper, Solen Lucca.  As always, the middle-aged elf was clean and proper, dressed in a colorful getup that would look more fashionable at a carnival than a barroom.  His blond hair was slicked back and hung down in back all the way to the collar of his blue jacket.

"Looking flamboyant today, Solen," Joella remarked, feeling flippant.  "How many Chinamen did you kill for that ensemble?"

"They were Frenchmen," Solen retorted, followed by a wry

grin. He knew Clan Talus had its origins in the south of France, so he was obviously feeding Joella's mockery back to her in kind.

"I'll take a plate of that slop you serve with cheese melted on top of it," Joella replied.

"And a glass of soda water?" Solen asked. Joella always had a glass with meals at the saloon, so it was really superfluous for him to ask, as he already knew the answer.

"Of course," Joella confirmed.

Solen scribbled the order down on a scrap of brown paper he had tucked in his shirt pocket, then shouted, "Fritz, order." A human boy scarcely old enough to grow facial hair rushed over and grabbed the note, then ran to the kitchen in back.

As the young waiter vanished behind a swinging door, Joella saw that Solen was still standing beside her table. "Yes?" she asked.

"Let's talk a moment," Solen said, grabbing a chair. "We've never had the time for polite conversation, have we?"

"I didn't think we had anything to say to one another," Joella replied, suspicious of the barkeep's intentions. He'd never had a good word to say about her before.

Solen sat down and gave her a funny look, then smiled. "So, when are you going to dump that midge and run off with me?" he asked unexpectedly.

It had to be joke, Joella knew, but he was so suave she could almost believe it was sincere. How utterly shameless of him!

"A Talus and a Lucca? What would the clans think?" Joella replied, mildly amused by his forward suggestion.

Clan Talus was a traditional rival of the Luccas, whose ancestors originally came from similar geographical locations. Historically, the Luccas considered themselves Swiss—though their ancient origins placed them from northern Italy—and as such they'd always had an attitude about the *French* elves, even after centuries of migration. Traditionalists amongst the clans might consider such a pairing to be almost as unsightly as an elf marrying a dwarf. *Almost.*

"Come on, you know we'd be perfect for each other." Solen persisted with his playful smile.

"I don't know if my husband would approve of your notion,"

Joella remarked.

"Please, we both know your marriage to the midge is all for show. Clever use of your Widow's Rights, by the way. Of course, you wouldn't have to use them if you'd just cast off the shackles of our antiquated traditions."

"Easier said than done," Joella answered. "The clan would never let me leave, no matter what. I am the chieftain's eldest heir, cursed by blood to obey at least *some* of our laws."

"Oh, don't play the victim. This isn't Europe. The clans have no power here—no more than we allow them. If you want to disregard Clan Law, there's nothing anyone can do about it. On the other hand, if you really like the midge, that might explain a few things."

"It's not like that," Joella blurted out, forgetting for a second that she had to pretend. After all the trouble she'd experienced in the past day, she was sick of lies, though that didn't mean she had to be entirely forthcoming. Her late husband Vint had taught her one thing; be honest, but never incriminate yourself. "I have an obligation to my people, and our ways."

"A shame," Solen said, leaning back in the chair. "If you ever change your mind, you know where to find me."

"Tending bar?" Joella mocked as Solen stood up.

"It's an honest living," Solen said, turning to leave. "And it's all mine!" he added, extending his arms triumphantly.

Joella felt like laughing, but wouldn't give him the satisfaction. She was used to guarding her gentler emotions, and it served her purpose to appear cool in this circumstance.

The saloon remained quiet for a few minutes, as Joella waited for her food. A couple of drunks were playing poker in the corner, but they knew how to keep their voices down. A couple of the working girls were lurking around, but they didn't seem interested in business—not that the handful of drunks were the sociable types. The ladies eventually migrated over to Joella's little table, though the elf would have rather avoided their company. It was one of those days where everyone wanted her attention.

"You're that lady sheriff, right?"

"Deputy sheriff," Joella corrected. She glanced up at the

young brunette with pink ribbons in her hair.

"Hi, I'm Sally."   The brunette motioned to her blonde companion and continued.  "She's Annie.  Some call her Sandy Annie, but that's another story."

"What's it like to be a gunfighter?" Annie interjected, flopping herself down beside Joella.

"I wouldn't know," Joella said.

"It must be glamorous," Sally mentioned.  "I mean, standing up to outlaws and bandits like that.  Doing everything a man can do, only better."

"Being a deputy is a job like any other," Joella replied, feeling awkward about having her ego stroked by the whores.

"What's it pay?  Good?" Annie asked, sounding like she might be interested in changing professions.

"Fifty cents a week with room and board, plus bonus pay for hazards."

Sally's expression changed and she shook her head.  "Is that all?  You go out risking your life and you can't even make decent money?"

"Oh, but the bonus pay must be something," Annie said, sounding hopeful.

"I pulled in five hundred for nailing a mad sorcerer a couple months back," Joella replied.  Thinking about the risks involved and the thrashing she'd endured, she knew she'd earned every cent of it.

Annie punched Sally in the arm and exclaimed, "See, I told ya we're in the wrong line of work."

"It's the only work girls like us can do to make decent money," Sally rebutted.

Annie guffawed at the assertion and argued, "Decent indeed. I barely pulled down twenty dollars last week after Solen's cut."

"You think getting shot will pay better?" Sally asked.

"Well, no, but a girl can dream, can't she?"

"Maybe you need a raise," Joella mentioned.  "What do you earn for... what you do?"

"Two dollars a poke," Sally replied.  "Solen takes half of it, but a girl can make ten dollars in tips on a good day."

"Yeah, on a *good* day," Annie added.  "Haven't seen much

more than barflies the last few weeks."

"If volume sales aren't doing it for you, why not raise your rates?" Joella suggested. "Two dollars seems pretty cheap if you ask me, especially if Solen takes a cut."

"You're so right," Annie said, sounding sweet as honey. "In fact, we ought to take in the full two dollars, before Solen gets a penny. Don't you think, Sally?"

Sally rolled her eyes, seeming annoyed by the suggestion. "You know what he'll say."

"So what? He doesn't own us," Annie said, pouting. "It's about time we started earning what we're worth."

"Planning to work for free, then?" Solen's voice announced from across the room.

"How does he do that?" Annie asked, slapping the table. "Those pointy ears don't give him special hearing, do they?"

"Nope. Some elves have good hearing, others don't, same as humans," Joella explained. "And some are also cheap bastards!" she said louder.

Solen grinned from behind the bar, and pointed obnoxiously. When the door to the kitchen swung open, he rushed over and grabbed the plate of food from the waiter, so he could carry it over to Joella, himself.

"Stirring up trouble with my girls, are we?" Solen mentioned as he set Joella's plate down in front of her.

"They approached me," Joella said, looking at the steaming plate of meat and beans covered in melted cheese. She quickly noticed there were no utensils. "What, am I supposed to use my fingers?"

"Sally," Solen said, hooking a thumb toward the bar. The brunette sighed and got up to retrieve the flatware.

Taking the newly vacant seat, Solen sat down and looked at the blonde. "Annie, have you been bothering our guest?"

"Who says you should set our rates?" Annie asked in a snit. "Seems it's our business, so we should decide what we charge."

"We've been over this before," Solen said. "Higher rates discourage customers. Discouraged customers visit less often. Fewer visits means fewer drinks sold, so I lose business, too."

"Your sales won't drop if we get paid more, and you're not

the one who has to wash off the filth of all those men every morning," Annie complained.

"She has a point," Joella remarked, feeling her mood improve. Seeing Solen flustered was doing wonders to relieve her tension.

"Stay out of this," Solen snapped, then turned back to his employee. "Annie, I've bent over backwards to accommodate you and the other girls. Have I ever laid a hand on any of you? Have I ever let anyone else abuse you or cheat you out of your earnings? Don't I chase off the riff-raff? I care about you girls. I paid your way out of that Kansas City slum, remember?"

"And I repaid you ten times over already," Annie persisted. "What have I got to show for it? Nothing. How's a girl supposed to save for the future?"

"Like everyone else. Work harder."

"You try getting poked ten times a day. See if you want to work harder."

"Oh, please. When was the last day you had half that many?"

"I hear the brothels in Carson City are getting five buck a poke these days."

"This isn't Carson City," Solen begrudged. "The clientele around here are a sight thriftier. You start gouging, they'll go somewhere else."

"And somewhere else will charge them more, too."

"She's got a point," Sally said, returning with Joella's fork. "Freelancer Bertha up the street charges three, and she got whacked with an ugly stick at birth."

"Enough!" Solen growled and stood up, knowing he'd been beat. He wasn't graceful with defeat. "Fine, you want more, charge more, but don't come crying to me when you can't round up enough work to pay your rent."

Solen stormed over to the bar to sulk.

"He charges you rent, too?" Joella asked.

"Five dollars a week, meals *not* included," Annie replied.

"No wonder you're broke," Joella said, stabbing at the chunky meat concoction. It didn't look good, but the flavor was spicy and satisfying. After all the excitement of the morning, she was famished, and wasted no time in polishing it off. All the while, the working girls watched her, as if secretly longing for different lives.

As Joella finished her meal, a commotion arose out in the street. People stuck their heads out of windows and doors all along the main drag to observe a large crowd coming up from the south. There had to be two dozen people riding into town, and right in the lead was the conspicuous form of Marshal Rodgers. The federally-empowered lawman dismounted in a hurry outside the Sheriff's Office as the crowd continued up the street.

As the crowd grew near, Joella noticed they were herding something peculiar. Flashes of alabaster skin and silver hair could be seen as the mob of riders moved, though the horses mostly blocked the view. Whatever it was, the men were keeping it penned in, and not with considerate prodding. A few times a man's foot jabbed at the white thing, and others poked at it with their Winchesters.

What had they captured?

Joella stood up from her seat, ready to go investigate, when she spotted Marshal Rodgers running out of the Sheriff's Office. He hopped on his horse and snapped the reins, racing up the street to pass the crowd. His destination was the Lucca Saloon.

Rodgers stepped into the saloon with his head held high and his collar freshly straightened. He had an air of superiority about him at all times, even when fresh off the trail, and he exuded confidence with every step.

As the Marshal came through the door, Solen ran up and greeted him. "Greetings, Marshal. How may I be of service today?" His words were amicable, though a hint of worry lurked as well. What did he have to fear from the law?

"Solen, it's so quiet in here," Marshal Rodgers remarked, examining the room. "Why don't you get a piano?"

"I'm not running some two-bit honky-tonk," Solen replied indignantly. "Unless you can find a classical pianist to accompany the instrument, I'd rather people drink and dine in peace."

"It's your business," Rodgers replied, sounding as if he disagreed with his own statement. "Now, where's the sheriff and his deputies?"

"Haven't seen Doliber or the midge all day," Solen remarked. "Deputy Talus is right here," he said as Joella walked over.

"Ah, there you are," Rodgers said, giving Joella a quick sizing-up. "So, where's that sheriff of yours?"

"Last I heard he was examining the train you cut loose from Yucca Junction."

"Any idea when he'll be back?" Rodgers asked.

"That's what I'd like to know," Joella said, growing concerned. It wasn't right that Doliber and Ron would run off without telling anyone, though it was possible they were on a hot lead. However, if that were the case, then what had the Marshal dragged in?

"I hope he sees fit to show up soon. We caught our man, such as it is," Rodgers remarked.

Joella was eager to see the killer, and followed the Marshal out onto the saloon's front porch to see what manner of man it was. Once they were at the top of the front step, the Marshal motioned for the men to spread out a little so Joella could have a clear look at the culprit.

Spotting its hunched white form, Joella felt her heart leap in awe. "A frost goblin? I thought they were extinct."

"Apparently not," Rodgers said. "But maybe they will be once we hang this one."

"Hang it? Why? You can't honestly think this sad little thing killed all those people."

"When we found it, the thing was gnawing on human bones, presumably someone from the train, hopefully not Miss Carter."

"Hopefully?" Joella asked.

"There twern't much left when we found 'im," one of the posse said, followed by a long spit.

"The creature is our killer. Look at those claws, and the way it's poised to attack, even now. The sooner we string it up, the sooner life can get back to normal around here."

It was clearly an attempt to glaze over the problem. The Marshal couldn't be that stupid, to think a goblin was responsible for such a massacre. They were scavengers, like crows or vultures. Sure, they'd eat a dead body if they found one in the wild, but they weren't the sort to hunt their own, and hardly the sort to smash up a train just for a snack.

The only reason to pin the blame on the goblin would be to lull the populace into a false sense of security—make them think the threat was gone. Once the angry mobs were satisfied, the Marshal could conduct a hunt for the real killer without civilian interference. Such a clever yet underhanded plan.

Grabbing the Marshal's arm, Joella pulled his ear toward her. "I know what you're doing, and it's a mistake," she whispered.

"I'm doing my job, mistake or not," Rodgers replied, then pulled away from her. Walking back to his horse, he addressed the crowd. "Get the judge. The sooner we try this semi-human killer, the sooner we can hang him."

A few in the crowd cheered, but most just grunted or nodded their heads. Two riders broke from the pack and raced further down the street, toward the courthouse.

"Somebody git a photographer while yer at it," one of the riders declared. "We gonna hang us the last frosty goblin. We done need proof!"

As the mob grew anxious, Joella wondered where the sheriff could be. A crime was about to take place, and he was the only man who could stop it.

## Episode 5:
## Recruiting the Damned

"Dismount, you maggot!" Ron shouted, jabbing Spencer in the side with the 1866 Winchester he'd taken from the kidnappers' possessions. The golden-receiver had corrosion spots on its originally polished surfaces, and a dent in the magazine tube reduced the maximum capacity by at least two rounds. Still, it wasn't a bad little gun, and the test shot Ron had fired earlier seemed dead on at fifty yards.

"Grimes, that's no way to talk," Doliber chided as he hopped down from his horse. "Even if it's true."

"All right, get down, you maggot, *please*," Ron said, leaning the rifle against his shoulder. He'd give an inch when asked, but only if it truly mattered. He saw no reason to play nice with these scumbags who'd conspired to waylay him and do untold harm to his wife—even if the marriage was a sham.

"That's better," Doliber said, as Spencer followed the order. His accomplice, Byron Burch, was still sleeping on his horse, tied to the saddle securely enough for a long ride. Whenever he woke up, he'd be in for a surprise. Those knots wouldn't be coming loose without outside help.

"What are we doing here?" Spencer asked, rotating his stiff shoulders as best he could with his hands bound in front of him.

"Seeing if we can arrange a shortcut," Doliber said, leading the men and horses into the livery stable. "Stay close, but keep your mouth shut. This is bound to be a precarious negotiation."

They'd been riding for hours, following the railroad tracks at first, but soon veering off the beaten path. The rail line between Tanner and Yucca Junction ran like a snake through the hills, doubling the distance in between. It was the only way for a train to scale the grade, though horses were not so limited. A more direct route would cut their travel time significantly, if another option didn't present itself.

Here they were, thirty miles southeast of Tanner, in a little mining camp called Goldwater. The boom town had been founded less than a year before, and there were already signs that things were petering out. Half the buildings in town were vacant, and the miners who remained didn't look all that prosperous. Still, there were people here, and one recent addition to the population interested Doliber—a curious individual with equipment that might get them back to Selwood in short order.

Ron followed Doliber into the livery stable on the edge of town, dubious about the value of this pit stop. Having heard Doliber's plan, the dwarf figured their odds of soliciting help were minuscule at best. Not only that, but knowing the sort of being they were trying to enlist gave him the creeps.

"All right, James, where are you?" Doliber shouted at the back of the stable. An annoyed horse whinnied in the corral beside him, yet no human answered.

"This is a waste of time," Ron said. "Looks like things are pretty dead around here. Your stableman's liable to have run off, left this dump for the miners to board their horses themselves."

"No, he's around," Doliber replied, looking around suspiciously. "James, show yourself. I'm not here to arrest you."

"Arrest?" Spencer asked, wondering what sort of fellow they were looking for. "This man some kinda outlaw?"

"Used to be," Doliber said, "but not in Nevada."

"Which don't mean you aren't looking for bounty, lawman," a peculiar voice replied from thin air.

Ron looked around, trying to get a bead on the source, even as the ghostly voice began to laugh. He held the Winchester at the ready, wondering if he might need it.

"If I wanted the paltry sum on your head, I'd have collected it months ago," Doliber replied to the ethereal laughter.

"Paltry?" the voice asked, sounding insulted. "I'd be worth

five thousand if anybody knew I was still alive. Besides, ain't you one of them damned Yankee Republicans?"

Doliber ignored the southerner's slur and replied, "I'm a man who keeps his word, and doesn't answer to Pinkerton."

"Which begs the question," the man said, appearing from behind a stack of hay bales. The clean-shaven gentleman in his mid thirties had slicked black hair and wore a peculiar grin on his lips. He kept his hands out in the open as he crept into view, consciously keeping them away from the twin pistols hanging from his hips. "Why wouldn't a sheriff want to bring in the notorious outlaw, Jesse James?"

"Jesse James is dead," Doliber replied without emotion. "He was shot in the back of the head at his home in Missouri nearly three months ago. It was in all the newspapers."

"Well, who am I to argue with the newspapers?" the man said, maintaining an uplifting demeanor. Turning to Ron, he offered his hand. "James Woodson, at your service."

Ron shook the man's hand, and sized him up. Was this truly the notorious outlaw Jesse James? How peculiar he'd all but admitted it; stranger still was Doliber's plan to recruit him, despite the extenuating circumstances. James was a robber and a killer, hardly the sort any lawman should want to tolerate.

The life and politics of Jesse James were a well-known fact, documented by newspapers and dime novelists across the country. He was a proud southerner, who'd made a career out of looting Carpetbagger trains, under the guise of exacting retribution for the Civil War—though many a sympathizer would have you believe he was a modern day Robin Hood, fighting for the well-being of his countrymen. Either way, Ron knew better than to mention that he'd fought for the Union Army during the war, or that he was still a "damn Yankee" at heart.

"Now, what business brings you to my little stable?" James asked, folding his hands together.

"For starters, we require the use of your translocator," Doliber replied.

James' demeanor shifted instantly, from one of overflowing gregariousness to more sedate suspicion again. "What would I be doing with a translocator?" His concern was warranted, as the mystical device was not only exceedingly rare, but highly illegal in Nevada. Only fully accredited warlocks were permitted to possess them, and their use was highly restricted, for a whole host of reasons.

"Don't play coy with me," Doliber said. "I've been keeping an eye on you since your arrival. A translocator leaves a unique disruption in the ether, something a trained warlock can detect. I know you've been using one, and I need to have it now."

"Just like that?" James asked, unclasping his hands and letting them slide down in the vicinity of his revolvers. "Assuming I have a translocator, that is a very pricey piece of hardware. Letting you *have it* would be costly. So, what's in it for me?"

"A chance at redemption," Doliber said, setting a hand on his own sidearm. "Lives are at stake, and I need your translocator to get to Selwood."

"That's all?" James asked, looking pleased again. "Well, if you'd like a one way trip, I'm sure something could be arranged, for the right price."

"The price is a job, assuming you're interested," Doliber said.

James broke out laughing and almost fell over. "You want me to work for you? Like a deputy?" He gasped for breath as the humor continued to resonate with him.

"That's right. A *man* like you has a lot to account for in this life, and what better way to atone than to help others by working for the law?"

"Who says I want to atone for anything?" James asked, still laughing.

"You're a shadowganger!" Doliber snapped.

As the word was said, James staggered back, as if he'd been slapped.

"What did you say?" Spencer asked, disinclined to believe it.

"You heard me. He's a shadowganger, a hollow copy of a man; a soul trapped in a lifelike shell, cursed to linger after a man's death."

"Naw, they're just an old wives' tale," Spencer said, shaking in his boots.

"Oh, they're real," Doliber said, closing in on James and staring into his eyes. "It's a very rare enchantment, and there aren't many mystics capable of this sort of spell. Needless to say, it doesn't come cheap, nor is it officially sanctioned by the Guild except in the rarest of cases. But Jesse James wronged so many people, I can imagine somebody was willing and able to make it happen. You are cursed to exist, Shadow, until all of Jesse's debt has been repaid, with interest."

The look of dread slowly melted off of James' face, as Doliber's words sank in. As his expression lightened, he gently said, "Thank you."

"For what?" Doliber asked, keeping his face shoved in front of the living effigy of Jesse James.

"For laying it all out for me," James explained. "These last few months, all this guilt has been rolling around in my head, like I'd never felt before, and I never knew why! Now it all makes sense."

"Then you'll accept my offer," Doliber said, backing off.

"Hardly," James replied, grabbing his jacket lapels.

Doliber stood silently, waiting for an explanation. It was so still in the stable, you could hear the individual breaths of each man.

"Seems to me I've got it made, so long as I lay low and mind my own business," James finally replied. "If I'm a shadow, then I'm already dead. That means I can't grow old, and if anything unfortunate should befall me, I'll simply rise anew the next day. That is, if what they say about shadowgangers is true."

"Oh, it's true enough," Doliber said. "As a shadowganger, you can't die until you make up for all the wrongdoing you did during your normal, mortal life."

"Then why would I ever dream of doing that?" James asked.

"Because you feel it, even now," Doliber said morosely. "Every moment of your current existence, you see them—the faces of every person you ever wronged, nagging you, tormenting you, making you feel guilt beyond anything you've ever felt before. Those thoughts and feelings will keep plaguing you until you start to make amends."

"It beats the alternative," James said, turning away from Doliber to face the hay bales. "If I really make amends, this shadowganger dies, right? I'll 'move on.' Well, I tell you death is nothing to be looking for."

"You're already dead," Doliber said. "The only question now is whether you'll choose the path to redemption, or wallow in eternal damnation."

"Oh, are you going to get all religious on me. Want me to get right with Jesus?"

"No, it's not that simple," Doliber said, looking at the floor. His eyes were worrisome, as he contemplated his next course of action. "I'm not supposed to tell you this. You're supposed to make the decision on your own, without foreknowledge of the true consequences... but I need you. If it costs me later, so be it."

Placing a hand on James' shoulder, Doliber breathed deeply and began. "You have a limited window to decide if you want redemption. Very soon, those nagging voices and memories—all that guilt you're feeling—it will get to the point where it consumes your every waking moment. You won't be able to think rationally. Your mind will delve into eternal torment, experiencing all the pain and suffering you've inflicted upon your victims. Your living hell will last untold centuries, until the mystical energy binding your soul to this shadow finally fades, releasing you to whatever afterlife awaits you. That is the end most shadowgangers experience, because they think they can outrun their own conscience!"

James glanced back at Doliber, looking mournful. "It has been getting worse," he admitted, clenching his fists in frustration.

"It'll keep getting worse unless you come with me," Doliber said.

"And you say just trying to make amends will shut it up?" James asked. "If I work for you, doing whatever lawful stuff, it'll get better?"

"As long as you are sincere," Doliber assured him.

James thought on it quietly for a moment, and eventually said, "Then we'll ride." He stuck out a hand for the sheriff.

"The translocator first," Doliber mentioned after shaking James' hand.

"That might be a problem," James said, returning his hand to his side. "See, I don't happen to have this translocator in my possession."

"Don't lie to me, James," Doliber said. "I am a certified warlock. I know a translocator signal when I sense one, and that thing has to be nearby."

"I didn't say it wasn't near," James defended. "I merely said that I am no longer the owner. But I can take you to the man who is."

"Good," Doliber said. "That'll be a start on your road to redemption." With a wave of his hand, he beckoned his crew to move out of the stable.

James smiled as they reached the horses. "If you don't mind my saying, I'd prefer it if this redemption of mine takes some time. When I'm paid up, that's the end, and I do not fancy dying under any circumstances."

"I wouldn't be so worried about dying if I were you," Doliber mentioned, mounting his horse. "Something tells me you have a long way to go."

* * *

"You can't let him do this," Joella said, rushing to catch up with Judge Raymond and Marshal Rodgers, who were marching out of the courthouse.

"Nothing I can do, Mrs. Grimes," Raymond said flatly, slowing down to let Joella catch up. The Marshal kept on walking, eager to find a rope.

"How can you justify hanging a man without a trial?" Joella asked.

"I'm afraid that thing isn't a man, not by any legal definition," Raymond said, tucking his hands into his trousers. His bulbous belly kept his wrists bent as he stood to face the elvish deputy.

Joella growled and rushed off to catch the Marshal. The situation was burning her up, as she knew the whole thing was a spectacle. Hanging a frost goblin for mass murder would serve nothing in the long run, and it had the very dangerous chance of backfiring. The real killer would still be at large, and if the people were lulled into a false sense of security someone might be caught off guard. Death might result because of this reckless subterfuge, and that was reason enough to challenge it.

The aging Marshal wasn't fast enough to get away from the young elf, though he didn't seem to mind her constant pestering.

He seemed more than happy to hear her pleas, even if he didn't really listen.

"You can't do this," Joella snapped. "I don't care what rationale you're using. Hanging an innocent man is wrong."

"Goblins aren't human," Marshal Rodgers rebutted. "Hell, they're more rodent than man."

"So that gives you the right to kill it, and trick the people into thinking it's dangerous?"

"And you've got a right to make people think you're married?" Rodgers said quietly.

"You can't threaten me," Joella said, feeling bold. Bright or not, she couldn't let anyone coerce her in such an underhanded manner. If that meant the truth coming out, so be it.

Marshal Rodgers shook his head and walked off. He didn't head back toward his posse, but instead took a detour in front of the mayor's house. No doubt, he wanted to inform the Atwoods about his "success." Whether they would buy it or not was another matter. No scholar would believe that a frost goblin could pull off such a massacre, and Charles Atwood was by no means an ignorant man. He'd been to college back east, as had his son, and neither were likely to be fooled by the Marshal's ruse.

It occurred to Joella that all she needed was one educated individual to speak the truth about frost goblins, and it could put an end to the Marshal's plan.

Turning the corner onto Main Street, Joella saw the angry mob had thinned. Most of them were probably in the saloon getting drunk, celebrating their glorious manhunt, while the dozen or so steadfast guards kept the goblin safe, waiting for the go-ahead from the Marshal. Nothing would happen until Rodgers was there to grandstand, assuring much needed time to see the mayor.

Hurrying over to Atwood's home, Joella saw a pair of ugly fellows staring at her from across the street. She'd recognize those goons anywhere; the boastful bastards who'd held her arms during the botched rape attempt. Were they following her, waiting for a second chance? They didn't know when to give up.

The Atwood residence was a non-descript whitewashed building with clapboard siding and a roofed porch ringing three sides. A knee high wrought-iron fence ringed a small yard in front, and sheets of sandstone led from the street to the porch steps. The house was a little larger than the others on the block, though nothing else alluded to the occupant's social status.

Joella's first instinct was to knock on the door and request an audience with the mayor. Her formal, elvish upbringing had taught her the customs of polite society, and left her with a lingering affinity for those in leadership positions. However, recent years had tempered her judgment, and prompted her to perform some reconnaissance first. There was no telling what the Marshal and Atwood were discussing, or who was commanding whom!

Slipping around back, Joella found the rear door unguarded and unlocked; an easy point of entry. Despite the look of the locals, Selwood was a very law-abiding town, and people were mostly trusting. Break-ins were virtually unheard of, and most men would gladly see a burglar hanged for his disgraceful actions. Local pastors claimed their good preaching and the fear of God kept men straight, though fear of a warlock sheriff didn't hurt, either.

While the exterior of the mayor's residence may have been ordinary, the interior was a show of extravagance. Plush rugs lined the hallways, and glossy floorboards shined underneath. Colorful paintings hung on the walls as Joella followed the faint sounds of voices. Two doors down, across from a flight of stairs, she spotted the back of Mayor Atwood's head, as the man sat in a patent leather chair in a room lined with bookshelves.

"Are you sure it's him?" Mayor Atwood asked.

"The leprechaun thought so," Marshal Rodgers replied. "Looks like your note was right."

"But why him, after all this time?" young Fletcher Atwood asked. "Why kill all those people on the train, and why nab Bettina of all people?"

"I'm not sure," Marshal Rodgers answered. "Though, it was old man Carter who shot Raethanon's son. There's a blood debt there, so the train passengers may have simply been in the way."

"Don't let the murdering swine off so easy," the mayor grumbled. "Raethanon never killed anyone without enjoying it."

Before Joella could listen further, a heavily accented lady's voice startled her from behind. "Kin ah help ye?"

Joella turned around to see a young, red haired woman wearing a plain black dress with a white belt around the waist; the standard coverings for a maid.

"I'm here to see the mayor," Joella said calmly, covering her eavesdropping.

"Talus, is that you?" the Marshal's voice blared out from the adjacent room.

Realizing she'd been exposed, Joella walked into the room, and locked her eyes onto the Marshal.

"Why, Deputy Talus, what can I do for you this afternoon?" Mayor Atwood asked cordially.

"I was hoping to have a word with you about the train massacre, but it's clear you've started without me."

"Oh?" the mayor said, sounding obtuse.

"You're holding a closed door meeting about the train massacre," Joella challenged. "I should have been invited."

"Why?" Marshal Rodgers interjected.

"How am I supposed to help solve this case if you're hiding things from me?" Joella asked.

"You are a deputy, paid to uphold the law and do as you're told," the Marshal said sternly. "It is not your place to be involved with every facet of the investigation."

"This is Sheriff Doliber's jurisdiction," Joella challenged. "His county, his town! In his absence, I represent him, and as such should be kept abreast of all matters pertaining to law enforcement."

"She's got a point, Ned," Mayor Atwood said.

"This was *our* town long before Doliber and his misfit deputies arrived," Rodgers said. "And as a U.S. Marshal, I am the law above and beyond any elected magician. Thank you, Mrs. Grimes-Talus, but we won't be needing your assistance."

Joella was flush with rage, unlike anything she'd felt before. This petty Marshal knew how to get under her skin, and he wasn't afraid to do it. Worse still, he seemed to enjoy it. The utter contempt he held for her, and for Sheriff Doliber, made her wish she were an outlaw. Her law-abiding conscience sadly prohibited her from giving the arrogant Marshal what he deserved.

Mayor Atwood was clearly in collusion with the Marshal, so

it seemed there was nothing more she could do. Leaving quickly seemed the best way to save face.

"Now, hold on just a minute, Ned," Mayor Atwood said, standing up as Joella turned to leave. "I understand how you feel, and agree we have to deal with things ourselves, but that doesn't mean slapping away a helping hand." He took Joella's hand and held it reassuringly. "Never mind the Marshal. He does get protective at times."

While Marshal Rodgers frowned in disapproval, Mayor Atwood walked Joella over to an empty seat beside the small reading table. Fletcher waved at her awkwardly, looking like a discouraged schoolboy being held after class for a lecture. The young man was caught in the middle of everything, but had little say.

Joella felt funny being led by the hand like a little girl, though it was only customary. Atwood was treating her with the same consideration he would any lady, though it had been a while since anyone had treated Joella that way. How the years had toughened her, leaving her uncomfortable to be treated so gently.

Mayor Atwood returned to his seat. "Now, where were we before the unpleasantness?"

"You were saying about someone called Raethanon," Joella said, wishing to know what they knew.

"Yes, Raethanon," Atwood said, his face growing stiff at mere mention of the name. "The bastard son of a Mexican and a Paiute. He made a fortune robbing stagecoaches during the California gold rush, and later sought to plunder Selwood during its infancy. The Marshal was just telling us that he is the likely culprit of the train massacre."

"Then you know the frost goblin didn't do it," Joella said, restraining her upset.

"There's no telling what creatures Raethanon has recruited to do his bidding," Rodgers said, defending his position.

"Oh, stuff it, Ned, of course the goblin didn't do it," Atwood snapped. "Don't think the good deputy can be fooled as easily as that mob you recruited. She's not some rube, and neither are the people of this town. Pinning the blame on some scavenger isn't going to solve anything."

"Don't tell me how to do my job!" Rodgers shouted.

"Then do it!" Atwood said, slamming his fist against the arm of his chair. "Get out there and find Raethanon, and bring back my son's fiancée!"

The marked division between the men brought joy to Joella's heart, and she couldn't suppress a growing smile. She turned to hide it from the mayor, but ended up giving the Marshal a clear view, which further enraged the man. He bared his teeth and stood up in a huff, heading for the door. Before leaving, he leaned down and whispered in Joella's ear.

"Thanks for your assistance, Deputy Talus," Marshal Rodgers said in passing. "I'll be sure to tell Mactus you said hello."

Joella turned her head, and resisted the urge to spit in his face. The man had no honor or shame! If defying him meant facing Mactus, so be it, but she would not give in to his tyranny.

"Don't mind Ned," Mayor Atwood said. "He has a lot on his mind."

"So have I, Mayor," Joella said, getting up to leave. She'd heard enough, and wasn't going to sit around while the Marshal roamed the town, seeking another way to enact his diabolical subterfuge. He wanted that frost goblin dead, and she somehow doubted the mayor's objections would perturb him.

\* \* \*

Goldwater was a dump of a town. Even the sparse foliage, while in full bloom, had a dead and drab look to it, giving everything a bleak feel. Dust and rocks dominated the landscape, and the hastily constructed homes and storefronts were built out of whatever the miners had scrounged. A couple of saloons stood at the center of town, and they appeared to be the only buildings of merit.

Sheriff Doliber led the way down the main drag, glancing at the handful of whores and shopkeepers who had nothing better to do than to gawk at the new arrivals. It was disconcerting the way the locals studied them, like ghouls looking for fresh prey.

"Tell us again about this Nash fellow," Doliber asked James as they trotted along.

"Percival Nash, goes by the name of Val," James said. "He's

a professional gambler, the type with the silk shirts and a set of aces waiting up every sleeve. He's been hanging out at the Midas Tooth Saloon the past month, doing his best to hustle the miners with pretty good success."

"What would a professional gambler want with a teleporting device?" Ron asked.

"He likes to travel on weekends, visit some neighboring mining camps and bigger towns where the pickings are richer. That's why he eyed my translocator."

"So, what, you lost it in a game?" Ron asked impertinently.

"Hell no," James said, sounding amused by the assumption. "I sold it fair and square. How do you think I could afford the stable?"

"You own the livery stable?" Ron asked incredulously. He'd thought James was little more than a hired hand from his cavalier attitude toward the business.

"Free and clear," James replied. "Nash won it at poker, but really had no need or want of it. So, for that and a couple of fine horses he bought my translocator."

"Sounds like Nash got a bargain," Doliber said, knowing full well the value of such a rare and illicit artifact.

"Can't say I haven't had my regrets," James added. "Though, I figured I could always take it back if I ever really needed it."

"Speaking of which," Doliber said, reigning his horse to a stop outside the saloon, "how'd you ever end up with a translocator in the first place?"

James glanced at Doliber with a smug look on his face. "The Pinkerton I shot didn't need it anymore."

Doliber nodded his understanding, but didn't smile. He'd never liked the Pinkerton Agents—what few of them he'd met. They were lawmen for hire, little more than enforcers for the railroad companies. They seemed to feel as if they were above the law in enforcing the law, which made no sense.

Still, that didn't give you the right to kill them.

Doliber dismounted and tied his reins around the hitching post outside the Midas Tooth. James followed suit, while Ron dealt with their conscious prisoner.

"Come along, maggot," Ron said, poking the young man

with the '66 Winchester.

"The name's Spencer."

"Your name might as well be hanged highwayman for what you've done to us," Ron snapped, jabbing him in the side again. "I swear, if anything happens to Joella..."

"Let's get moving and make sure nothing does," Doliber suggested as he climbed the steps to the saloon's covered porch.

After Spencer got down to follow, Doliber and James walked into the saloon. The barroom was dead at midday, as the prospectors were all in the hills looking for their big score they knew was out there, waiting for them to dig it up. That left a handful of lonely working girls and a few stray gamblers hiding at a corner table.

The leather-faced bartender paid more attention to the glass he was polishing than to the strangers who entered his establishment. He obviously wasn't eager to serve.

James led everyone over to the corner table, where three men were sitting. Two of them looked as dusty and haggard as the landscape, though one was a pinnacle of style. The well-dressed man tipped his bowler hat and smiled as the four new arrivals surrounded him, and his grungy companions took their leave.

"Hey there, Nash," Jesse said as the well-kept man remained silent behind his grin.

"Why, Mr. Woodson, what an unexpected surprise," the gambler replied, shifting his glance back to his hands. He picked up a deck of cards and began to shuffle. "Finally worked up the nerve to lay odds against me at the table?"

"Hardly," James rebutted. "I'm afraid I've come to reclaim the translocator you so artfully bargained off of me."

"Why would you do that?" Nash asked, setting the cards down and sliding back away from the table.

"Seems I've no use of a stable anymore."

"Well, that's your problem," Nash replied, slipping a hand under his jacket. "A deal's a deal."

"Then we have a problem, as I'm much in need of a translocator at the moment."

"Too bad," Nash answered with narrowed eyes.

"I figured you'd say that," James said, followed by a quick

grin.

In a split second, James' face went blank, and his body surged into motion. His hand yanked the revolver out of his holster and cocked the hammer in a single move. His finger was on the trigger before anyone could blink.

Nash had clearly expected the maneuver, and drawn a derringer simultaneously.

Armed and ready, neither man hesitated to pull the trigger. Two loud shots sounded, and both men recocked and fired again, eager to finish one another.

On any other day, under any other circumstances, one of the men would have died—perhaps both. But that wasn't the case when Sheriff Doliber was on the scene. As those bullets exited their gun barrels, the warlock sheriff froze them in mid-air with a simple spell. The bullets hung in front of their respective targets like eerie specters of doom, waiting to continue onward, into each man's face.

"All right, you've both made your point," Doliber said. "Now it's time I made mine."

"Who the hell are you?" Nash asked, trying to smack the bullets out of the air, only to have his hand bounce back with each swing.

"I'm the sheriff of this county, and you are in possession of a contraband magical device. Hand it over, and we'll be on our way."

"What?" Nash said, stepping away from the hovering bullets. "But I paid squarely for it!"

"Bet you wish you'd taken my offer of a refund," James replied jovially.

"Don't worry, you'll get your property back," Doliber answered. James started to protest, but the sheriff cut him off. "The trade was not legal, so the payment shouldn't be binding in my opinion. We could take this to court, but that might result in *other* charges being filed against both of you."

James grumbled and kicked a chair. "Fine, he can have the stable back, but I'm keeping the horses."

"One horse," Doliber replied. "You'll need it." Turning to Nash, he added, "I assume that is amenable."

"Fair enough," Nash answered, looking nervous.

"Good," Doliber said, relaxing his spell over the bullets. Without his influence over them, the lead slugs clacked harmlessly to the floor. "Now, let's see that translocator."

## Episode 6:
## Hanging Party

They were a riotous crowd, eager for blood. The mob holding the frost goblin knew what to do, and learning that Judge Raymond had just signed off on the hanging made them all the more willing to get on with it. All that stood in their way was the Marshal, who'd had a sudden change of heart. Little did they know he was under orders from the mayor, or he'd still be spoiling for an execution.

"Come on, Rodgers," a scraggly prospector grumbled and pouted. "A few minutes ago, you wuz all fer hangin' this here goblin!"

"Yes, and I still think it is guilty, but others have doubts, and I cannot ignore them. Therefore, I believe a little discretion is in order. We should lock this goblin up until we can confirm it is our killer."

The crowd shouted protests, and a muscular ranch hand shook his fist. "We don't need your say so no more, Marshal. The judge says the goblin ain't even semi-human. That means we can do whatever we like to it!"

More voices from the crowd called for a hanging, and most of the men were well armed. It seemed hazardous to obstruct them in their frenzy, so the Marshal stepped down from the front steps of the Lucca Saloon. He could say no more. The mob would do what it desired, and his opinion be damned.

"Let's string it up!" someone shouted, and the whole crowd began marching down the street. The frost goblin was trapped in the center of the mob and was dragged along with no means of escape. Death seemed to be its inevitable destination.

Joella came running up to the crowd, but couldn't even get their attention. Their focus was set, and their intentions clear. Nobody would deter them.

Spotting Marshal Rodgers at the back of the pack, Joella accosted him. "What are you doing? You were supposed to talk them down!"

"They're not much interested in talk at the moment," the Marshal remarked, keeping his eyes on the mob he was following.

Joella persisted. "You are a United States Marshal, as you're so eager to remind everyone. They *have* to listen to you."

"Apparently not," Rodgers said.

The crowd turned at the end of the street, marching around the courthouse to the gallows out back. The sturdy wooden frame was set to accommodate two at a time, though hangings were fairly rare. An occasional horse thief and a few stray bandits had swung from the heavy hemp nooses, but this would be the first goblin hanged in Selwood. The scrawny creature was lighter than most men, so there was no doubt the facilities could handle the job.

Six men marched the goblin up onto the stage and prepared the noose. The thing didn't even fight them as they slipped the rope over its head and snugged it against the throat.

It was a crying shame, but Joella could do nothing but watch. The badge pinned to her jacket didn't mean much in the face of such overwhelming opposition. The citizens en-masse were the true power, and their will would not be denied.

Two men up on the scaffold completed their adjustment of the noose and stepped back with their comrades, who lurked at the trap switch. Once the hatch mechanism was inspected and deemed functional, one of the men gripped the lever, waiting for the right moment to send the vile creature to its maker.

"You're killing an innocent being!" Joella shouted, wishing someone would listen to her.

As the tall man at the lever flexed his hands, eager to pull the switch, a group of riders came thundering around the courthouse. The crowd turned and locked their eyes on the men, and an eerie silence ensued.

Of course, the sudden arrival of the county sheriff tended to have that effect.

"What are you men up to?" Doliber demanded from atop his horse.

As the guilty mob remained silent, Joella walked over to the sheriff. "They're lynching a frost goblin," she said.

"Where in God's name did they find a frost goblin?" Doliber asked emphatically. "Those things are one step away from joining the dodo."

"You should ask the Marshal about the particulars," Joella said. "He led the posse that captured it."

"I see," Doliber said, processing the information. "Then I suppose this whole spectacle is his doing."

"I told them to cease and desist," Marshal Rodgers rebutted, storming over. "Not that it's any of your business."

"The hell it isn't." Doliber snapped the reigns of his horse and ran it straight into the tick of the crowd. Nearing the gallows, he swung his free right arm, sending a ripple of glistening magic through the air. The mystic blade sliced the rope above the frost goblin's head, freeing it from certain doom. The frightened creature stayed in place, unwilling to make a sudden move.

Doliber turned his horse around, making a small clearing amidst the mob. "Listen up! I don't care what fairy tales your mothers told you. Frost goblins are nothing more than scavengers. They don't possess magic powers, and they can't commit the sort of mass murder we found aboard that train."

"We caught it dead to rights!" a deep voice from the crowd replied.

"Gnawing on a human arm, it was," a whiny older gentleman added.

The crowd started to get spirited again, as they convinced themselves of the convenient truth. They were eager to believe that they had their killer, and they could put an end to things nice and neatly.

"Like I said, it's a scavenger," Doliber continued, "like a vulture or a rat. It could've picked that arm up anywhere, perhaps from the real killer who dropped it."

"But the Marshal swore he knew," another man said.

"The Marshal..." Doliber wanted to say "lied," but opted for a more diplomatic reply. "The Marshal was mistaken."

Whispering and mumbling erupted from the crowd, as people discussed the matter amongst one another.

"Then the real killer's still out there," someone said above the din of the crowd.

Amidst the bewildered mass, a loud snap sounded, and Doliber felt a stabbing pain in his back—the burn of hot lead as it burrowed into his flesh! The shock of the attack caused him to drop the reins and grow unbalanced in the saddle. As he fell from his mount, he wondered how this was possible. His mystic wards should have protected him from such an attack by summoning a force barrier to deflect it. There were only a few firearms capable of countering his brand of magic; the guns he'd personally enchanted for his most trusted allies!

The shocking truth struck him as he hit the ground. He'd been shot by one of his own weapons. Only a handful of Selwood's most upstanding citizens were entrusted with such guns. How could one of them turn against him so wickedly?

A new wave of anger and confusion washed over the crowd. More than half of the men were outraged or concerned about the underhanded assault against their sheriff, while a sizeable minority took it as an excuse to run. Amidst all the confusion, it was unclear where the shot had come from, or who had fired it.

Ron jumped off his horse and ran over to Doliber as the crowd thinned. Suddenly, a new series of shots sounded, and Ron flinched, fearing the assassin was firing anew, but the true shooter turned out to have an angry Southern accent.

"You Yankee cowards!" James shouted as he fired at some fleeing cowboys. "Shoot a man in the back! You all oughta die!" A few of the cowboys fell, as James' bullets struck them.

"Woodson, stop!" Doliber struggled to shout.

In seconds, Joella was on top of things. Running up behind James, she whacked him over the head with the butt of her pistol, knocking him out cold.

The mob continued to disperse as Ron and a few concerned citizens came to Doliber's aid. All the while, Marshal Rodgers shouted orders, seeking to regain control over the situation. A few of his men listened, and helped to restrain the frost goblin, which looked ready to bolt amidst the chaos.

Doliber's back felt wet, and he knew it was his own blood soaking through his shirt. His arms were shaking and his legs were feeling cold. It couldn't be a good sign.

"Hang in there, Doliber," Ron urged as two men lifted the sheriff off the ground. "We'll get you to the doctor."

Doliber thought about saying something, but he was so tired. Better to keep his mouth shut and get some sleep.

* * *

Ron was used to the sight of blood. He'd seen enough of it over the years that it didn't bother him much anymore, but today was different. This blood wasn't from some bandit or outlaw. It belonged to a friend.

Doctor Wilson pulled the forceps out of the wound in Doliber's back, extracting a small metal slug. He dropped the lead into a surgical pan and washed the wound with another splash of whiskey before stitching it up.

"What's the verdict, Doc?" Ron asked as he walked up to the table.

"He's lost a lot of blood," Wilson replied in a dull monotone.

Ron felt like smacking him for giving such a vague and non-committal response. If the odds weren't good, why didn't he just say so? People had a bad habit of avoiding the obvious and sugar-coating cow dung. In Ron's opinion, the ugly truth couldn't be made beautiful with semantics, and folks ought to just be up front about it.

Avoiding reality was one problem Ron had never had. He'd always told it like it was, and expected the same of others. Facing the truth no matter how nasty was the story of his life. It didn't make him the most popular dwarf on Earth, but it made him practical.

It also meant he couldn't deny the likelihood that Doliber would die.

Ron stood there, looking at the sheriff's blank expression. Less than three months ago, this man had coerced Ron into his service, but it hadn't taken long for the dwarf to realize how important and worthwhile that service could be. After all they'd been through in such a short amount of time, they were now close colleagues. Working together, they'd seen so much, gone so far. It wasn't an exaggeration to say they'd even saved the world together.

Now, Doliber lay here on his death bed. What a crying shame.

Ron wasn't one for sentimentality—at least, he would never admit to any—so it astonished him how attached he'd become to his current station in life. This land, this life, this boss; he didn't like the idea of losing any of it. Yet, that unwanted change seemed inevitable, and what made it worse still was the nature of the change. It was all so pointless—a senseless act of betrayal.

Ron promised himself, no matter what happened, that he'd find the man who'd done this, and give them a traitor's death.

"Grimes," a voice echoed inside Ron's mind.

Ron looked around, startled by the sound. He saw Doctor Wilson washing blood off his hands over by a shaded window, but nobody else was around. The voice repeated, and he recognized who it was.

"Doliber," Ron replied vocally, drawing Wilson's attention.

"Don't speak," Doliber replied telepathically. "There isn't much time. There are things that must be done, things only you can do. Listen carefully."

\* \* \*

Joella found herself waiting alone.

The doctor's parlor was neat and orderly, with a few paintings hanging on the walls. It would have been a nice place to visit, if not for the reason she was here. Waiting to hear word of Doliber's condition was nerve-wracking. They'd been in there for over an hour, Ron and Doc Wilson. If they were taking so long, it was most likely bad news.

A door opened, and for a moment Joella's heart jumped, thinking it might be the doctor coming to share some good news. Though, her hopes faded when she realized it was the outside door, and she saw the spectacled face of the town's chief telegraph operator, Henry Currant.

"How's he doing?" Henry asked, taking a seat beside Joella.

"I have no idea," Joella replied, slouching in worry. "They haven't told me anything yet." Wishing to change the subject and take her mind off the tragedy, she asked, "How are things outside?"

"They're getting things covered. The Marshal's recruits have rounded up a few suspects, and locked up the two men Doliber and Grimes brought back with them from who knows where."

"Have you asked those two about it?" Joella asked.

"Oh, plenty of us have asked, but neither man is talking. Somebody said they might be punchers from the Silcox spread, up on the Flat."

"If so, Silcox has got some explaining to do," Joella said. "What about that Woodson fellow?"

"He's still out cold," Henry replied. "The Marshal's got his eye on him, won't let him out of his sight."

"The man did wound three people with that shooting frenzy," Joella mentioned.

"True, but I have the feeling it's more than that. The Marshal's pretty eager to question him about something, but he's keeping pretty quiet, too."

"I wouldn't mind getting in on an interrogation or two," Joella said, troubled by the holes in her knowledge. What had Ron and Doliber been doing all morning, and who were the strange men they'd brought back? In all the madness, Ron hadn't told her, and Doliber obviously couldn't at the moment. Of all the things that irked her, ignorance was the worst.

At times like these, Joella regretted not having telepathic abilities. Everyone else in her family had some sort of mental talent, whether it was basic mind-reading or remote viewing. Yet, she had none. Her only mystical talents involved teleportation, and that was somewhat limited. What she wouldn't give now to spy on the operating room, or sneak into Woodson's mind for answers.

Alas, she was condemned to wait for answers, like everyone else.

"He'll be all right," Henry assured her, seeing the worried look on her face. "The sheriff always pulls through."

Joella wanted to believe him, though in her heart she couldn't repel her doubts. Over the last few months, she'd come to respect and admire Doliber in so many ways. His mastery of magic had made him seem invulnerable, the perfect lawman that no bullet could harm. It was hard to see such a good man fall, and she didn't want to face it.

Needing to get back to work, Henry patted Joella's shoulder and left. The Telegraph Office wouldn't run itself, and his assistant was still pretty green.

Once again, Joella found herself alone with her own thoughts, with nothing to do but worry and wonder.

The time passed slowly, and it seemed like days before the door to the operating room creaked open. Lifting her head, Joella saw Ron's stout form stomping out. From the solemn look on his face, she already knew what he was going to say.

"No," she whispered, as if her hopeful denial could change reality.

"He's dead," Ron said blankly.

Joella stood up and stormed over to the operating room door. "I want to see him."

"You can't," Ron said, pulling her away. She shoved him aside and grabbed the door knob, but it wouldn't open. The doctor must have locked it from the other side.

"Why?" Joella asked, tears welling up in her eyes.

"Nobody's allowed to see the body, not until it's properly prepared."

"What does that mean, *'properly prepared?'*"

"It's a stupid Guild thing. Some highfaluting warlock has to show up and perform some mystic rites. While we wait for that to happen, we have a job to do."

"How's that?" Joella asked, finding herself growing distraught. Doliber was dead, and in her mind her deputization had died with him. She had no desire to continue—at least, not immediately. She needed time to mourn, and when that was over she doubted the next sheriff would be interested in having a female deputy, elf or otherwise.

"Doliber may not be around, but we've still got our badges and our orders. We owe it to him to complete our mission, and bring his shooter to justice."

Ron's gruff and grumbling diatribe wasn't much of a pep-talk, but Joella knew he was right. Deep in her heart, she wanted to keep going, and assure that Doliber's death did not go unavenged. "You're right," she said, wiping her tears. "Where do we go from here?"

"First we see Judge Raymond," Ron said. "Then we're going to have a little chat with the Marshal about jurisdiction."

\* \* \*

Marshal Rodgers flipped open the full box of cigars sitting on Doliber's desk. They were cheap, nothing fancy, but it had been a while since he'd had a smoke. Rodgers stuck one of the brown tubes in his mouth and searched the desk for a match, but couldn't find one. Of course, Doliber didn't need matches to light his cigars. Damn warlocks and their magic tricks! He tossed the cigar on the floor in frustration, deciding he could continue to live without tobacco.

The cells at the Sheriff's Office were packed. After the shooting, Marshal Rodgers had taken the most trusted members of his posse and arrested the less respectable volunteers. Some threats had been made, but nobody else was shot during the arresting-spree.

Now, two dozen men populated the cells, but only one really interested Rodgers, and that man had nothing to do with the attempted assassination. The mysterious "Woodson" who'd arrived at the hanging with Doliber looked suspiciously familiar, and the Marshal wanted to get to the bottom of that mystery before continuing with anything else.

The man began to stir, but the Marshal decided he needed a little additional stimulation to bring him around. Grabbing a glass of water off the desk, he tossed it in Woodson's face.

"Wake up," Rodgers ordered, setting the empty glass down but staying on his feet. "It's answer time."

Woodson blinked his moistened eyelids and tried to move his arms to wipe his face, only to find his wrists were tied to the chair. He struggled vainly a little before shooting the Marshal a bitter glare.

"What do you want?" Woodson grumbled.

"For a start, what the notorious outlaw Jesse James is doing alive and well in Nevada, running around with the Nye County sheriff."

"I'm afraid you've mistaken me for someone else."

"Bull," Rodgers said, locking eyes with the man.

Seeing there was no sense denying it further, Jesse James smiled and asked, "What gave me away?"

"I've seen enough wanted posters of you, and by God you sure do resemble Jesse Woodson James. Couple that with the rumors I've heard about a 'James Woodson' roaming around the mining camps west of the Yucca Flat. To be fair, I hadn't given those rumors much credence before seeing you for myself."

"Perhaps it would be best if you forgot you did," Jesse suggested, "especially considering that I'm already dead."

"Can't do that," Rodgers said with a sour inflection. "You've killed a few too many good men for me to let you walk."

Jesse scoffed at the assertion. "Weren't too many good men among them. Yankee carpetbaggers and Pinkerton thugs, mostly. Either way, I never killed except out of necessity."

"You wouldn't have had a necessity, if you hadn't gone stealing," Rodgers countered. "Don't play innocent with me. You used your personal grudge against the Union to justify robbery and murder, and that sure doesn't make you Robin Hood."

"Sounds like you're one of them Yankee Carpetbaggers, yourself."

"You're damn right," Rodgers said. "I served under General Sherman during the war, and fought to rid the world of the small minded whims of you secessionists. Too bad we missed a few."

"So, how's it going to be?" Jesse asked. "You gonna keep me tied up until Sheriff Doliber is back in good health, or just shoot me?"

"Actually, I'm hoping to hang you before long, right and legal," Rodgers said with a straight face.

Jesse tried to keep his mouth shut, but after a few moments he burst out laughing.

"You think I won't?" Rodgers asked, insulted by the outburst.

After regaining control of himself, Jesse explained. "If you do hang me, I expect I'll be back in time for breakfast."

"How do you figure that?" Rodgers demanded.

"He's a shadowganger," a familiar voice announced.

Marshal Rodgers turned toward the front door and spotted Ron and Joella entering the office. The dwarf clomped over to the desk and sat down in the chair behind it. "Somebody was angry enough to cast an atonement tether on his sorry soul." He followed up with a smile.

"Superstitious nonsense," Rodgers countered, unwilling to believe in it.

"Doliber didn't think so," Ron said, losing the joy from his expression.

Rodgers frowned at the comment, but bit his tongue. Mention of the sheriff was an easy way to vex him, and that petulant little dwarf knew it. The Marshal had never cared for Doliber, largely because of the man's connection to that Guild of his. Manipulation of magical forces was beyond the Marshal's understanding, and much of it seemed contrary to rational thought. Part fear, part resentment, it all merged into a thorough dislike of all spell casters, certified warlock or not.

Rodgers couldn't stand Doliber because of who he was. The sheriff was a rogue element posing as a law officer, and therefore couldn't be trusted. The loyalties of anyone in a secret society like the Guild had no business being in such a vital and sacred position of trust and authority, in Rodgers' opinion.

Despite his personal feelings, the Marshal still had to work with the warlock sheriff, so feigning concern he added, "How is Doliber?"

"Dead," Ron said morosely.

There was no cheer in the Marshal's eyes to hear the news. The death of any lawman was no cause for celebration. Though, while it didn't please him, it did appear to make his job easier. With Doliber out of the way, he would be in charge, undisputedly, and could control the aspects of the current investigations without dissenting opinions taking precedence.

"Well, as troubling as this turn happens to be, I hope you will both continue to serve in the interim, and help me get to the bottom of the train murders, as well as Doliber's shooting," Rodgers said, seeking to be diplomatic. Honestly, he needed all the help he could get.

"We'll be staying on, that's for sure," Ron said, digging a folded sheet of paper out of his vest pocket. "Only not in the capacity you might favor."

Rodgers took the paper from the dwarf and read it. The letter was penned by Judge Raymond, and cited State Statutes regarding legal authority and the appointment of sheriffs. The letter of the law was spelled out in black and white, but the Marshal could hardly believe what he was reading. "This can't be," he said, bewildered.

"Yes, it is," Ron said, regaining a certain smugness. "I'm the new sheriff."

Rodgers wiped the surprise off his face and tried to appear confident again. "Well, no matter. I am a federal law officer, after all. I will continue to head-up this investigation."

"Under my supervision," Ron corrected. "This is my town, and my county. All lawmen answer to me now."

"The devil they do!" Rodgers shouted, losing his cool. "I am the Marshal. My authority comes directly from Washington!"

"And mine comes from the State of Nevada, and according to the Constitution that authority supercedes yours."

Rodgers bent down to stare into the dwarf's face. "You sound like a no good secessionist," he sneered.

"Funny," Ron replied. "I fought for the Union, as I recall."

"So did I," the Marshal said, straightening up.

"Then you're used to taking orders," Ron said. "Now, cut James loose, and go get your posse. We'll be hitting the trail in the morning."

Rodgers couldn't believe he was being ordered around by Doliber's former lackey, a hairy midge! He wasn't going to take it lightly. "Free him yourself, and get your own posse," he said, storming out of the office.

As the Marshal left, Joella removed the six-inch bowie knife she always kept under her jacket and used it to cut the ropes holding Jesse to the chair.

"Much obliged, ma'am," Jesse replied, rubbing his wrists. Once his legs were free, he stood up in a hurry. "Now, if you'll excuse me, I believe I'd best get out of town before that Yankee Marshal comes back with his friends."

"You're not going anywhere," Ron said, standing up to block Jesse's retreat. Though nearly two feet shorter than the outlaw, the dwarf was able to make himself seem imposing. "Dead or not,

Sheriff Doliber is still your boss, understand?"

Jesse James looked down at the little man, reading his body language as the practiced student of human behavior that he was. Dwarves were basically the same as humans in regards to mannerisms and emotions, so he could tell what Ron was getting at, and knew how serious he was.

"We're both going to see this thing through for him, agreed?" Ron pushed.

"Agreed," Jesse replied, slipping a hand into his pants pocket nonchalantly. "Say, you're not really a Yankee fighter, are you?"

"Drafted," Ron said, failing to disclose how eager he had been to fight. At eighteen, he'd been eager to preserve the Union, though he wasn't about to admit it to a proud rebel.

"Well, in the spirit of cooperation, I will forgive your unwitting sin. Can I have my guns back?"

"As soon as I'm confident you aren't going to shoot any innocent bystanders," Ron said.

"Innocent, my ass!" Jesse burst out. He took a breath and calmed himself before continuing. "I'm sorry if I overreacted, but I do take great offense at seeing a man shot in the back, for obvious reasons."

Joella chose that moment to chime in. "Personally, I'm glad somebody did something. As far as I'm concerned, most of the men in that mob were willing accomplices to Doliber's murder."

Jesse faced her and nodded appreciatively. "Why, thank you again. I do not believe we've been properly introduced."

"Joella Grimes-Talus," she replied, offering him a hand to shake.

In chivalrous form, Jesse took her hand and kissed it. "Pleased to make your acquaintance. Knowing elf custom as I do, Grimes would be your husband's name, correct?" he said, glancing over at the dwarf.

"Yes, Ron is my husband," Joella confirmed. "You seem surprised."

"I have many elf cousins," Jesse explained. "While some are willing to pair themselves with humanity, I have never met one interested in marrying a dwarf."

"Our relationship is complicated, and private," Joella

answered.

"In that case, I shall pry no further," Jesse said.

"Good," Ron said in his regular, dismissive tone. He went over to the desk and began opening drawers until he found one containing pistols. Removing four of the firearms, he handed two to Jesse and said, "Come on, we've got work to do."

As Jesse examined his returned weapons, Ron examined the two he'd kept for himself. The bulky Colt single actions had never been his style, though they'd served Doliber well enough. After removing the Hopkins and Allen revolvers he'd borrowed from his would-be kidnappers, he strapped Doliber's spare gun belt around his waist. They still didn't feel right. He was eager to get his own pistol back, the trusty Remington that had never let him down. Whether he could do that without bloodshed was still anyone's guess. It would all depend on Silcox.

Ron and Jesse headed for the door, and Joella moved to follow them, but the dwarf quickly stopped her. "Not you, Joella," he said.

"No, you're not sticking me here," Joella protested. "I need to get out there and help!"

"Someone's got to stay here and guard the prisoners."

"Anyone can guard the cells," Joella complained. "Pick any of the names on Doliber's trusted citizens list."

"Problem is, one of those 'trusted citizens' shot him," Ron said. "At this point, we don't know who to trust. It's just you, me, and Jesse James."

Hearing his name, Jesse took the opportunity to reinsert himself into the conversation. "I'd gladly stay behind, though the Marshal might feel inclined to haul me away. Though, perhaps you would be more suited to guard duty, Mr. Grimes. The lady and I could go out, instead. No need to delegate such a lowly task to a beautiful woman, after all."

"Thank you, Mr. James," Joella said appreciatively.

"No deal," Ron countered. "Joella's got all the qualifications to safeguard the jail cells until we get back. You and me, we've got a tougher job to take care of."

"What job is that?" Jesse asked as he opened the front door.

"We've got to deal with a devil."

## Episode 7:
## Death on the Flat

It was hot and desolate on Yucca Flat, an arid waste of sparse vegetation—a no man's land where even the wildlife was nothing to speak of. Though, in recent years, people had come. A handful of ranches had sprung up in this inhospitable place, bringing with them herds of special cattle designed for the desert terrain.

The Sandy Cows, or "Sandies," were almost indistinguishable from ordinary bovines, except for their curled, ram-like horns and their ability to live on dirt. These magically engineered cattle could feed off the minerals in the sand and dust of the hottest desert, though they preferred to snack on cacti and tumbleweeds where available. Water wasn't an issue, as they had the unnatural ability to condense moisture straight from the air through their mouths. Modern science called the creatures impossible, but the mystic arts had made them a reality, nonetheless.

Introduction of this new breed was bringing life to the wastelands, turning places like Nye County into a booming place for ranching. While mining was often an unstable and fleeting concern, raising cattle was a constant that enticed people to put down roots.

Dale Forgison trotted along the range, surveying the free-range herd with his co-worker, the gruff Max Bellair. Both men were hired hands of the Silcox Ranch. Old man Silcox had been the first to introduce the Sandies to Nevada, and now he owned half of Yucca Flat, with his eye on acquiring the rest of it. That didn't sit too well with the dozens of small ranches that bordered his vast spread, as they weren't keen on selling out.

Silcox wasn't one to take no for an answer. As it stood, his men were under orders to seize any opportunity to cut the competition, though most of the time they were too busy performing their honest jobs to harass the neighbors.

Dale and Max had the good fortune to be watching one of the center spreads, far away from any property lines. They wouldn't have to hassle with any moral quandaries, or feel they were disobeying their boss. For the time being, all they had to do was mind the herd without any funny business.

A commotion caught Dale's attention. A cow was snorting and shaking its head near the ground, and by the time he got over to it the young animal had collapsed.

Seeking an explanation, Dale hopped down from his horse to investigate. Checking the cow over, he soon found the culprit.

"What happened?" Max asked as he arrived, reigning his dark horse to a halt.

Dale hauled the torn carcass of a snake from the cow's mouth. "The dumb thing tried to eat a rattlesnake."

Max made an amused sound. "I didn't rightly know there was any of them rattlers around the Flat."

Dale just shook his head. Max had been riding this range for over a year now, and the old geezer still didn't know the wildlife. The white-haired Texan was an absent minded fellow, never minding his surroundings. His inattention bordered on idiocy, and if he didn't know a fair share about animal husbandry and gunplay, he'd have been just about useless.

"Aw, she'll be okay," Max remarked about the cow. "Venom will make her sleep fer a few hours, but then she'll be right as rain."

"Speaking of rain, I could use a drink about now," Dale mentioned, grabbing the canteen off his horse. He took several good swigs, wishing he could down the whole thing. The heat of the day was just starting, so he had to conserve on fluids. It would be hours before they hit another watering hole.

It was a rough life, but Dale was used to it. He'd grown up

all over the frontier, as his father roamed around, looking for work while trying to land "the big score." He'd seen ranches and mining camps straight from Missouri to California, and worked alongside men twice his age since as long as he could remember. Nothing much in the way of possessions, so long as he had a job that fed him, he was satisfied.

Another commotion started amongst the herd, only much farther away. A few dozen head of cattle began snorting and stampeding off in the distance, and there was something else, a pale figure roughly the size of a man. It was beating on one of the cows, and the animal promptly collapsed under the assault.

"Did that son of a bitch just knife one o' our herd?" Max asked, squinting his eyes to study the distant scene.

"Better go find out," Dale said, spurring his horse to a run.

The horses crossed the short distance like lightning, and as the two men approached they saw a horrific sight. The cow that had been stabbed was being torn apart, its blood and meat spread out upon the sandy ground. The pale attacker continued to burrow into the flesh of the animal like a vicious dog, hiding its head within the cow's stomach. It wasn't until the men were within striking distance that the vicious being poked its head out to see the approaching cattlemen.

"Jay-zuss!" Max exclaimed.

The bony creature may have held the general shape of a human, but its skeletal form and bony protrusions were far different. The sunken eye sockets and protruding cheeks glistened as the blood of the cow dripped from its face. The evil grin on its sharp fangs shouted danger.

"That some kinda hairless werewolf?" Max asked, drawing his Colt.

"Never heard of one," Dale said, reaching for his own pistol.

"Ain't never heard o' nothin' like that, neither," Max said, firing at the creature.

The shot was accurate, and struck the creature directly in the forehead. Where a bullet would ordinarily punch right through bone and brain matter, that was not the case against this beast. While the skin peeled away, the bone was too dense to crack from the hot lead, and seconds after the blow the skin healed over the wound, leaving no mark at all.

Frightened to see his shot deflected, Max kept firing, and Dale joined him, blasting the creature with a dozen rounds from their respective guns. Some bullets ricocheted off bone, while others sank into soft flesh, yet none had any lasting impact on the terrible thing.

Responding to the attack, the creature leapt at Max's horse, killing it with two swipes of its long talons. Max collapsed with the falling horse, but managed to roll and avoid injury.

Dale wasn't about to leave his partner there to face the creature alone, but he knew they had to get away. "Come on," he said, offering Max a hand.

"Naw, that horse can't run with two," Max said, pulling the knife from his belt. "Go on and git. I'll deal with this little darling."

Dale wanted to argue, but his good sense told him to run. Whipping his horse around, he forced it into a gallop, fearing for his life like never before. He looked back to see Max sparring with the pale creature, deflecting its clawed arms with great skill, but there was no way he could hold out against such a foe. The next time Dale glanced back, he saw the old man lying on the ground, and the creature crouched over him.

This thing wasn't anything an ordinary cowpuncher could kill. He needed to get back to the ranch, tell old man Silcox what had happened. If anybody would believe him, maybe they'd be able to get the right kind of help before the killer struck again.

* * *

"Would you stop that scratching?" Ron complained.

Jesse James pulled the hand away from his face and returned it to the reins of his horse. "You should've given me time to shave," he responded, feeling the tingling return to his chin.

"I told you we'd be heading out in the morning," Ron said. "It's not my fault you don't get up before dawn."

"And it's not mine that you wear that carpet down to your ribs."

The men hadn't said much during the morning's ride across the arid expanse. It had taken them two hours to reach Yucca Junction on horseback, and the Silcox ranch house was twenty miles northeast of that. They were down to the last few miles and their individual idiosyncrasies were grating on one another. Of course, their divergent backgrounds were bound to cause trouble, and Ron wondered how long it would be before the Rebel outlaw decided to turn the tables on him.

Coming over the sandy hill they'd been climbing, the landscape took an abrupt turn for the better. Where the desolate wastes had greeted them the whole way, now before them sat a lush, green oasis nestled within a bowl-shaped valley. A small field of tall grass waved with the breeze on either side of the road leading up to a palatial ranch that more resembled a wealthy plantation house than a western farm. A small orchard was planted all around the western quarter of the valley, and beyond the house and barn, the foliage turned to thickets of ponderosa pines and blue spruce.

"This sure looks like a civilized spread," Jesse remarked, slowing his horse to stare at the scenery.

"Silcox must have a freelance magician on staff," Ron said, unable to fully fathom the number of spells required to maintain such an environment in the dry land. That element left him wary of the ranch mogul's true power, and what he'd do when confronted about the past day's scurrilous actions.

Before they could get halfway across the lawn, a pair of armed riders came out from the ranch to greet the new arrivals. Ron flashed his badge and asked to see Albert Silcox. The riders agreed, but maintained a chilly exterior as they escorted Ron and Jesse to the old man, who was taking lunch on the back porch.

"Ah, Deputy Grimes," Silcox greeted the dwarf as he marched up onto the porch.

"Mr. Silcox?" Ron greeted, having never met the man before. He was surprised that the ranch tycoon knew him, and it certainly left him at a disadvantage.

"Please, call me Albert. Have a seat, Deputy."

"It's *sheriff* now," Ron said with a twinge of resentment. "Doliber was shot yesterday."

"Sad news," Silcox said, sounding mildly concerned. He picked up a tray containing sandwiches and offered them to Ron and Jesse. Neither man accepted.

"Afraid we've got no time for idle pleasantries," Ron said.

"Oh," Silcox said with obvious disappointment.   "So, what can I do for you?"

"I reckon you have something that belongs to me, namely a Remington revolver your employees stole from me yesterday."

"Former employees," Silcox corrected.   He snapped his fingers, and one of the armed escorts clomped over.   Silcox whispered in his ear and the man hurried into the house as the old man continued.   "Believe me, I had no foreknowledge of their activities, and have discharged every man involved."

"Really?" Ron said dubiously.

"Of course.  Do you really believe that I would sanction the kidnapping of lawmen as part of some petty personal vendetta? I'm a businessman and a gentleman.  I have no time for such illicit trifles."

"Then why'd Spencer and Byron say you were in on it; that you'd smooth things over when they rode us back to Selwood?"

"I   fear   they   misjudged   their   importance   among   my operations," Silcox said.

Ron didn't believe him entirely, but accepted that the old man was smart enough to be covering his ass in the aftermath. Things hadn't gone as planned for the kidnappers, and it didn't serve to side with them now.  Still, it was hard to believe such a complex and dastardly plan could have been undertaken without his knowledge and endorsement.

"Nice spread you've got here," Jesse remarked after a terse silence.

"Indeed, uh, mister..."

"James. Deputy James," the outlaw said with pleasure.

"Yes, Mister James, this is a fine setup I've built, and much of it with my own two hands.  The plants and other greenery you see is what I personally planted.  I've done my best to bring a touch of comfort to this otherwise inhospitable land."

"A lot of work for your little oasis," Ron said.  "Some might ask why you wasted all the effort to build in the middle of nowhere.  Why not set up shop somewhere more friendly, like in Oregon, or just up-state a piece?  There must have been plenty of good  claims  waiting  to  be  snatched  up  back  when  you  started here."

"And why would I want to be anywhere else?" Silcox asked, looking a bit insulted.

"Oh, I just figured you might've liked someplace with a bit more real water," Ron said.

"Where's the challenge in that?" Silcox asked, grabbing a glass of brown liquid sitting on a nearby table. He took a sip and continued. "Any ordinary man can eek out a mediocre living plowing the fields where nature provides, but it takes true ambition and wherewithal to bring life to a lifeless place. Can you not see the shining jewel here, amidst the wastes?"

"I can only imagine the expense to create and maintain it," Ron remarked, knowing how pricey freelance magicians tended to be. A place like this had to have a full time caretaker, and daily magic treatments to keep it from blowing away with the sand.

"It is no more expensive than any other ranch of comparable size. As I said, this is all the fruit of my own labors."

Ron's eyes flashed with surprise, as another piece of the puzzle fell into place. "You're a warlock?" he asked, knowing such extensive magical abilities were hard to find outside of the Guild.

"Unofficially," Silcox replied. "Even as a child, I was gifted with certain talents, though I didn't have the opportunity to attend a Guild Academy. My skills are my own."

While Ron continued to consider the implications, a ranch hand returned with his Remington, and the pair of Colts Doliber had been wearing at the time of their abduction. The weapons appeared undamaged, though they had been unloaded.

"I hope you will accept my sincere apologies for the actions of my former employees," Silcox said as Ron put on his gun belt and removed the loaner guns he'd taken from the Sheriff's Office.

Under the circumstances, Ron felt he had no alternative. There were more pressing matters to attend, and he could live with the satisfaction of having Silcox's lackeys pay. Those directly involved with perpetrating the plot would be nailed to the wall, and if one of their associates had shot Doliber they'd all hang.

For now, Ron was just happy to have his favorite gun back.

Ron considered their business at the ranch finished, and was about to take his leave when a new rider came charging around the house. Once the horse swung around in front of the porch, the rider yanked it to an abrupt stop and hopped off in a hurry. The man was frantic as he climbed the steps and rushed over to speak to Silcox.

"Forgison, what's the matter, man?" Silcox asked as the youthful rider gasped for breath. "You're supposed to be watching the center spread with Bellair."

"Max is dead," Dale said urgently, clutching his knees for support. "Some... *thing* killed him."

"A thing?" Ron asked.

Dale looked at his employer, seeking permission to continue in front of the strangers.

"Go ahead, Forgison, tell the sheriff here all about it."

Dale's face twisted up in a dubious expression. "Sheriff? You?"

"Yep," Ron said smugly.

Dale's momentary surprise at the dwarf sheriff faded quickly, and Silcox asked him to sit down as he related his tale. The young cowpuncher was careful to stick to the facts and tried not to exaggerate anything. The story was pretty fantastic on its own, and didn't need embellishment.

As Dale wrapped up his story, Ron had a sick feeling growing in his gut. After all he'd heard recently, all the facts he and Doliber had been able to uncover, this new creature could very well be what they were looking for.

"You say this thing had claws?" Ron asked for clarity. "About yea big?" he held up his thumb and forefinger.

"Half the length of each finger, yeah," Dale replied.

"Have you heard of such a creature before?" Silcox asked, looking at Ron with suspicion.

"Maybe," Ron said, standing up. "We'd better check this out." He waved for Jesse to get up and follow him.

"Perhaps you're right," Silcox said, climbing out of his chair and turning to one of his ranch hands. "Saddle Reba, and get my Henry," he ordered.

The man nodded and disappeared into the house to fulfill the request.

"You treat all of your hands like servants?" Ron asked, feeling a tinge of resentment for the man's tone.

"Only when necessary," Silcox said.

Ron and Jesse headed off the porch and unhitched their horses from the rail. They were mounted and ready to ride, but waited for Silcox's horse to arrive.

"You sure you want to ride out with us?" Ron asked, wishing he'd change his mind. The wealthy cattleman was a rogue element with questionable motivations.

"This is my range, and I'll be the one to defend it," Silcox answered. Turning to the man still sitting on the porch, he shouted, "Forgison, get down here!"

"Sir, you know whereabouts we was," Dale said, fighting back a stammer. "Do you really need me to come along?"

"If you want to keep your job I do," Silcox stated.

Dale fidgeted a little, but came down and got on his horse. It didn't seem like he'd be much good if they ran into trouble, but men did have a way of surprising you in the thick of it. At the very least, he'd be an extra snack to distract whatever creature they found.

"Get off that thing," Silcox grumbled to his subordinate. "He's all played out. Go get a fresh mount from the stable!"

Dale snapped the reigns and trotted his exhausted horse over to the stable, where he quickly exchanged it for a fresh ride.

Ron thought about the story Dale had told, and the fact that his partner had died. Though the young man said his older companion had sacrificed himself willingly, the presence of a dead man left no credible witnesses to corroborate the claim. An old adage from his childhood came to mind; you don't need to outrun the bear, just the other guy being chased by it. Though a cowardly tactic, it was often effective.

After a few minutes, Silcox's horse arrived. Reba was a jet-black mare with a stubby body and long legs, which made her look like a pony on stilts. Though awkward, she was young and fast, so the old man was devoted to her. "I named her after my late wife, as they've got about the same temperament. This girl will never do me wrong."

Reba was saddled and ready to go, but Silcox double-checked everything. He took exceptionally long checking the well-used Henry rifle. The firearm might have seen service in the Civil War from the amount of wear on it. There was hardly a speck of finish left on the wood or metal, though it obviously was in working order. He cycled the action a couple of times, and then loaded it before sticking it back into its rawhide scabbard.

They hit the trail, and Dale led the way through the orchard and up a gradual slope that led back to the sands of the Yucca Flat. It was a sudden change at the crest of the hill—one minute, they were surrounded by apple trees and meadow grass, the next, sand and rock dominated the landscape for as far as the eye could see. Miles of nothing welcomed them into the heart of Silcox's spread.

The trail was ill-defined, as the sand blew around and the rocks didn't hold tracks. Landmarks were mostly in the distance, hills and mountains that you'd be hard pressed to reach in a day. A few dips and valleys pocked the flat terrain, though it was difficult to tell position from them, as they all looked similar. Silcox knew where they were heading, though, as did Dale Forgison.

An hour's ride didn't change much, though Dale said they were getting close. "The herd's up ahead there, see?" He pointed to a few specks in the distance. They might have just been a bunch of rocks from the looks of them, but they were several miles away.

They kept going, trying not to push the horses too hard in the hot sun. As they got closer, the animals Dale said were cattle appeared pretty still. If they were the herd, they weren't roaming very much. The reason for their inactivity became clear as the men rode up to the many limp carcasses lying on the Flat. Blood and entrails were strewn about the large bodies. Nothing stirred, and the kills were still fresh.

"My God," Silcox mumbled, eyeing the herd. "Two hundred head lost, at least!"

"Yeah, never mind the man," Ron grumbled, directing his horse away from Silcox. The dwarf felt like surveying the slaughter without the wealthy cattleman's commentary. Though, he couldn't ditch his deputy.

"What you figure did something like this?" Jesse asked. "Werewolf, maybe?"

"Nah, I've seen werewolves," Ron replied, remembering a

short and hectic encounter with the creatures a few months back. "This is something completely different."

"Over there!" Dale shouted, pointing toward the far side of the herd.

Ron squinted hard to see across the distance, and spotted something white and red wiggling around behind one of the dead cows.

The four men rode over toward the movement, watching for any sudden change. As they neared, they could see its arms lifting and falling, as it hacked at the cow's flesh with its clawed hands. Most of its white skin was covered in blood, as it continued to flail in a wild fury.

"Careful," Dale mentioned as they got closer. "That thing took a dozen bullets, and it didn't even slow her down."

"Her?" Silcox asked.

"She's got the parts, Sir," Dale answered.

"I don't care if she's got the finest rack west of the Mississippi," Jesse said. "Let's figure out how to kill this bitch." Without warning, he drew his revolver and fired at the creature, managing a solid hit to her chest, which quickly drew her attention.

"Damn it, James!" Ron shouted as the lady creature hyperventilated into a hissing chant.

After working herself up into a fit, the creature charged forward at the riders, darting across the ground with lightning speed. As she came within a few feet of the horses, she leapt forward and stabbed both sets of claws into the chest of Reba. The dark mare snorted and collapsed with Silcox still in the saddle.

As the horse rolled over onto Silcox, Dale turned around. "You don't pay me enough to git myself killed," he said, snapping the reins to run away.

The bony female creature turned her attention to the fleeing target, and slashed the hind quarters out of the horse before Dale could get thirty feet. He managed to hang onto the saddle's horn as his ride dropped out from under him, and with adrenaline-amplified strength he leapt clear of the animal, into the waiting arms of the slaughtering beast. His scream only lasted a second, as the sharp talons quickly tore out his throat.

Jesse sent another bullet at the creature, but it deflected

against bone. "Serves him right trying to run like that."

Several more bullets did nothing but aggravate the bloody hag, who charged forward and leapt onto Jesse's horse. The claws tore the outlaw's face apart, cheek bones shredding like paper under her furious fingers.

As Jesse's lifeless body slid from the saddle, Ron pulled out his Remington, wondering what good it would do against this frightening foe. "Damn it, Doliber, I could really use your help about now," he said. But no help was coming, and he knew it.

Nowhere to run and no way to hide, Ron knew he was about to die. He wasn't going to do it sitting down, either, so as the creature hacked up Jesse's body, the dwarf hopped down onto the ground and stood on his own two feet, ready to face his demise standing.

The lead balls blew out of Ron's revolver, each one striking the skeletal creature with precision. Three landed right between the eyes, and three more went for the heart—at least, where a heart would be if the creature shared humanoid anatomy. If it had any vital organs, they weren't harmed by the shots, and the angered creature moved toward her next target. Ron deflected her initial swings with his pistol, but she was incredibly strong, and knocked the empty weapon from his grasp. The next blow was a slap against his chest that sent the dwarf onto his back.

The horrific lady creature stood over him, sunken eyes staring down at him with bestial passion. "Life!" she seemed to hiss as she raised one arm, preparing to strike. Before the blow came down, a bright light smacked into the creature's belly, and she staggered away from Ron, screeching madly. A second blow made her cringe and pant, hugging her belly as if she'd been stabbed.

Ron rolled to his feet and looked over at Albert Silcox, crouched beside his dead horse, flailing bolts of light at the vicious creature.

"These are heavy stun bolts," Silcox said, throwing another at the creature. "One ought to be enough to paralyze a horse for hours."

Looking over at the creature, Ron saw she was only dazed by the blows. Was it pain she felt, or simply frustration at having her strength sapped?

"Got anything stronger?" Ron asked, picking his empty pistol off the ground. He holstered it and went for a spare in his saddle bags.

"I'm trying!" Silcox said as he let loose a ball of yellow energy.

The creature shrieked with the impact, and fell onto her side. A second ball of the yellow magic made her flinch, but her movements slowed. Two more blasts, and she finally stopped fighting and fell asleep.

"Is she dead?" Silcox asked, trying to stand, he cried out as he put weight on his left leg, and fell against Reba's corpse. "I think I broke my ankle."

"Well, she's still breathing," Ron said, walking over to the slumbering beast. He dared to poke her with the toe of his boot, but she didn't respond to the provocation. "Got enough to finish her off?"

"I doubt I have enough to mend my injuries," Silcox replied, grimacing in pain.

"You can do that?" Ron said.

"Muscles and bones are easy to knit," Silcox said. "Hurting people is hard. I won't be casting much of anything for a while now."

"A shame," Ron said, returning to his horse. "I don't think she's going to be too hospitable when she wakes up, and I don't feel right leaving her alive." Taking the loaner gun out of the saddle bag, he aimed and fired at the unconscious creature, only to see the bullet deflect.

"It must be an inherent enchantment," Silcox said. "Something that requires no conscious component. Her form is naturally impervious."

"Wonderful," Ron said, kicking a pebble in frustration. This was a damnable situation, one with no clear solution. He couldn't run away, and leave this creature to kill again, yet he had no obvious means of stopping her. What could any ordinary law man do against such power?

"I suspect she'll sleep a good while," Silcox said. "That magic would've put the toughest human to sleep for a month."

"Ain't nothing human about that," Ron said, walking over to give Silcox a hand. He supported the old man's leg as they walked over to Jesse's horse, that had been spared during the fracas. She was a tough old girl, fearless in the face of gunfire, and she could easily support the cattleman with a bad leg. Ron then went over to his own horse that had been left unscathed and said a mental prayer for small favors. That stallion had seen him through some tough trails over the years, and it would've been a shame to see him go.

Grabbing a length of rope from under his saddlebags, Ron went over and began binding the blood-soaked creature. He doubted it would do much good if she woke up, but it made him feel better. Once she was restrained, he carried her over and flopped her on the back of Silcox's ride, then went over to his own horse. A quick climb up the custom double stirrup, and he was back in the saddle.

They started maneuvering around the field of dead cows, and came upon the mutilated body of Jesse James. "You aren't going to leave your colleague here to rot, are you?" Silcox asked.

Ron sighed. "Probably not," he said, hopping down off his horse to retrieve the body. He wasn't sure what was going to happen with Jesse, as shadowgangers were little more than myth to him. Would this body regenerate, or would a new Jesse James pop up somewhere else? Either way, it was wise to take the corpse along, just in case.

After tossing Jesse's body onto the back of his horse, Ron asked, "What about that Forgison fellow of yours?"

"He cut and run on me," Silcox said. "Let him find his own way off the Flat."

Ron accepted it, seeing it would only burden one of the horses to carry the extra weight of the body. He didn't know much about Dale Forgison, only that his last act had been one of cowardice. It was a common affliction among men, and one Ron could not abide.

With everything set, the men started on their long ride across the Yucca Flat. It was going to be rough, but if they rode straight they might hit Selwood by nightfall. Then maybe they'd find someone who knew what the hell to do with the thing they'd found.

## Episode 8:
# Nobody's Child

Joella wanted to kick someone.

The cells were mostly empty now, the twenty or so members of the mob having been released by Judge Raymond. A crafty lawyer had worked out a deal, and since they'd all been serving as Marshal Rodgers' deputies at the time of their arrest, it was deemed unnecessary to hold them further. Never mind that one of the rabble may have shot Sheriff Doliber; no evidence meant no charges.

In addition to one harmless frost goblin, there were still five men behind bars. One was a surly barfly who'd tried to rough up one of Solen's girls; two others were Spencer and Byron, the pair that Ron and Doliber had brought in. And of course there were the would-be rapists who'd accosted Joella. With all the chaos that had come about, their trial had been postponed. It would be another day before they'd face judgment, so she was stuck guarding them still.

It was getting close to lunchtime, and Joella wished for a break. Yet, after Doliber's assassination, she had no idea who she could trust. Most likely, the shot had been fired from one of the guns Doliber, himself, had enchanted. That pointed the finger toward those most-trusted men who had been tasked to defend the town in the case of mystical banditry. That helped to narrow the pool of suspects, but still left a dozen men to investigate, none of whom would take kindly to being called an underhanded murderer.

The train massacre was also a pressing concern, which had

everyone on edge, and there was the mounting power struggle between Marshal Rodgers and the Sheriff's Department. It was never good when lawmen fought over jurisdiction, and Joella feared for her safety. The Marshal had made some ominous proclamations, and she half-expected to see Mactus Sellius show up before long. Mactus was the man who would have had legal right to claim her as an unwilling bride, if she hadn't married Ron all those months ago. Elvish Clan Law was a deplorable thing in some ways, archaic and backwards, treating women like property, yet she could not escape it.

With everything going on, Joella had to be stuck behind a desk, guarding prisoners. The tension was unbearable.

"Joella."

The voice was incredibly faint in the back of her head, and at first she couldn't distinguish it from her own thoughts. Yet, after hearing her name a few more times, she could tell someone was talking.

Getting up from her seat behind the desk, Joella moved over to the small archway that led to the holding cells. Glancing around, she wondered if one of the prisoners was taunting her, but as she looked at the men she heard the voice again, beckoning her, and saw none of them speak a word.

It wasn't an outward voice, she realized. Someone was trying to communicate telepathically.

"Who are you?" Joella asked in her mind, focusing the thought so it could be easily perceived by whoever was tapping her brain.

"Ron needs help," the voice whispered.

"What?"

"Help Ron," the voice persisted.

"Who are you?" she asked again, trying to sound forceful in her own thoughts.

"Help him," the voice said, fading out.

"Where is he?" Joella asked.

The voice didn't answer. The mysterious contact had ended.

Joella shook her head, frustrated by the ambiguous message. Without knowing who was talking, she couldn't be sure if she could trust it. Was someone seeking to pull her away from her post and make a move on the prisoners, or was it someone genuinely concerned for Ron Grimes? If it was an honest plea for help, how could they know of Ron's need?

As she put the facts together, a hopeful thought crossed her mind. "No, it can't be," she mumbled.

The possibility that Ron might actually be in trouble outweighed the risk of deceit. If she didn't try to help, she could never forgive herself if something happened to him.

Running out of the Sheriff's Office, Joella looked around for the nearest citizen she could trust to guard the prisoners during her absence. Nobody immediately stuck out, only a few strange drovers trotting down the conspicuously empty streets. It didn't look promising. Then, the perfect candidate came out of the barbershop across the street. It was someone she wouldn't have considered drafting a day ago, but under the circumstances he was just the man she was looking for.

"Solen!" Joella shouted, catching the barkeeper's attention.

"Mrs. Grimes-Talus, how lovely to see you, as always," Solen said, sounding in a good mood as he approached. His face appeared freshly shaved, and his hair showed signs of slight trimming, though it remained fairly long.

"I need your help," Joella said, digging into her pocket.

"Really? I was just about to go set up for the lunch crowd, but for you I might make the time."

"Good," Joella said, pulling a tarnished star from her pocket. With swift fingers, she pinned it to his shirt. "You're on guard duty, Deputy."

"Hey, now, I didn't mean..."

"Solen, this is important," Joella said, trying not to sound needy. "Ron might be in trouble, and with everything that's happened lately, you're the only person I can trust."

"Trust? Me?" Solen said, beaming with pride.

"Don't get too full of yourself. We both know you're still a scoundrel," she said, stepping back. "Now, get inside, and stay there until I come back."

"Aye, aye!" Solen said with a mock salute.

Joella waited for him to enter the Sheriff's Office before activating her lone mystical power. Her teleportation talent allowed her to travel dozens of miles in the blink of an eye, though without knowing of Ron's exact location she'd have to search a bit. First stop would be the Silcox Ranch. Hopefully, someone would be able to point her in the right direction.

Closing her eyes, white light surrounded her body, and she was off.

* * *

The horses weren't making great time in the desert climate. Their loads were heavy and the midday sun was roasting their hides. After an hour, they were ready to drop, so there was no choice but to rest.

Albert Silcox led them to an old watering hole at the base of a hill. There were a few patches of moss around a depression in the ground, but there was nothing to drink. Nobody had used this water source for years, and Ron figured it had dried up, though Silcox knew better.

"It's just silted up," he said. "Dig down, and you'll hit the spring."

Ron hadn't been in the arid climate long, so he accepted the older man's word. He hopped down off his horse and retrieved a small hand-spade from his saddle bags. It wasn't much, but it beat using bare hands.

Of course, Silcox's busted ankle prevented the old man from helping. It was all on Ron. The soft dirt came up quickly, and about a foot down the soil got sticky and clumped from the moisture. Two feet down, water began pooling up in the bottom of the hole, and Ron widened it out for a suitable basin. He waited for it to fill, and then led the horses over to drink. They didn't mind that it was dirty, and after they drank their fill he let the reservoir replenish itself and clear up, so he could refill the canteens.

Once they had their water and the horses were satisfied, they resumed their trek. It was still a long ride off the Flat, and the deadly creature they carried with them could awake at any moment. The sooner they got to Selwood, the better.

Ron had done many dangerous things in his life, but this topped them all.

Looking over at Silcox's horse, seeing the pale, skeletal beast hanging behind the rider, he caught a brief sign of life from the creature. A few brief spasms from her bound arms, and a twitch of her neck. The thing was waking up, and there was nothing to be done about it.

Options were nil. They'd passed on the chance to run away, choosing to not leave the unconscious killer amongst her slaughter. Braving the odds, they'd gambled on getting her back to Selwood to find help in time. Once she awoke, no ordinary bonds could restrain her, and Silcox's magic was exhausted. They couldn't subdue her again, and when she broke free she'd cut them to pieces. So much for protecting the public at large; she'd be wild and free despite their attempt at containment.

The creature's eyes popped open, and they locked onto Ron. No emotion lurked on her face, just a blank stare of heartless intent. She aimed to kill him, just as soon as her body recovered enough to snap the ropes tying her down.

End of the line, Ron thought. How sad that it had to end so suddenly, and in failure. He'd always thought his death would be for something. First time death had stared him in the face it had been on the field of battle, fighting to preserve the Union. Other times, he'd been up against cattle rustlers, wild Indians, and more recently a mad sorcerer; but all those times when death seemed near it had come with the benefit of knowing he was accomplishing something; that he'd die a winner. Now, facing this bloodthirsty being, he didn't feel he'd succeeded at all. He would die in failure, and nobody would be there to finish the job.

The creature growled as its strength returned. Silcox turned around and started to panic, as he felt the squirming creature rub up against his back. The old cattle baron had nowhere to run, and his ankle prevented him from dismounting. Realizing he was out of options, he quickly regained control over his emotions. He would meet his doom with dignity.

Ron reigned his horse to a halt, and Silcox did the same. The men looked at each other, as the creature began to thrash. The rope still restrained it, and held it tightly to the horse, but it wouldn't be long before the bonds snapped under her inhuman strength.

It seemed like something ought to be said, but Ron couldn't

think of anything.  Words were lost to him as he pondered the limits of his existence, and the regrets that lingered.  So many things he'd done, yet others he'd never gotten around to.  Most unexpectedly, he found himself worrying about what he *wouldn't* leave behind.  No family, no children, no legacy.  In the grand scheme of things, the world would forget him, and nobody would care he ever existed.  It had never bothered him before.  Why was it plaguing him now?

He would leave a widow, but would she really grieve?  As he thought of Joella and their sham marriage, he wanted to laugh, but it also left him yearning for more.  The superficial show they'd been putting on for the past few months had given him a desire for the real thing, and he was beginning to realize how nice it could be to have a marital bond, and the prospect of children.

Why did he always have to realize things when it was too late?

A snap sounded, and Ron looked to see the creature's arm flying upward, as her hand was freed.  With several swift swings, she cut the remaining bindings with her claws, and then sank them into the hind quarters of the horse under her.  The mare whinnied and staggered back as the creature jumped off.

Sitting atop the crippled horse, Silcox turned to Ron and tipped his hat.  "It has been less than a pleasure to know you, Sheriff."  Obviously, he was not a man for idle pleasantries in the face of impending death.

The creature was pacing around like a wolf, sizing up her prey.  There was more than basic animal instincts in her; there was joy in her killing.  She was savoring this moment, eager to kill those that had tried to capture her.  When she could wait no longer, she would pounce, only would it be Silcox she killed first, or Ron?  Either way, both men were doomed, and it would only be a matter of moments separating their deaths.

"Dear God, forgive me," Ron whispered, feeling there was nothing else to say.

A sudden flicker of light flashed in front of the creature, and Joella appeared out of thin air.  Before the creature could respond to her arrival, she raised her hand and blew a cloud of red dust into the killer's bony face.  The pale being began sneezing uncontrollably.

"Come on, get over here!" Joella shouted.

Ron turned his horse around and trotted over, as Silcox limped up beside Joella. They were all standing in front of the sneezing creature, not three feet away from it.

Squinting her eyes and summoning all the strength she had, Joella enveloped them all in a teleport, taking them away from the bright desert into the dark confines of the Sheriff's Office.

It was fortunate the room had a tall ceiling, for Ron was still atop his horse. How the animal would get out the door was a problem that could be solved later. A more immediate concern was the killer they'd brought with them. The bony creature continued to sneeze frantically, and seemed wholly unaware of her surroundings.

"Bravo!" Solen said, standing up from behind the desk to give applause. "That's quite an entrance."

"Not now, Solen!" Joella snapped, grabbing onto the sneezing creature.

"What did you give her?" Ron asked, dismounting.

"Essence of Red Moon," Joella answered, as the creature continued to sneeze uncontrollably. "It should've knocked her out cold."

"At least she's distracted," Ron mentioned.

"That thing is deadly," Silcox said. "I hope you've got something to contain it."

"The anti-magic cell's our best bet," Ron mentioned.

"Assuming her strength is mystically derived," Joella countered.

"Let's herd her in there and find out."

As Silcox found a place to rest his leg, Ron and Joella dragged the sneezing creature into the back, toward the last cell on the right.

Silcox dropped himself down into the chair in front of the sheriff's desk, and saw the prim and proper elf sitting across from him, smiling with a peculiar smirk. "I know you?" he asked, searching for a name."

"Albert, it's been quite a while," Solen said, offering the old man a hand to shake. "Tell me, how is that wife of yours?"

"Dead," Silcox said.

The news didn't sadden Solen in the least, and he showed it. "Well, in that case, perhaps you'd enjoy the company of one of my ladies for an evening? No?"

Silcox sneered at the elf and turned his face away. "Solen," he grumbled, finally recalling the saloon owner's name.

A woman's shrill scream echoed out from the cell block, and Solen jumped to his feet to investigate. "Joella, are you all right?" he asked, daring to move forward, despite the potential for danger ahead. He wasn't timid, and was willing to stick his neck out if it could benefit his self-interest. The prospect of garnering Joella's favor was reason enough, at the moment.

"It's not me," Joella replied. "Something's happening to our prisoner!"

Solen ventured down the hallway, passing the different cells and their captives until he reached the back of the jail, where Ron and Joella were gazing at the creature they'd just thrown into the anti-magic cell.

"What are you doing to her?" Solen asked as he looked at the screeching and writhing creature.

"Nothing," Ron said. "We just tossed her in there."

Solen stared in awe, as he witnessed the happenings inside the cell. As the creature continued to scream and lurch in agony, a transformation was taking place. Her bony features were filling out, as fat and muscle tissue returned. The claws retracted and became ordinary fingernails, hair shot out of her head, forming a long mane of brown locks, and her pasty skin turned a rosy pink. The whole process took less than a minute, and the end result was both miraculous and stunning.

"Oh my," Solen said, eyeing the dazed woman in the cell with lecherous thoughts. She was completely naked and very attractive.

"Peep show's over," Joella suddenly said, grabbing Solen's arm to escort him away.

"Wait a minute," Solen protested. "Don't you realize who that is?"

"You know this broad?" Ron asked, averting his gaze out of modesty.

"It's Bettina Carter!" Solen replied.

\* \* \*

Word spread quickly in Selwood, and the story of Bettina Carter's miraculous reemergence was the talk of the town within the hour. It didn't help when Solen started speaking of his experiences to any customer who was willing to buy an extra drink. Gossip was worth money, especially when it was true.

There were still many unanswered questions about her disappearance, and of her possible role in the train massacre, so her presence was making quite a stir. It was a safe bet that people were going to keep talking, and exaggeration and hyperbole made for a dangerous mix.

The mayor and his son rushed down to the Sheriff's Office right after Joella brought them the news of Bettina's return. They were in such a rush, the rest of the story had to be related to them in-transit.

"You're saying Bettina was turned into some kind of monster?" Fletcher said as they stepped into the Sheriff's Office.

"It looks that way," Joella confirmed. "We're still trying to figure out what happened, though we've ruled out lycanthropy, as well as necromancy and demonic possession."

"Demonic possession, no, but Shamanic possession, yes," the mayor said with absolute certainty. "This is Raethanon's work, I'm sure of it. He cast some sort of spell over Bettina, forced her to commit these crimes."

"We haven't been able to prove anything yet," Joella said, trying to keep an open mind. The mayor had his assumptions, but there was no evidence to back up his claims.

"It would help if we still had a warlock on the payroll," Mayor Atwood mentioned, sounding rather incensed by Doliber's death. "How goes the investigation into his shooter?"

"We've hardly had time to look into it," Joella admitted. She paused as they reached the archway leading into the cell block. Glancing at the floor, she fought back her own solemn emotions and said, "I can't say that we'll ever know who did it."

"Buck up, Deputy," the mayor said, patting her shoulder. "I'm sure you'll do everything you can. Now, about my son's fiancée."

Joella led them down the hallway to the cell in back, where Ron was still standing guard. He kept one hand on his revolver as he watched the woman sitting on the hardwood bench. She seemed harmless enough, cuddled up under a woolen blanket, but he'd seen something else from her, and wasn't about to let his guard down. He kept one eye on her, even as he addressed Joella.

"Where's Silcox?" he asked.

"With Doctor Wilson," Joella replied. "The ankle's pretty bad, and I didn't want to wait around. I figured Fletcher here would want to see his lady."

"I thank you for your diligence in the matter," Fletcher said. "May I see her?"

"She's right there," Ron said, waving a hand at the woman behind bars.

"I mean go inside, visit her properly."

"I wouldn't advise that," Ron mentioned. "Not if you value your hide."

"Ron, it's fine," Joella chided, reaching for the lock.

"Hey, we've got no idea what's going on here," Ron said, stepping over to stop Joella. "We've got no idea what made her change, or what made her revert to human. For all we know, she could be contagious!"

"I accept the risks," Fletcher said loudly, "as you did bringing her here."

Ron rolled his eyes and stepped back, allowing Joella to open the cell door. "It's your funeral."

Fletcher moved into the cell as soon as Joella opened it. "Thank you, I am in your debt," he said, and shut the door behind him.

"Yeah, don't you forget it," Ron said.

Fletcher ignored the bitter dwarf and hurried over to his beloved's side. As he came to her, Bettina sat up and threw her arms around him, allowing the heavy blanket to slip off her shoulders in the process. The young man gave her a reassuring hug, but soon recoiled, blushing at seeing her naked flesh. It was hardly seemly for a man to see his bride nude before their wedding night, and he had been sure to preserve the morality of their relationship. There was far too much sin and debauchery in this day and age, and he'd have none of it.

Bettina clearly understood his concerns, and promptly pulled the blanket over herself again. She blushed sheepishly at the gaffe, but smiled at him reassuringly.

Recovering from the awkward moment, Fletcher looked down at his shirt and saw a spattering of red specks clinging to the fabric. He brushed away the dried blood and tried to ignore the horrific tale he'd been told. That wasn't Bettina's doing, not really. How could it be? A woman possessed and transformed by a supernatural force could not be held accountable for such actions. She hadn't been in her right mind.

"How are you doing?" Fletcher asked clumsily.

"I don't know," Bettina answered, squirming a little under the itchy blanket.

"Tell me, what happened?" Fletcher pleaded.

"I don't remember much," Bettina said, fighting back tears with every word. "I remember the train. Something attacked it. And then I was in this hole, in a cave, and then... I don't remember!" She broke down in tears, and leaned on Fletcher's comforting shoulder.

It was the most he could expect from her under the circumstances, and he didn't wish to pressure her further. As far as he was concerned, this was all an unfortunate happenstance, something best forgotten in the grand scheme of things. All he wanted now was to take her out of this dismal cell, and get her to the church as planned. Their wedding wasn't scheduled until tomorrow, so there was still time.

"Come, let's get out of here," Fletcher said, helping Betting to her feet. He walked her over to the cell door, but it remained closed.

"Sorry, that ain't gonna happen," Ron said.

"Really, Sheriff, you can't keep an innocent woman locked up like this," Fletcher protested. "You can see she is no longer a threat. Whatever form of mysticism was plaguing her, it's gone now."

"We don't know that," Ron rebutted. "For all we know, she could relapse at any time, maybe right in the middle of yer honeymoon. You wanna risk that?"

"It's my risk to take," Fletcher said, refusing to back down.

"Well I ain't!" Ron snapped.

"Let's not get all up in arms," the mayor interrupted. "I'm sure the acting sheriff is only trying to do his job as he thinks it should be performed. However, under the circumstances, I believe it would be in everyone's best interest to allow my son to take his fiancée home, where she will be properly cared for."

"That woman killed three men, and slaughtered a herd of cattle," Ron said, placing himself directly in front of the mayor, but too short to get in his face. "I ain't letting her out of my sight until we get to understand why and how she did that."

"Then you may accompany her to the Carters' residence, and see that she is no threat," Mayor Atwood stated. "Perhaps then you'll be able to get on with more important tasks, such as finding your predecessor's killer."

"What about tracking down Raethanon?" Joella asked.

"Leave that to the Marshal," the mayor said. "Now, do as I asked."

Joella started to unlock the cell, but Ron grabbed her hand and yanked the keys from her grasp. "No way am I cutting that woman loose."

Mayor Atwood stormed over and grabbed Ron by the collar. "Look here, little man, I am the mayor here. Selwood is mine. I built it, I fought for it, and I'll not have some uppity midge show up and tell me what to do in my own town!"

"Get your hands off me," Ron grumbled, fighting the urge to punch the man in the gut.

Atwood released Ron and stepped back, keeping an incensed expression on his face. "I'll have your badge for this."

"I'm sure the voters will have a say in that," Ron replied. "Think how they'll feel when they hear you ordered me to release the prime suspect in the train murders case."

"Bettina didn't do that," Fletcher interrupted. "She just said..."

"Shup up, Fletcher!" Atwood snapped, then wagged a finger at Ron. "You're crafty, almost as crafty as Doliber. But you've got a lot to learn about greasing the wheels, son. Now, how about we forget this little spat and agree to a compromise."

Ron was never one to acquiesce, and he didn't see how there could be any give and take under these circumstances. Either Bettina stayed behind bars, or she didn't. It was that simple, and there was no middle ground to be had. Yet, when the mayor makes a suggestion, you at least have to hear him out.

"I believe it is in everyone's best interest to release Bettina," Atwood persisted. "At least, let her visit home for a few hours. Her poor mother has been bedridden for years, and her younger siblings have been worried sick. I urge you, in the name of civility, to agree."

Ron glared up at the mayor. The man wasn't going to take no for an answer, and it was pointless to further anger him. His middle ground might make a modicum of sense, after all.

"Two hours, and Joella sticks with her the whole time," Ron replied, feeling it was the best possible answer.

"I suppose that will have to do," Atwood said.

Joella grabbed the keys from Ron and quickly unlocked the cell door. Pushing the bars open, she waved Fletcher and Bettina to come forward. The happy couple hurried through the door without hesitation.

As Bettina passed through the door, she staggered forward and fell to her knees. Before Fletcher could reach down to help her up, she began to scream. Tossing her arms up, she gripped either side of her head, and her body began to spasm as the transformation overtook her. Skin started to tighten, and bony protrusions began to emerge. The hair on her head shrank, as if being sucked into her skull, even as her skin turned deathly pale. In seconds she would once more become the monster!

Ron realized he didn't have much time, and took the initiative. Running forward, he threw himself against Bettina, pushing her back into the cell and tackling her to the ground. As soon as she was back within the anti-magic confines, the transformation stopped and she quickly reverted to her human form.

"So much for your little outing," Ron said, standing up.

Joella tossed the blanket to Bettina, and the dazed woman grabbed it in a hurry, but remained on the floor, too scared to move.

Both Atwoods kept their mouths shut, seeing their plan had failed.

"This tells us something important," Joella said, trying to break the tension. "The anti-magic field within the cell neutralizes the source of her affliction. That means there is an exterior source generating it."

"And if we find it, we can make her normal again," Fletcher said, teeming with hope.

"Probably," Joella answered. "I'd say our next step is to resume the search, see if we can track down Raethanon, or whoever else is behind this."

"The Marshal is taking care of that," the mayor said.

"Forgive me, but I don't have much faith in that Marshal," Ron remarked.

Mayor Atwood shook his head and stormed out, having done as much sparring with the dwarf as he cared to this day. His son lingered, and leaned against the bars to the cell.

"We're going to get you out of this, Bettina," Fletcher assured her. "I swear, I won't rest until we are together."

"I know," Bettina replied wistfully.

There was nothing else to be said, so Fletcher turned away, wishing he could do something. There had to be a way he could help, to stop the man who had taken his bride and turned her into a mindless killer. Though a peaceful, Christian man, Fletcher felt the burning desire to take up arms against the individual responsible. He felt shame, both from his sinful hatred and because he lacked any practical skills to fulfill his vengeful desires. He'd never learned to shoot straight, and he remained wholly oblivious to the ways of magic. Without those tools, he was no good to anyone in a fight.

Fletcher's education had taken a purely academic path. History, literature, philosophy; they were all very good things to study, but when it came down to it, they had no practical applications in a situation like this. He could lecture on the fall of Carthage, speak about the campaigns of Washington and Grant, speak of Napoleon in the man's own words, but could he deign to fight as those men had? He could recount the history of the Knights of Wallace, but could he harness their mastery over magic? Hardly. Knowing something was far different than doing it.

It was too late to learn, Fletcher knew, but he vowed to remember this day, and rectify his ignorance. In the meantime, he would have to make do with what he had.

"I wish to help," Fletcher said, as Ron and Joella escorted him out of the cell block.

"Like your father helped?" Ron said, shaking his head. "The best thing you can do is go home and stay out of the way."

"I know I'm not a fighter, nor am I a politician as my father," Fletcher defended. "But surely, there must be something I can do to help you save Bettina. I could guard the jail here, leave you both to continue the search for Raethanon."

As they exited the cell block, Joella remarked, "That isn't a bad idea."

"You really want to get stuck here behind a desk?" Ron asked, agreeing with Joella's assessment, though not eager to relinquish his gruff demeanor.

"Just let me get a few books to bide the time," Fletcher said with great enthusiasm. He hurried toward the door.

"Sure, but I haven't said yes yet," Ron rebutted.

Fletcher ignored him, and ran out of the office, eager to get a treatise on martial combat from his father's library. It seemed an opportune time to rectify his ignorance in the ways of the world, even as he made himself useful.

It was a short walk to "Atwood Manor," as Fletcher liked to call it. Though the exterior resembled the other houses found in Selwood, it had the largest interior layout, and the most capable staff in all of Nevada. It was no surprise an educated young man would romanticize his family home with a superficial moniker.

A brief visit to his father's study provided him with several texts on fighting and a primer on mystical physics. Though they would bring little more than academic knowledge of the concepts, it would be a start on his path toward becoming a Western warrior. Suddenly, it didn't seem wrong to acquire such knowledge, as he'd always have his scholarly background. He could still teach and preach however he desired, but also be able to defend those he cared about.

With the books tucked under his arm, Fletcher smiled as he walked back toward the Sheriff's Office, feeling things were going to be okay. With the combined forces of Marshal Rodgers and Doliber's deputies, Raethanon would surely be found and brought to justice.

Fletcher was gleefully dreaming of his coming wedding day as the bullet burned into his back. The sharp penetration struck a second before the gunshot sounded in the distance, and he felt his stomach dampen with his own blood. The books slipped from his grasp and hit the ground before he did.

Several people rushed out into the street to see what had happened. A small crowd quickly assembled, as Fletcher continued to bleed, soaking the ground beneath him. He was getting cold in the middle of a hot summer's day, and he feared he would no longer be of help to anyone.

## Episode 9:
## And The Dead Shall Rise

The surgery went as well as could be expected. After being shot, Fletcher Atwood had been brought to the town's most renowned physician, the venerable Doctor Wilson. Though, the prognosis was not good. The bullet had blown right through his abdomen, and expansion of the bullet had caused some collateral damage. Though death was not immediate, the chances of long-term survival remained slim.

"Why are there no medlocks in this blasted town?" Mayor Atwood shouted.

"I'm sure Doliber could explain better than I about the self-imposed limits of the Guild," Wilson said as he washed his hands. "With the exception of war triage, warlocks with medical talents are generally restricted from practicing their healings abroad."

"The Guild and their sanctimonious pledge of non-interference," Atwood sneered. "What good is having such power if you will not use it for the betterment of others?"

"I guess they deem the risks of abusing that power aren't worth the benefits of using it in most cases," Wilson replied.

The mayor had heard the explanations before, and didn't care to rationalize the Guild's behavior any further. The elite organization of warlocks did not concern him. That they barred their members from healing his son was a minor irritation, for even if they permitted such healings it was doubtful a medlock would be in the area. There were far too few warlocks with medical aptitudes to go around.

Fate refused to be kind, and Atwood wondered if Solen hadn't been right all along. The "curse" was punishing him.

Stepping out into the late day sun, Atwood walked home. There was nowhere else to go, really. He didn't feel like socializing with the townspeople at a time like this, and he'd worn out his welcome with the deputies. He still couldn't believe that the dwarf was acting-sheriff. It was like a bad joke. How would a midge ever instill fear into criminals?

Atwood crossed the short path to his front door, and went inside without ceremony. A maid hurried over as she spotted him, but he dismissed her and hung up his own suit jacket on the stand, ignoring the collection of ladies jackets already hanging there. Marjorie must have company, but he didn't care to intrude. His wife was not one for his company these days, despite their sharing a bed at night.

The study was a quiet refuge, a few steps away from the front door. He opened the door and locked it behind him, seeking absolute privacy. The chair in front of the fireplace was calling to him, but before sitting down he retrieved a quart bottle of scotch whiskey he had tucked in the bottom drawer of his desk. No glass was needed as he sought to drink himself into oblivion. It seemed to be the appropriate response to the day's events.

After several deep swigs, Atwood was getting the familiar buzz, but feeling no better. Tears began to run down his cheeks, as the liquor weakened his emotional control, and allowed him to surrender to the pain. He knew he wouldn't feel much of anything by the time he found the bottom of the bottle, and the best he could hope for was to be finished with the task before his eyes got too red.

Before he could drink further, a thumping sounded at his door. The voice of his wife accompanied it. She hammered and pleaded for him to see her, with all the upset of a grieving mother. There was no way he could get drunk, not before dealing with her.

Pulling the door open, Atwood looked at the distraught face of his wife. "Charles, is there word of Fletcher? Will he be all right?"

"I doubt it," Atwood said, staggering back into the room. He returned to the chair and picked up the bottle for another taste.

"Don't you have guests to entertain?"

"Meredith's with them," Marjorie replied, referring to their Irish maid.

"Good," Atwood said, taking another swig from the bottle.

"Curse you, Charles. You know what I think of the drink!" Marjorie chided, wiping her tears. "And at a time like this, when our son may be lying on his death bed!"

"I'm in no mood for your lectures," Atwood replied after a swig. "I'll not hear your Methodist nattering this day!"

Marjorie came into the room and sat down next to her husband. The dark dress she wore was cumbersome in the small seat, but she managed to push it off to the side as she settled in. "Please, Charles, we can't be like this. Not now."

"Like what? At odds? We're always at odds."

"Only since you turned your back on the Lord," Marjorie corrected. "What happened to make you hate God so much?"

"I don't hate God," Atwood rebutted. "I don't believe your interpretation of His wishes. You take everything to extremes. No liquor, no gambling, no fighting. You give no exception to the rules, and that I cannot abide." He concluded his point with another swig.

Marjorie sat silently, lost for words in the face of his obstinacy, wholly ignoring her own.

"You should understand my objections," Atwood said, feeling inebriated enough to argue with her. "These beliefs of yours, they're futile. According to that preacher of yours, we ought to be a humorless race, devoid of pleasure or vanity. Not only that, but he calls justice 'unholy retribution.' He'd have us sit on our hands and do nothing, rather than find Fletcher's shooter. Forgive me for thinking we ought to get drunk once in a while, and go out and hang the bastard who murdered our son!"

Marjorie turned her head away and wiped at her cheeks. "It's not as simple as that."

"Yes, it is," Atwood persisted. "You know full well what Pastor Jameson would say—that it's sinful for us to judge, even under these circumstances. Hanging a man is never right, he'd say. Damn him and his pacifism to hell! An eye for an eye, that's the Lord's way. The only fools who think different are a bunch of overly-educated philosophers who've never had to live in the real world."

Marjorie stood up and glanced down at her husband, looking every bit as tormented as he did. "Like Fletcher," she said, and then walked out, shutting the door behind her.

"Yeah, look where it got him," Atwood said to himself, looking down at the bottle in his hands. It was still pretty full, and he realized he had a long way to go.

* * *

The undertaker's office was shut for the night. The aging fellow who ran the place had whiffed enough noxious fumes for one day in his preparation of three bodies. One had been an old man, dead from natural causes. Another had been a drover accidentally trampled by a herd. The third had been a deputized outlaw fresh off the Flat.

Jesse James lay flat against the table, a full bottle of formaldehyde sitting at his side. All the materials for preserving his body lay in wait, but none of it had yet been used on him.

Jesse's face had been pretty clawed up when he'd arrived. The claw marks went straight through the skull, carving large gashes from nose to both ears. The undertaker had gone about preparing the other two bodies first, and during the afternoon he kept glancing back at Jesse's face, and noticed something different each time. Whenever he'd glance at the wounds, he thought they appeared less and less severe, until they were hardly there at all. As the sun went down, the undertaker decided to call it a day. Clearly, his perceptions were being distorted by fatigue, and his imagination was playing tricks on him. Best leave one body for the morning.

As the first rays of moonlight began streaming through the windows, Jesse blinked his eyes and took a deep breath. The fading memory of a second death now lurked in the back of his mind as he shivered. The heat had yet to return to his body, and his cold blood was just beginning to circulate.

As feeling returned to his extremities, he forced himself to sit up. As the fog lifted from his eyes, he studied his surroundings, spotting several coffins within spitting distance.

"Well, this is new," Jesse remarked, recalling the last time he'd awakened from death. He'd found himself on the floor of his living room, seemingly unscathed. He'd recalled the shot, but been able to dismiss it as a false memory. There'd been no hole in his back where he remembered Ford shooting him, and decided that God had given him a reprieve. It didn't take him long to grab his translocator and get out of town, before anyone discovered he was alive and well.

Now that he knew the truth, he wasn't in such a hurry to run. Where could he go that his personal penance wouldn't find him? The voices in his head, the magically-enhanced guilt, wouldn't leave him alone even now. The mental strain was made bearable by acting for the greater good of others, and being deputized was his ticket to the next life. If it took him a few centuries to get there, he wouldn't complain about the delay.

Walking over to the door, Jesse found the shop locked from the outside. It had to be a padlock, for there wasn't a means of unlocking it from the inside. Why would an undertaker lock his shop? Was he afraid someone might want to steal a body?

Jesse used his shoulder as a key, throwing himself against the door several times until the screws holding the locking clasp pulled out. As the door opened, he managed to right himself to prevent a fall. Brushing the wrinkles out of his blood-stained suit, he shut the broken door and walked down the road, smiling at a couple of streetwalkers who gave him funny looks. No doubt, it was the first time they'd ever seen a man break out of a mortuary.

Selwood was pretty quiet after sundown. The residents were on edge after the recent killings, and nobody felt safe. If both the warlock sheriff and the mayor's son could be gunned down in broad daylight, there was no telling who else would bite a bullet in the coming days. People who didn't have legitimate business to attend were staying indoors.

Rising from the dead seemed like a good occasion for a drink, so Jesse headed straight for the most active establishment in his path, the Lucca Saloon. No doubt, someone there could front him a dollar. The sheriff was good for it.

As Jesse came through the doors, half the patrons turned to look at him, and an eerie silence fell upon them. He smiled, and wondered why they were staring at him until he looked down at his suit in the lamplight. The red stains ran in thick streams down his chest, making for a pretty gruesome sight. It looked like someone had dumped a bucket of blood over his head, and he'd neglected to change the shirt after washing his body.

"Do any of you happen to be a tailor?" Jesse asked. "I believe I'm in need of a fresh set of clothes."

A few people laughed, and life returned to normal. Clearly, the rowdy crowd had better things to do than concern themselves with a stranger's affairs.

Jesse walked over to the bar and slapped the counter. "Bourbon!" he commanded.

Solen walked over, polishing a shot glass with a rag. "Aren't you dead?" he asked nonchalantly.

"I believed as much, but I must have been mistaken," Jesse joked.

"Two bits," Solen replied, setting the glass down and turning to retrieve a brown bottle from the rack behind him.

"Charge it to the sheriff," Jesse replied. "It would seem he is in my debt."

Solen looked Jesse in the eye to size him up. After a few moments, he shrugged his shoulders and poured the drink, deciding the man could be trusted.

Jesse threw the shot back and cringed appreciatively. "Ah, that's the stuff." Solen moved to refill the glass, but Jesse halted him. "Say, why's it so quiet in here? This is a saloon. Why no piano?"

"As I recently reminded a certain Marshal, this is not some low-rent honky-tonk," Solen replied, corking the bottle and putting it back on the shelf.

"Don't any of you boys have a fiddle, at least?" Jesse asked the crowd. They all ignored him and kept to their eating, drinking, and gambling.

"Care for some dinner?" Solen asked as Jesse turned back around.

Thinking about it, Jesse realized he wasn't hungry in the least. It was quite surprising, as he felt the process of being killed and revived would have brought him an appetite. The mysticism involved clearly didn't work on that principle, and he now wondered if he needed to eat at all. His body was no longer bound by physical laws. It was some form of magically contrived imitation.

Regardless of any need, he had felt the desire to eat regularly since his first death, only at the moment his hunger was satisfied.

"No, I should probably be going," he told Solen, sliding off the barstool.

As Jesse turned to leave, Solen grabbed his arm gently. "You'll have to stop by when I'm not so busy, and tell me your secret."

Jesse laughed at the barkeeper's forwardness and walked out.

The air was still warm, though it tended to get cool after dark. Even in the summer months, temperatures could be chilly at night in the desert climate, as there was little to hold in the heat.

Jesse walked down the road, sticking close to the buildings and their boardwalks whenever possible. There were a few people out, but none paid him any mind as he made his way to the Sheriff's Office. Though, as he came within sight of the nondescript two-story building, he saw someone else running across the street toward the front door. Whoever was heading there was in a hurry, and Jesse wondered if that might spell trouble, so he hastened his own pace. He rushed up the front steps and lurked outside the front door, eavesdropping on the conversation.

"I reckon he's comin' here," a voice said.

"Thanks for the information," the familiar voice of Ron Grimes responded.

Assuming the conversation was about him, Jesse opened the door and announced himself with a cough and a grin. He stepped over to the desk, as the dwarf watched with a young man wearing leather chaps and a patchy beard.

"Miss me?" Jesse asked as he tossed himself down in a chair in front of the desk.

"Coulda used you earlier," Ron replied, leaning back in his chair. He nodded to the young informant, and the fellow hurried off on his business.

"So, what'd I miss?" Jesse asked.

"Too much," Ron replied, and then informed him of the

latest developments.   With the dwarf's regular brevity, he got through the story of Bettina being the monster and Fletcher Atwood getting shot.   The whole retelling lasted less than two minutes, leaving Jesse with a vengeful anger.

"Another cowardly back shot!" Jesse cursed.   "Can't anyone have the decency to shoot folks in the face anymore?"

"The caliber of bullet that dropped Fletcher was the same size as the one we pulled out of Doliber, so it's probably the same shooter.   Either way, we've got no leads, other than this Raethanon fellow the mayor keeps spouting off about.   Seems to me he's some kinda local folk legend more than a man."

"I wouldn't discount it," Jesse warned.   "Nothing's more dangerous than the truth behind a legend."

"Agreed," Ron said before a yawn overpowered him.   It was getting late, and he'd been up since before sunrise.

"If you would like, I could stand watch tonight," Jesse offered, feeling wide awake after his mid-afternoon death nap.

"Considering all that's going on, I'd like to guard things myself," Ron said, followed by another yawn.   "But my body has other ideas."

Ron got up and walked over to the stairs on the wall opposite the desk.   He took his time climbing the steps, but made it without incident.

"I'll holler if there's any trouble," Jesse assured him.

Things were suddenly very quiet.   The prisoners were asleep, and weren't much for snoring.   Jesse looked around for something to distract himself, and started reading the local paper sitting on the desk.   It was a week old, and had nothing about recent events, which left him irritated.

Tossing the paper aside, he spotted the box of cigars sitting on the desk, and thought he might indulge himself.   Popping the lid open, he grabbed one of the long brown tubes and found the end had already been bitten.   He didn't care to share another man's saliva, so he grabbed another one and began hunting for a pack of matches.   When none could be found, he turned to the lamp. Removing his suit jacket, he used the sleeve to protect his hand from the heat of the glass as he lifted the chimney to get at the flame.   A few quick puffs brought the cigar to life, and he returned the lamp's chimney, having only slightly smoked the glass with the maneuver.

Sitting in the sheriff's chair, savoring his cheap cigar, Jesse looked down at his blood-stained shirt and wondered when he'd be able to afford a change of wardrobe.

* * *

Ron relieved Jesse from guard duty at dawn. The dwarf was usually up before the sun, but liked to eat breakfast and clean up a bit before coming down from his room. This morning, he brought a clean set of clothes along with him.

"I figure you could use something fresh to wear," he said, handing the bundle to Jesse.

"Like you read my mind," Jesse said, still looking wide-awake despite being up all night.

"It's one of Doliber's," Ron said. "You're a bit smaller than him, but I figure it'll fit all right."

"Then I'll go put it on," Jesse said, heading for the stairs.

"There's still some warm coffee in the pot up there," Ron shouted after Jesse went upstairs.

It was bound to be a big morning, Ron realized, as he settled into the chair. As soon as Joella got up and came in, they'd start hauling their prisoners over to the courthouse for their hearings. There were a whole host of charges, from kidnapping to attempted rape, and Ron felt confident they'd all be working a chain gang before nightfall. Considering the evidence against them, it was a done deal.

As he waited patiently, a knock came at the door, and a young blonde walked into the office. She was dressed formally, in a long, black skirt and matching blouse, and the broach on her chest gave her a sophisticated look. Ron looked her in the eyes as she neared the desk, and she blinked uncomfortably.

"Sheriff, I feel I must have a word with you," she said sheepishly.

"Sure," Ron said. "What about?"

"Well, Sir, it concerns my boss, Mr. Alvin Faust, owner of Selwood Savings Bank."

"Go ahead," Ron said after she stopped talking for a considerable spell.

"It's a rather sensitive matter," she said.   "I'm afraid your inmates may overhear us."

"Would you like to go upstairs?" Ron asked.

"That may be best."

Ron led her up the stairs and brought her to the kitchen where Jesse was pouring himself a cup of coffee.  The reformed outlaw offered the lady a cup, but she declined.

Realizing he'd left the office unmanned, Ron asked Jesse to head down and wait for Joella to arrive.  He agreed without objection, and took his coffee with him.

Once they were alone, Ron initiated the conversation.  "I don't believe I caught your name," he said, sitting down at the small table by the window.

"Myrilla Frost," the lady replied sitting down across from him.

"Like your employer?" Ron asked.

The lady's face went blank for a second before she caught his meaning.  "Oh, no, he's Faust.  I'm Frost.  I know, similar," she said, sounding chipper.

"So, why are you here, Miss Frost?"

"Well, like I said, my boss, Mr. Faust.  He's missing," she whispered, growing nervous again.

"Missing, you say?" Ron said.

"Yes, since Tuesday.  He and his wife went on a day trip to Yucca Junction, but they never came back."

"I see," Ron said, quickly shuffling the new information into current events.  The train massacre had happened on Tuesday, and it was an interesting coincidence that this banker had gone missing on that same day.  "Do you think he may have been involved with the murders aboard the train?   Perhaps another unfortunate victim?"

"Well, maybe, but that's only part of why I'm here.  You see, I think Alvin might have been responsible for Sheriff Doliber's death."

"Why would you say that?" Ron asked, feeling stung by the suggestion.

"Well, I can't be certain, but I do know he had a gun, a special gun.  He showed it to me, an ugly little thing with the shiny finish flaking off. He said it had the power to kill a warlock, even."

"Why did he show it to you?" Ron asked, feeling suspicious. "Did he make a habit of showing it off?"

"Oh, no, I don't think he showed it to anyone else except me. He liked to impress me like that, but he really didn't need to."

"I see," Ron said, somehow doubting the gun was much of a secret. Any man who'd brag about his "special" pistol to an employee was likely in the habit of flashing it all around town as a matter of pride. Assuming Faust was telling the truth, and he did have one of Doliber's magically enhanced firearms, it wouldn't be much of a stretch to assume someone had killed him for the gun.

Still, something didn't add up about Myrilla's story. If a prominent banker went missing, why did it take three days for her to come forward? And why her, of all people? Ron dared to ask as much, which brought another blank stare, followed by an explanation.

"Oh, well, I'm the only one who knows, I think," Myrilla said awkwardly. "You see, Alvin likes to take trips. A lot of times, he'll say he's going away for a day or two and be gone a week, off to someplace like San Francisco or Carson City, just for a change, you know. Everybody else at the bank thinks this is just one of those trips, but I know better."

"How so?" Ron asked.

"Oh, he told me he'd be back."

"Really?" Ron said dubiously. It looked like a false alarm, a worrisome employee exaggerating the situation.

"Yes, he did," Myrilla assured him. "You see, Alvin and I had plans on Wednesday, and he never stands me up."

"Plans?" Ron asked.

"Well, yes. Please don't make me say more," Myrilla urged, looking sheepish all of a sudden.

"Right," Ron said, reading between the lines. It wasn't hard to surmise that the young lady was having an affair with her married employer, and that gave her story more credibility. It was still possible the man had simply skipped out on his mistress, or that his wife might have waylaid him for a few extra days, though it was worth investigating.

"I'm glad you came by," Ron said, standing up to escort her out. "I'll be sure to look into Mr. Faust's disappearance."

Myrilla thanked him as they headed for the stairs. When they reached the front door, the lady leaned over and kissed him on the cheek. "Thanks for listening." She hurried out the door, leaving Ron blushing behind his beard.

"Aw, that's sweet," Joella's familiar voice said from across the room.

"Laugh it up," Ron said, stomping over. He saw Jesse standing in the corner, smirking as he often did. "I may have got us a lead on Doliber's shooter."

* * *

Bettina was alone, again.

The jail was quiet by nine o'clock. The prisoners who had been occupying the ordinary cells had been hauled off by the sheriff's men. The dwarf warned the criminals, each in-turn, that their day of judgment was at hand, and his elvish deputy made a point of mocking one scruffy character in particular.

They'd cut the frost goblin loose hours ago, and now the only other person in the whole building was some kid, barely old enough to shave. He'd introduced himself as Gary Britton, but hadn't said much else. He was supposed to be a short-term guard, and acted it. No motivation whatsoever, he just sat at the desk, looking bored. He was due to be relieved within the hour, and had other things on his mind.

So, Bettina sat in the cell with the itchy blanket wrapped around her, wondering what would become of her. She still didn't know if Fletcher was alive or dead. All she'd been able to learn was that he'd been shot. The dwarf sheriff didn't really care for her, that much was obvious, and none of her siblings had bothered to pay her a visit, either, not even to bring her a set of clothes. They were like that, self-absorbed and wholly disinterested in her. She hadn't talked to them much since leaving for college, and she knew they resented her for leaving. They were a different sort of people, more rugged and wild like this western land.

Bettina had never cared for Western life, and after several years back east she had grown a taste for a more sophisticated life. She and Fletcher had both been anomalies in this rural land, growing up with a thirst for knowledge and a disdain for country life. They'd come home to get married, but their plans after that were destined to lead them into more civilized settings.

Though, it was all falling apart.

There was nothing else for Bettina to do but wallow in self-pity and worry about the future. The life she had known seemed over, as she stared at the walls of her cell, sensing the horror that awaited her if she ever stepped outside again.

Dragging her attention away from her inner musings, Bettina heard a door open, and she wedged herself against the bars of her cell to peer down the hall into the office up front. There, she saw a darkly tanned man with white hair, wearing a tasseled rawhide jacket adorned with turquoise jewelry. He moved toward the desk with a slow and careful stride, keeping his eyes locked on the young guard sitting there.

"Can I help you?" Gary asked.

"No," the old man said, pulling a small pistol from his belt. The gun made a weak popping sound as he fired, and after a few moments he reached over and pried something away from the guard's body. Bettina saw it was a key ring as the old man clutched it in his hands and walked down the hallway toward her cell.

"Hello, señorita," he said with his scratchy voice. "It is time you were free again."

"No, I don't want to leave," Bettina said, fearing the horrid transformation that awaited her beyond the protection of the anti-magic cell.

"Do not be silly," the old man said, turning the key in the lock. "No one wishes to be caged. You have a grandeur purpose to serve, one you cannot fulfill in this place."

The door swung open, and Bettina backed away. She kept moving until she was up against the wall, and the wrinkled man was breathing in her face, grinning with his brown and crooked teeth.

"Who are you?" Bettina asked faintly.

The old man grabbed her arms and answered. "I am Raymondo Theonés, but you may call me Raethanon."

His arms were strong, and Bettina could not break away.

Her bare feet were ineffective against his torso as he carried her out of the cell, and then it was too late. As soon as Bettina passed beyond the protective cell, the enchantment reclaimed her. In seconds, the painful transformation began, stripping her humanity away, replacing it with mindless, animal desires. With her body transformed, she became the killer once more.

Seeing his task accomplished, Raethanon made a discreet exit. Utilizing his shaman powers, he teleported away moments before Bettina's clawed hand could slice him in half.

Infuriated by her captivity, and mentally conditioned to destroy, Bettina ran down the hallway and rushed out of the sheriff's office, eager to kill anyone who got in her path. A young couple was coming out of the barbershop across the street, and they were her first target. Leaping into action, she was across the street in seconds and pounced on top of the man first, sinking her fingers into his chest as her teeth clamped around his throat. One bite and two strokes of the hands turned him into a bloody lump on the barber's porch.

Before the lady could screech in revulsion, Bettina swiped her clawed hand across the lady's neck, severing her vocal cords. The hacking and slashing that ensued was superfluous, merely sport of the animal Bettina had become.

A blast sounded, and bestial Bettina felt a load of buckshot sting her side. Looking up, she saw the barber leveling a single barreled shotgun at her, and another blast erupted. A spray of lead smacked her face, but did no lasting damage. Taunted by the attack, Bettina lunged forward and knocked the shotgun from the barber's grasp, then tackled him to the ground. She raised her right hand, ready to plunge it into the man's chest, only to find it pinned in mid-air.

"That's enough out of you," a voice said.

The invisible force yanked Bettina off the man, and dragged her out into the street. Struggle as she might, the mystic bonds prevented her from breaking free. Her animal mind continued to stare at the barber, eager to spill his blood.

A crowd gathered quickly to witness the man who had restrained the beast.

"That's enough gawking," Sheriff Doliber said, putting a foot on Bettina's chest.  "I've got a killer to arrest."

# Episode 10:
# Shaman Hunt

Doliber tossed Bettina Carter back into the anti-magic cell, and once again her body returned to normal. The pale, bony creature vanished, replaced by the beautiful young lady who had grown up as a stableman's daughter in Selwood.

Her bare flesh wasn't hard on the eyes, and Doliber found his libido stimulated. He had to turn away before his mind was distracted with impure thoughts. Locking the door quickly, he kept his eyes on his hands at much as possible, and left the naked woman as soon as she was safely put away.

His inability to curb his hormonal reaction to the sight of her bare body frustrated him, and he swore he'd revisit some meditative suppression techniques whenever he had the chance. Warlocks were taught to transcend desires of the flesh. That wasn't to say they weren't allowed the pleasure of physical intimacy, but casual affairs were frowned upon, and sexual fantasies were equally shunned.

As he walked away from the cell and neared the office, Doliber saw the outside door fly open, and Joella came running toward him. She didn't stop until she had her arms wrapped around his shoulders in a reassuring hug.

"You're alive!" she said, squeezing him.

"For the moment," Doliber said, cringing at her grip.

Joella backed off, and Doliber raised his shirt, checking the bandage on the right side of his stomach. It was still clean and tightly wrapped.

"Sorry," Joella said, regaining a professional detachment.

"It's all right," Doliber said, looking pleased. "Where's Grimes?"

"At the courthouse," Joella said. "We have four men on trial for waylaying you and trying to rape me. He'll be along as soon as he can."

"Of course. I hope my reemergence hasn't disrupted the prosecution," Doliber mentioned, feeling in the mood for a hanging. Though, those men were liable to get jail time, at most. Their attempted crimes had posed more of a nuisance than anything else, so they couldn't be punished too severely.

"There's so much I have to tell you," Joella said, eager to share the latest developments with him.

"It's all right, I know everything," Doliber replied, having been remotely observing events as they unfolded.

Joella smiled again as she came to a realization. "I knew it. You were the one who told me Ron was in trouble yesterday."

"It was risky, but it had to be done," Doliber replied, thinking Joella was showing far too much emotion over their reunion. It was one thing to be happy about a colleague returning from the dead, but she was practically fawning over him. Maybe it was just his imagination. His emotional control wasn't what it should be since the shooting.

"Risky? I assume you had a good reason for making everyone think you were dead," Joella said, her pleasant demeanor remaining in tact.

"A very good one, and I'll tell you all about it later. Right now, we have to catch Raethanon."

It had been a tricky gamble, playing dead, but it had paid off. From the moment he'd felt that bullet in his back, Doliber knew he needed to hide, and wait for the culprit in this affair to show himself. His opponent had clearly sought to remove his greatest threat from the scene, so Doliber had obliged him, allowing him to tip his hand. As expected, Raethanon had let his guard down after thinking the mystically endowed sheriff was out of the picture.

Now the villain had given Doliber all he needed to find him. A teleport out of jail gave him a trail to follow, or so it seemed. The warlock sheriff wasn't going to take anything for granted until this vile shaman was behind bars or under boot hill.

Exposing Raethanon hadn't come without a cost. Several people had died because of Doliber's inaction, and one of those victims was slouched over his own desk. The limp form of young Gary Britton was a nagging reminder of the villain's ruthlessness, and the ultimate cost paid when good men did nothing.

Doliber swore he would not let Gary's death be in vain. None of those who had died during his absence would. They had all paid for Raethanon's hanging with their own blood.

"Someone will have to guard Bettina," Doliber mentioned, getting back to business. "Someone who won't let their guard down this time."

"You think Raethanon will come back?" Joella asked.

"He has to. Whatever his ultimate plan is, he needs Bettina out on the loose to complete it. If we don't catch him quickly, you can bet he'll return for her. Either way, I'm taking no more chances."

Clambering boots drew Doliber's attention, and he turned to see Ron Grimes escorting a pair of handcuffed men into the office. The scruffy cowpunchers slouched along as the dwarf kept a gun pointed at their backs.

"Ron, hold down the fort," Doliber said, grabbing Joella by the wrist.

"Good to have you back, boss," Ron replied as he nudged his prisoners back toward the cells.

Doliber nodded, and then vanished with Joella in a flash of light. The scene around them changed quickly, and the gloomy Sheriff's Office was replaced with the sands of the high desert. Barren hills greeted them, as a westerly wind threw dust in their faces.

"This was unexpected," Joella said, looking around.

"As I said, we have to act fast," Doliber replied, looking at the ground. "There." He pointed to footprints in the sand, leading down the slope.

They charged down the grade, Doliber taking the lead. As they followed the trail, he expanded his mental perceptions, sensing the residual traces of magic energy in the area, seeking out any ruse or trap. He found nothing out of the ordinary, telling him that Raethanon was near. The shaman had teleported to this location from the Sheriff's Office, and hadn't cast another spell since.

The trail of footprints started to curve, as the sandy soil turned rocky. Coming around a bend, they saw in the distance the entrance to a cave, a black patch amongst the yellow and brown landscape. That had to be his hideout. It was a satisfying discovery, but it meant increased danger. The shaman would likely know they were coming, and he still possessed a pistol capable of blowing right through magical defenses. Doliber wasn't in the mood for taking another slug, so he had to think fast, and come up with a viable plan of attack.

"Think you can teleport yourself to the top of that ridge?" Doliber asked Joella, pointing to a hill just to the right of the cave.

"I've still got a few miles in me," she replied. "What's the plan?"

"I need you to set up a covering position. Be ready to pick Raethanon off once I drive him out of there. You'll only get one shot at him, so make it count."

"I'd be more comfortable with a rifle," Joella said, drawing her revolver. "Either that, or have a closer shot."

"I wouldn't advise getting closer than fifty feet," Doliber suggested. "If you can make the trip back to Selwood to pick up your rifle, go ahead."

Joella closed her eyes and promptly shook her head. "No, it's too far. I'll just have to make do."

"All right," Doliber said, slapping her shoulder. "When we're through here, we'll have to work on expanding your mystical reserves."

Joella smiled, then disappeared. Doliber peered across the desert, and tried to spot her on the hill, but it was over a mile away and the sun was in his eyes. He would have to take it on faith that she was waiting there, prepared to take the shot.

It was time to chase the villain from his lair.

Closing his eyes and rolling them up into his skull, Doliber reached his mind out to the world around him, sensing the Earth's crust beneath him, seeing the many layers of dirt and rock, leading down toward the burning mantle. Straining his consciousness to perceive the minor faults and cracks within the outermost layer of the planet, he reached out with a stream of energy to manipulate them. With practiced care, he vibrated the proper lines, and caused the ground beneath him to shake wildly. The tremors became a full-blown quake for miles around, sending rocks and dust sliding down the hillsides. The loose particles buried his feet before he realized it.

The summoned quake had the intended result. The caverns up ahead were growing unstable as the shaking continued. Hunks of stone started to fall from the mouth of the cave, and sand threatened to bury it completely.

Doliber felt the sand burying his legs, and he knew it wouldn't be long before the growing landslide dragged him down, but he couldn't stop yet. Raethanon hadn't come out yet, though he had to be inside. Was he willing to risk being trapped in that cave, rather than expose himself?

It all depended on how powerful the shaman truly was. Did his teleportation energy extend to the point where a trip out of the cave wouldn't be a problem after being buried alive? Mystics who weren't affiliated with the Guild generally lacked such powers, so Doliber didn't consider it a probability, though he couldn't deny the possibility.

As he felt himself being forced down the hill with a wave of sand, Doliber relinquished his mystic hold on the fault lines and allowed the Earth to calm. He had failed to flush Raethanon with his first stunt, but there were others to be tried. Only, the risk of injury would increase with his next attempt.

After climbing out of the sand, Doliber reached his mind out again, this time sending his consciousness wandering. He left his body huddled behind a pile of rocks as his astral form surveyed the landscape leading up to the cave. As he neared the dark entrance, he sensed Joella's presence right where she was supposed to be. It was reassuring as he ventured into the darkness of the cavern.

There were no signs of life at first. The earthquake had hidden many of the subtle signs of activity, spreading dirt and hunks of rock to cover any tracks. Though, as he went deeper into the space, he started to see bits of trash, an empty bottle, the bones of small animals, and finally a small fire pit. A large stack of wood filled up a wide crevasse, alluding to the presence of a highly talented teleporter. There wasn't much in the way of native firewood nearby, so that pile had to be brought in from miles away, and your average magician wouldn't have the strength to move such volume.

The coals in the fire pit were cold, but a faint flickering could be seen deeper inside the cave. Doliber sent his astral form further, and as he came around a corner he spotted his quarry. Standing in the dim glow of several torches was Raethanon, and he was not alone. Standing not five feet in front of him was another transformed creature. The pale skin and bony protrusions were identical to the alterations that had overtaken Betina, only this specimen was clearly male.

What was Raethanon really doing? Trying to breed a new race of enchanted beings? For what purpose?

Doliber wanted to peer into the shaman's mind and get the answers he sought, though his power was weakening. The distance shouldn't have been an issue for him, so there had to be some magic at work within the cave, sapping his strength. He was finding it harder to remain in this place, and having pinpointed Raethanon's position there was no need to linger. In the blink of an eye, he returned to his own body. The sudden shift in scenery was disorienting, but he was used to it.

Knowing Raethanon's position, Doliber tried his next best trick, attempting to teleport the shaman out of his lair and into Joella's waiting sights. Though, the same interference that had blocked his telepathic probes made it impossible for him to lock onto the shaman's form. There was no way he could drag the madman out of the cave, not without dispelling the magical interference field first. That was currently beyond his skill-set.

Another option came to mind, but it would only work if Doliber was right about the field's properties. Peering into his memories of the cave, he locked onto a piece of firewood and tried to move it. The maneuver was difficult, and it took ten times the effort it should have, but he managed to teleport the chunk of tinder. The strain of hauling the object distorted his accuracy, however, and he cursed as the wood fell on his foot.

A couple more teleports allowed him to compensate for the

interference field, and after placing one hunk of wood right in front of the cave, he knew he was ready.

Doliber grabbed the pasty creature standing with Raethanon. The careful direction of the spell caused the creature to materialize directly in front of the cave, and before it could react to its rapid relocation, the warlock sheriff wrapped it up in a mystic bond, leaving it trapped in plain sight.

That was the bait to lure Raethanon out into the open. The creature was clearly important to him, and with any luck its abduction would cause him to slip up.

It was a strain to hold the creature. Its strength was incredible, and the mystical interference was mounting. Raethanon had fashioned the field to protect himself first and foremost, but objects around him were still difficult to handle with mysticism.

Doliber felt the strain in so many ways. A burning sensation started behind his eyes, as he continued to exert all his strength to hold the thrashing creature in place. He didn't notice the blood soaking through his shirt until it got thick enough to run. All this time, since waking from his surgery, he'd been keeping himself together with carefully maintained magic fields. Distracted and strained as he was now, his control had faltered, allowing the wounds to reopen. It was all too much, but he wouldn't give up. Releasing the creature now would put Joella at its mercy, and he wouldn't let another innocent person die this day!

Struggling as he was, Doliber didn't notice the man standing behind him until he felt a gun barrel poking him in the shoulder.

"Good morning, Señor," Raethanon said. "You are looking well for a dead man."

Doliber's concentration snapped, and the creature escaped his bonds.

"Raul!" Raethanon shouted, then whistled.

The creature was over a mile away, yet it clearly heard its master. Bounding forward over the desert sands, it was in front of Doliber within a minute, hissing and growling like a mad dog. Yet, at Raethanon's command, the creature stayed its hand.

"Sheriff, I would like to introduce my son, Raul Jose Theonés," Raethanon said with great pride.

"Your son?" Doliber asked, looking at the grimacing beast.

"As an educated wizard, you should understand," Raethanon said. "The conservation of life is a fickle thing, difficult to overcome, yet hardly impossible."

Doliber finally understood. As horrible as the truth was, he could not deny it. Raethanon was being literal when he called this creature his *son*. It was, in fact, the same son that had been killed by the residents of Selwood over thirty years ago.

Resurrection was a forbidden magic, for various reasons. The first being that it was impossible to raise someone from the dead outright. The laws of life and death were still largely unexplored, but what little was understood precluded man from snatching a soul from the afterlife without great expense. Freelance witches and sorcerers occasionally practiced the dark art of raising the dead, but it never came without consequences. For one life to be restored, many more had to be sacrificed, and there were often unforeseen side-effects—such as the risen being transformed into a half-dead monster!

So, Raethanon's son lived again in this horrid shell. It also meant Bettina Carter was equally cursed. Though, that led to more questions.

"Why did you bring Bettina Carter back from the dead?" Doliber asked.

"She is not dead, Señor," Raethanon said, surprised by Doliber's assumption. "She is a living conduit, the only chance my son has at reclaiming the life that was stolen from him!"

"Spiritual transduction?" Doliber said, shocked by the revelation. It was another rare, forbidden magic, scarcely more than legend among the Guild. The concept of siphoning off mystic energy from one cursed individual to another; it was unthinkable!

"Now you understand why I need señorita Carter to be freed. So long as she remains isolated in your cell, she cannot take my son's curse upon herself, and he cannot be a man!"

"Why her?" Doliber asked.

"Transduction is such a delicate process, and so is retribution! To satisfy my needs, I chose the blood that stole my son's life in the first place. It was Virgil Carter who took my son away from me, so it is the blood of his child who must bring Raul back to me!"

It was all clear now, and Doliber knew his time was short. Raethanon was bragging, and that could only mean one thing—he had no intention of leaving Doliber alive. Everything was revealed, so there was nothing left but a bullet.

"Under other circumstances, it would have been a pleasure to know you," Raethanon said, cocking the pistol. "Sadly, it is time we say adios."

Doliber closed his eyes, fearing he had played his hand, but hopeful that he still had an ace in the hole.

A shot sounded, and Doliber felt the pistol barrel scrape against his shoulder blade as it was pushed away. Raethanon threw out a few Spanish curses as he stepped back, and Doliber turned to look at the shooter. As he'd hoped, Joella was there standing a few feet away, her pistol in hand. The shaman was clutching his bleeding wrist, and glaring at her angrily, clearly caught off guard by her presence.

"Raul!" Raethanon snapped, and the creature charged at Joella. She vanished in a silent burst of light, and reappeared fifty yards away in the opposite direction. She shot again, putting a bullet into Raethanon's left knee. Raul ran at her again, and just as he came within striking distance she teleported out of his path, reappearing beside Doliber.

Joella and the sheriff both aimed their pistols at the shaman's head.

"I'll give you one chance to surrender," Doliber said, his aim shaking a little as the pain in his side grew intense.

"It is you who will surrender; surrender Bettina Carter to me!" Raethanon growled.

"Not a chance," Doliber replied, ready to fire.

Raethanon vanished. No light show, no sound, no transition. One second, he was there, the next he wasn't. Raul had disappeared, as well. The shaman's teleport was seamless, the sort of skill you would only expect from a Guild Master.

Doliber was ready to perform another resonance trace, to detect where Raethanon had gone, but his strength had left him. Struggle as he might to activate the magic scan, his mind was blank, and his body was fading fast. He felt his legs give out from under him and before he knew it he was on the ground. The sand was so hot against his cheek, and the pain in his gut was like a million pins tearing out his guts.

How foolish he'd been to hesitate. One bullet could have ended Raethanon's reign of terror, yet he'd tried to be chivalrous. It wasn't his worst mistake, but it looked to be his last.

Joella fell to her knees and rolled Doliber onto his back. She tried to get a response out of him, begged him to get up, but he didn't answer. He knew what she was saying, but it didn't seem important to talk. So much effort for a few worthless words. What could he say to relieve her distress? There was nothing he could do at this point. Better to shut up and accept the inevitable at last.

"You're not going to die on me again!" Joella shouted, tears forming in her eyes. He knew she truly meant it, and he continued to ponder the depth of her feelings. How much did she really care, and what could that mean for him? What a shame he wouldn't live to find out.

Wrapping her arms around him, Joella utilized the last remaining remnants of her teleportation power, and they vanished in a flash.

* * *

The jail cells were pretty empty now, as only two men remained in custody following the preliminary hearing. After hearing the testimony of both Ron Grimes and Joella Grimes-Talus, Judge Raymond had decided to empanel a jury for the perceived ringleaders of the conspiracy, Byron Burch and his scrawny associate Tom Sheldon. The youthful Spencer Davis was released as an unwitting accomplice, as was the lop-eared Mr. Lockward after Joella testified on his behalf.

Albert Silcox had been there, but only to disavow any connection to the men and their crimes. He wanted to be on the record in opposition to their actions, and made a public apology to Joella for the behavior of his former subordinates. The open display of remorse would assuage the guilt he must have felt, whether he were directly involved or not. After satisfying his conscience, he'd limped out of the courtroom to a wild commotion out in the street.

That commotion had turned out to be the return of Sheriff Dolbier, and shortly thereafter the judge adjourned court for the day, allowing Ron to escort the defendants back to their cells.

Doliber and Joella were gone before Jesse James showed up to help Ron with the prisoners. There was no telling where they'd gone or when they'd be back, though Ron had his suspicions, and knowing the sheriff's ultimate plan he was content to sit behind the desk and wait for news.

Leaning back in his chair, Ron realized this was the first time he'd felt normal since Doliber's shooting. It had been awkward to hold the sheriff's secret, and play the boss for a while. It was a familiar experience, being underestimated and derided by all comers who felt a dwarf was incapable of handling the job of a man. He'd shown them all during his short stint, though it felt good to be second fiddle again. Let Doliber handle all the hassles that came with the job of sheriff. Ron was still getting used to being a deputy.

Seeing Ron had everything well in hand, Jesse went upstairs to grab a bite to eat.

Just as things seemed to be settling down, the door to the Sheriff's Office flew open, and in stormed the leather-clad Marshal wearing a scowl on his face. Something had upset him more than usual, and it didn't take a genius to figure out what.

"Hey, Rodgers, where have you been hiding?" Ron asked as the man marched over to the desk.

"I hear Doliber's still alive," Rodgers said sharply. "I'd like to see him, now."

"He's not here," Ron said. "But I'm sure you'll be seeing him real soon."

"Look at you," Rodgers said. "Sitting there, all full of yourself. You think this is all some sort of game. You and that sheriff of yours have a lot to answer for!"

"How do you figure?" Ron asked.

"People are dead, people Doliber could have saved if he hadn't been playing dead these past two days. He'll answer for his negligence."

Ron was sick of his tone and wasn't going to take it sitting down. Scooting his legs under him and standing up on the chair, he got right back in the Marshal's face. "Now you look here, Neddy, the way I see it a lot more people would be dead right now if Doliber hadn't gone under for a spell. This was all to find out who was responsible for these crimes, and I dare say he's done it. I expect we'll see him hauling the guilty party in any time now, all thanks to this 'game' as you call it. Now get out of my face!"

Pushed over the edge by his inner rage, the Marshal lashed out. He shoved Ron with both hands, knocking the dwarf off balance. Ron flipped over the back of the chair and came down on his back, barely avoiding a nasty head injury.

The click of a cocking hammer snapped the Marshal out of his rage. He turned toward the staircase to see Jesse James aiming at him.

"That's enough out of you," Jesse said, maintaining his aim.

The Marshal put his hands up and backed away from the desk. He kept his eyes locked on the deputized outlaw with an itchy trigger finger, knowing full well how dangerous the man could be. He didn't speak again until he was able to grab the door knob and was assured a swift exit.

"You've got a bad habit of coming back, Jesse," Rodgers said as he opened the door. "One of these days, you're gonna stay dead, and by God I swear you'll burn in Hell!"

"Then I'll see you there," Jesse said, pleased with himself.

The Marshal slammed the door as he left, giving no effort to hide his disgust.

"You okay?" Jesse asked Ron.

"Better than him," Ron replied as he retrieved his hat. The wide-brimmed thing had rolled halfway across the room after his tumble.

"I oughta shoot that Yankee bastard," Jesse said, losing his lighthearted expression.

"Hey, watch it," Ron chided. "I'm a Yankee, and we ain't all bastards."

"Fair enough," Jesse said, not sounding terribly convinced. Heading back up the stairs, he added, "I need to take a bath."

Ron just smiled and sat back down behind the desk, satisfied.

Things were quiet again—for a few minutes at least. The still atmosphere couldn't last, not with two angry prisoners in residence, along with Bettina Carter crying on and off in the anti-magic cell. As the surly cowboys started heckling and bickering amongst themselves, Bettina's sniveling grew louder, and Ron felt the start of a headache.

After a few minutes, Bettina's crying turned to screams, and the men grew silent. As Bettina's screams persisted, Ron felt he should see what was troubling her. When he came within her field of vision, she shrieked, and pointed at him frantically.

"Hey, calm down, lady," Ron said. "What's the matter?"

"Stay away!" Bettina shouted. "Please, stay away!"

"Fine," Ron said, turning to leave.

"No, not you. Him!" Bettina shrieked, wedging herself against the back of the cell and pointing her arm at thin air.

She had to be nuts, Ron thought. There was nobody there, though she kept on panicking as if there were. Could an expert illusionist be masking his presence? No, impossible! The anti-magic properties of the cell precluded that, and the door was locked tight, so how could anyone get in there?

"Help me!" Bettina begged, her eyes growing wide. She began gasping, and sliding forward, as if someone were dragging her by the waist. The blanket was bunching toward her middle, further alluding to that likelihood. Impossible may have been too strong a word, Ron realized, as he saw the woman slammed up against the cell door, even as the lock clicked open.

"Save me!" Bettina pleaded as the door swung open.

Ron wasn't going to stand idle while a woman under his protection was abducted! Yet how could he fight this invisible enemy? Dare he shoot at thin air? There was no telling if there were truly a cloaked individual there, or there was an external magic affecting her. Either way, he had to stop it!

As Bettina was dragged out of the cell, the door slammed shut behind her. Ron felt himself pushed aside as the woman fell to her knees and began transforming before his eyes.

Time was short, but Ron saw an opening. Whatever magic had taken her from the cell seemed to be gone, and he understood what had to be done.

Moving quickly, Ron used his key to unlock the cell door, hoping to get Bettina back inside before her transformation was completed. That was the plan, anyway, but the moment the cell door came open, Ron realized what a fool he had been. In an instant, the scene changed around him. Bettina wasn't outside the cell at all, but sitting on the bench in front of him, still safe inside the anti-magic prison.

It had all been an illusion, a trick played inside the dwarf's mind to make him open the cell!

Then, he was there; the wrinkled old man with tan skin and white hair. Though, he didn't look too healthy. He was bleeding from his knee and wrist, yet somehow he was still able to walk.

"Gracias, enano," Raethanon said.

Ron suddenly felt something hit him, a magic force that pinned him against the wall, and kept him stuck there. It wasn't enough to really hurt, but he wasn't able to break loose. He could do nothing but hang there, watching as Raethanon entered the cell and hauled Bettina out once more. This time, it was real. Bettina was turning into the monster.

As Bettina continued to transform, three loud shots sounded from down the hallway. Raethanon froze for a moment, then his head slowly turned around, glancing toward the office. There, standing in the archway, was Jesse James, a smoldering six-gun in his hand.

Before he could do more than see the shooter, Raethanon collapsed on the floor.

The force holding Ron against the wall vanished, and being unprepared for the sudden weight of his own body, he stumbled to the ground beside Raethanon. The old shaman was breathing his last, yet still a twisted smile was on his lips.

"I give the parting gift of death to all the peoples of Selwood," he whispered to Ron. Once the words passed his lips, his facial muscles relaxed and death claimed him.

Ron got to his feet in time to see Jesse throwing Bettina back into the cell. He'd managed to reach her before the transformation was complete, though her claws had already formed, and she'd lashed out, leaving bloody gashes down both of his arms. He held up his hands and screamed after shutting the cell.

"You gonna be okay?" Ron asked, seeing the long red grooves hiding under the tattered shirt and jacket.

"I hope," Jesse said, cringing in agony.

"Might want to see Doc Wilson," Ron suggested, wondering

what good medical treatment would be for a shadowganger. He was already dead, wasn't he? His body was more magical than physical, though it looked real enough. A few stitches might be in order, just the same.

Ron was ready to accompany Jesse to the doctor's, but somebody had to guard the prisoners. After the latest fracas they were unusually submissive, but still...

"I can find my way," Jesse assured him, trying to open the front door, but the blood on his hands made it too slippery.

"Yeah, sure," Ron said, hurrying over to open the door. Before he could, Jesse collapsed.

"Aw, shit," Jesse said, laughing before he slipped unconscious. The wounds on his arms stopped bleeding once his eyes closed, and as Ron stood and watched, the wounds started to heal themselves. In moments, the deep cuts were gone, yet Jesse remained unresponsive. He was deep asleep, and there was no telling how long he would remain in that state.

At least he wasn't going to die, again.

Ron was ready to head back to the desk when another disturbance began. Glancing out a window, he saw people running down the street, looking panicked. Concerned that another transformed creature might be rampaging through the streets, Ron dared to leave the office manned by sleeping Jesse, and investigated the latest happenings.

Rushing outside, he grabbed the first person he could. "Hey, there, what's going on?" he asked the young man.

"The dead!" the man said, pulling away from Ron. "The dead are rising!"

## Episode 11:
## Raethanon's Revenge

Ron saw them coming up the street, the pair of corpses wearing their best suits. They were all prepped for a funeral to be the guests of honor, but they weren't supposed to be walking there. These men had died days ago, and had had their bodies pumped full of chemicals by the undertaker. There was no way they could be alive in any normal sense of the word.

Raethanon's final curse was unleashed upon Selwood. These dead men had risen, but for what purpose? And why was everyone running? They were just dead bodies reanimated by magic energy. Ron scoffed at how gullible some people were as he drew his pistol, ready to end the corpses' reign of terror.

Gripping the Remington with both hands, Ron sighted his targets and fired. One shot each, straight to the forehead. He expected that damaging the brain in such a manner would stop an animated corpse, though once he put a ball into each cadaver's head, the dead men kept on walking. This wasn't his lucky day.

They were thirty feet away, as Ron considered his options. These dead bodies wouldn't be easy to stop, and if their enchantment went so far as to make them impervious to a head shot, there was no telling what evil machinations were afoot. The true power of these cadavers was wholly unknown.

While most people were steering clear or running away from the walking dead, one chubby elf had different ideas. Ron quickly recognized him as the drunk he and Joella had arrested earlier in the week for disorderly conduct. The idiot had tried to shoot up the town, and might have hurt someone if they hadn't nabbed him. The judge had let him off with a cheap fine, and now he was here, ready to make a nuisance of himself again.

"I ain't a scared o' you!" the elf shouted at the dead men. He was clearly inebriated, and was reaching for his gun as he approached the corpses.

The dead men said nothing, but one promptly reached for the drunken elf. The elf shot the body in the chest, after which the unaffected corpse swung its cold hand at the shooter's face.

"Damn!" the drunken elf shouted, placing a hand on his cheek as the dead men continued past. He fired twice more, managing to place bullets in the back of the scratcher, though just barely. If it hadn't been point blank, there was no telling where his lead would've landed.

The dead men ignored him, and kept moving toward Ron.

The drunken elf kept rubbing at his cheek, feeling the sting of the scratch turn cold. The skin was going numb, and he started massaging his face to get the circulation back. It wasn't helping, and soon his hand felt strange. The fingers were no longer rubbing against soft flesh, but something hard and gritty. His head began to throb, and he started screaming from the growing pain. It didn't last long, and before he could realize what was happening his mind shut off, sending his dead body collapsing to the ground.

Ron saw the drunk on the ground, and his eyes widened. The elf's body was turning to stone!

These walking cadavers weren't just any animated corpses. They were avatars of Raethanon's revenge. Enchanted with magic beyond the purview of civilized wizards, only a pagan shaman would dare to use such a sinister spell!

Now Ron understood why everyone was running away. It seemed a prudent course of action to follow their lead, but it was nothing he could bring himself to do. This was his stand to make.

Three more shots from Ron's revolver sank into the approaching cadavers. The lead balls penetrated their flesh, and two exited through the other side, but the wounds did not slow these animated dead. However, they weren't invincible, and each bullet proved they could be stopped. Only, how much lead would it take to finally put them in the ground?

Ron shot his last load, and walked backwards as he started to dismantle part of his revolver. A spare cylinder sat in a pouch at his belt, and it was an easy enough task to swap out the part, thereby gaining six additional shots in a hurry. After locking the loaded cylinder into his pistol, he took aim and emptied all six shots into the dead men, but they kept coming!

Having used his spare cylinder, Ron was left to reload, which was a lengthy process for his cap and ball revolver. Each chamber had to be filled with powder, and a wad and ball rammed into place. Once all six were charged, he placed percussion caps on the nipple of each cylinder. Even with haste, it took him over a minute to complete the loading, and by then the dead were upon him!

One of the dead men swiped its hand toward the dwarf, and it was all Ron could do to slide away from the lethal fingernails. With his heart racing, he unloaded his entire revolver into the chest of the nearest dead, punching six more holes through it, but that was still not enough. Daylight was shining through the man's insides, but the flesh wasn't damaged enough to impede its movements.

The cadavers were looming in front of him, and there was no way to escape. Ron tripped over his heels and fell on his ass as he reached for his powder. There was no way to reload quickly enough for another strike, and he stared up as four arms swung back, preparing for a flurry of swipes.

Ron closed his eyes and awaited the final blows. He expected to feel their vicious claw marks on him at any moment, but instead he heard a thunderous blast, and felt the cold spray of blood and tissue splattering on his forehead. Opening his eyes, he saw one of the undead staggering around with only tatters of skin sticking out from where its face had been. A clear hole went through from the back of the head, and bits of brain dripped out of the wound.

A second shot sounded, and Ron scooted backwards as a large slug blew off the other corpse's right arm at the shoulder.

As devastating as the blows were against the cadavers, it still wasn't enough to stop them. The one-armed undead man turned around toward the origin of the shot, while his faceless companion staggered around aimlessly.

Ron got to his feet and looked past the dead men to see Marshal Rodgers standing ten feet away, sliding fresh shells into a massive double-barreled shotgun. It was the first time Ron had ever felt glad to see the Marshal, and he hoped he wouldn't regret it.

Two more blasts, and the one-armed undead man became armless. The crippled cadaver stopped advancing, uncertain of what to do about its impairment.

"Good of you to finally show up," Ron said as he hurried over to the Marshal.

"I never left," Rodgers said, pocketing a couple of empty shotgun hulls and reloading his double-barrel. "So, where's Doliber now?"

"Damned if I know," Ron said, eyeing the Marshal's shotgun. "That's a beauty. Ten gauge?"

Rodgers shook his head. "It's an eight. She kicks like a mule, but packs a real punch." He snapped the action shut and set the thing to his shoulder, aiming at the dazed dead. Two more slugs kept them stunned and confused.

"You might want to get yourself some stronger artillery," Rodgers mentioned as he ejected two more hulls. "I'm about out of slugs, and they're still standing."

Heeding the advice, Ron darted over to the Sheriff's Office, and made a beeline for the gun rack behind the desk. He surveyed the assorted weapons, and grabbed a twelve gauge coach gun sitting beside a pair of '73 Winchesters. The extra punch of a shotgun slug would be more effective than a rifle at short range, though there weren't many shells to be had. Checking the stash of ammunition beneath the rack, Ron found only half a dozen slugs. There was plenty of buckshot, so that would have to do if the first six shots weren't enough to stop the cadavers.

Stuffing the shells into his vest pockets and hoisting the shortened shotgun out of the rack, Ron was ready to face his enemies anew. Walking for the door, he saw Jesse James lying there, slumbering through it all. At least the wounds on his arms were gone, so he ought to be back in fighting shape whenever he awoke.

Stepping out of the Sheriff's Office, Ron saw the cadavers were on the move again. The pair was working en tandem now, the faceless one keeping a hand on his armless companion as they lurched toward the Marshal. Though ungainly in their strides, their legs were surprisingly fast, but Rodgers wasn't about to run for cover. He was still trying to knock them down, using shells loaded with bird shot. At close range, the eight gauge was still having a significant impact on the dead flesh, but not enough.

Ron had to get close. The smooth bore of a shotgun was not conducive to accuracy, and he didn't have enough slugs to spare, nor did he want to accidentally put one in the Marshal. Running up to the dead men, Ron stuck the shotgun right at the armless one's hips and pulled both triggers. The recoil pushed the dwarf onto his butt, but is also managed to shatter enough bone to plant the cadaver face first into the street. There wasn't much more the one-legged corpse could do, and is flopped around on its belly, vainly seeking to continue.

Without its armless companion to lead the way, the faceless one wandered around aimlessly, swiping its arms in the air, seeking prey it couldn't see.

Ron got back on his feet, and only then noticed the burning pain in his hands and forearms. For a moment he thought the recoil had shocked him worse than expected, but then he spotted the shattered end of the shotgun. The dual load had been too much for the Damascus steel, and the metal had been blown apart. The resulting shrapnel had scraped Ron's left hand and the trigger guard had broken two fingers on his right.

"I'm out of shells!" Marshal Rodgers shouted as the faceless cadaver bumped into the front steps of the Lucca Saloon. The thing climbed the steps and felt around for the door, eager to get inside.

Ron dropped the smoldering remains of the shotgun and hurried over to the saloon, uncertain of what he would do, but knowing he couldn't sit idle while innocent lives were at risk.

There weren't many people in the saloon as Ron burst in. The faceless cadaver was bumping into tables, as the working girls screamed and Solen fired a tiny handgun at the unwelcome guest. The shots were enough to draw the undead man's attention, and

Solen soon found himself in its path. The bar counter kept it from getting to the elf, as he wedged himself against the bottle rack.

Glancing over at Ron, Solen said, "Don't just stand there bleeding. Get this thing out of my establishment!"

Ron felt like leaving the arrogant elf to his own demise, though even he didn't deserve to die at the hands of this monster. If there was something Ron could do, he would do it, but with one hand bloody and another one broken, his options were nil. He could stand and watch, but do little else.

This faceless cadaver had to be put down once and for all, and it would just take a little more lead to do the trick. An idea came to mind, and Ron hurried out into the street, feeling it was time the citizens of Selwood did their civic duty.

Ron stood in the middle of the street and shouted at the top of his lungs. "Come on, people. Get your guns! These enchanted cadavers ain't gonna kill themselves!"

Nobody heeded his first call, so he continued. "You want Raethanon to win? Go ahead and hide. Me and the Marshal, we already took down one of these cadavers, but we're done played out. It's your turn to finish the last of 'em. I know there are enough guns around this town. Get armed and get on down to the Lucca Saloon here and shoot the bastard!"

He kept shouting for people to help, and after a minute the street filled up. Dozens of armed men, and a few armed women, ventured out of their homes and businesses, willing to take up the charge and do what was needed to safeguard their town. The armed citizens assembled before Ron, and he led the way up the saloon's steps, directing them to prevent chaos.

Stepping into the saloon, Ron looked at Solen and smiled. "Better duck," he said, stepping off to the side.

Solen spotted the angry citizens pouring into his establishment, and as the first ten men raised their guns, the elf dropped behind the counter.

The first volley of bullets hit their target, for the most part. A few stray shots shattered bottles of whiskey and blew hunks of wood out of the counter, but most sank into the dead man's flesh. The blasts drew the faceless creature's attention, and it turned around toward its new attackers, bloody arms outstretched as it approached.

Another dozen citizens entered the saloon and fired their weapons, as the first dozen fired again. The hail of bullets tore hunks out of the mangled cadaver's body, and after several more volleys the dead man's belly split off his torso, thumping to the floor. The legs took a few more steps, but then stopped, lurking five feet away from the angry horde of citizenry. After another dozen bullets shattered bones, the legs finally collapsed beside their other half.

Shots outside drew Ron's attention to the window, and he looked out to see another group of angry citizens putting an end to the crippled cadaver. The one-legged, no-armed thing kept flopping around as they pumped round after round into the gory mess, until it finally was too disintegrated to twitch.

Ron sighed with relief, seeing the end of the enchanted dead. The cries and cheers of the citizens were a faint echo in his head as a wave of giddiness swept over him, and he felt the need to sit down. His hands were throbbing pretty badly, and the blood loss from a deep wrist cut was sending him into shock. Adrenaline alone could no longer sustain him, and it was time he rested. Reaching a chair, he tried to sit down, only to slip off the seat and fall into the adjacent table.

"Somebody, get a doctor!" a concerned citizen shouted, hurrying over to help Ron up off the floor. Two of the working girls came and helped, though the dwarf was hardly heavy enough to warrant the extra hands. They just wanted to help. Once they had him situated, one of the girls tore a length of lace off her dress and tied up the bleeding wrist.

Ron's head was spinning, and he looked up to see the gathering crowd. These strangers of the town he was deputized to protect were showing genuine concern for his well-being, and for the first time in ages he felt appreciated.

The crowd parted, and Solen came over holding a bottle and a glass. "Hey, you gonna give me a whiskey, or what?" Ron asked, giddy from the blood loss.

"I believe this is more in order," Solen said, pouring a small amount of yellow liquid into the glass. He held it up to Ron's lips and poured it into the dwarf's mouth.

The liquid tickled the back of Ron's throat and he coughed as he swallowed. Though, once the substance was down, he felt his head clearing and a renewed surge of strength coursed through his veins. He perked up and shook off the delirium. His hands were completely numb, and the rest of him was feeling better.

"What is that stuff?" Ron asked, eyeing the unlabeled bottle.

"Sprite water," Solen replied, corking it. "And not the cheap knock-off stuff they slip into some sarsaparillas."

Ron had never bought into the boastful claims of the health water salesmen before, but after sipping Solen's sprite water he was having a quick change of opinion. That stuff had a real healing kick to it. He felt like he could take on another cadaver invasion, if only his hands weren't maimed.

"You'll still need time to heal," Solen said, seeing Ron moving his damaged hands. "It's not a miracle cure."

"Don't suppose any of you know a good Medlock," Ron said, finding himself wistful over the days when such minor injuries could be cured with the wave of a warlock's hand. The bloody Civil War had had its upsides, as few as they were. Medical care was the only thing he really missed about those days, and he felt like cursing the Guild for their current refusal to allow their members to practice healing abroad. How many lives could be saved, and how much suffering ended if they utilized their gifts for the benefit of others?

Without magic help, Ron's hands would heal on their own, and he expected the townspeople would see to his needs in the meantime. A deputy's hazard pay ought to kick in for his most recent services, so he didn't expect to be strapped for cash while he was laid up. The worst part would be sitting around, doing nothing. Idle behavior didn't suit him.

"Grimes, get out here," Marshal Rodgers shouted from the street.

The tone of his voice was angry and commanding, and Ron's short affinity for his presence was gone. It would be business as usual again, and the pseudo-feud between the U.S. Marshal and Sheriff Doliber's deputies would be back in full swing. Ron expected his current handicap would mitigate their dispute for the moment, as he made his way through the milling crowd.

As soon as he got down the saloon steps, he spotted Rodgers in the middle of the road.  "What do you..." he started, before following the Marshal's gaze and seeing the reason for the summons.  His heart almost froze as he saw what the problem was.

It was Fletcher Atwood.

The young man who had been shot in the back was standing there, not thirty feet away, only he wasn't really there.  Not the living, breathing man, that is.  Death had surely claimed him after all, for now there stood another animated cadaver, with pale skin and blank expression, ready to enact Raethanon's final will.

There were plenty of armed citizens on the street, and the rest were pouring out of the saloon.  It wouldn't be hard to take down this final threat, and put an end to Raethanon's wickedness.  Everyone was just waiting for the word.

"Stop!" a cry sounded from down the street.  Ron spotted Mayor Atwood rushing forward.  The older man placed himself between his undead son and the armed crowd.

"Out of the way, Charles," Rodgers cautioned.  "We've got to take him down."

"No, not like this," Atwood said.  "This is my son! He... he's still alive!"

Arguments to the contrary floated about the crowd, and Ron just shook his head.

"He's dead, Charles," Rodgers reiterated.  "The only thing keeping his body going is a trick of magic."

"Perhaps," Atwood conceded, shooting his hand up.  "But perhaps not!  My son was on his death bed, true, but he was not dead when this mystic plague came upon him a short time ago.  We could save him.  Somebody could save him!"

"Ain't nobody gonna save him!" Ron challenged.  "We've gotta end this now!"

A few dozen citizens backed up the statement, as they aimed their guns at the mayor's son.

Atwood refused to give an inch.  "You can't do this.  I am the mayor of this town, and I'm telling you people to put down your guns!  Do it!  Nobody's going to shoot my so—ahhhh!"  He shouted as stinging pain scraped across his back.

Atwood stumbled to the ground and turned to see his undead

son walking past. The scraping pain continued on his neck and upper back, and reaching to rub the wound he felt the gritty texture of stone forming on his skin. His final protest had cost him dearly, and in seconds his body transformed into solid rock, sending his soul flying.

With the mayor out of the way, the enraged townspeople fired on undead Fletcher. The hail of bullets pelted him, blowing off chunks of cloth and flesh with each impact. A hundred or more rounds went through his body before enough tissue was damaged to stop his movement. A bloody pile of hamburger was all that remained of the mayor's son, a sad but necessary end to Raethanon's revenge.

The scene was too much for Ron. He'd seen enough death and gore to last two lifetimes, so he chose to take his leave. "Somebody find Doc Wilson and tell him to meet me at the Sheriff's Office," he said, passing through the crowd.

It was a short walk down the road to the Sheriff's Office, and Ron managed to open the door with his bloody left hand. There weren't any broken bones in that one, and he could take the pain of pressing the cuts against the knob as he turned it. That sprite water was good stuff, but the numbness wasn't complete, and he still needed to get bandaged up.

Shutting the door behind him, he glanced over and saw Jesse slumbering still. He decided to head back to the cells and check on the prisoners, Bettina in particular. Through all the chaos, nobody had been guarding her, and he had a bad feeling about it. The disturbance would have been the perfect opportunity for another escape attempt.

Stepping up to the archway beside the desk, Ron locked his eyes on a conspicuous figure at the end of the cell block. The tall, broad-shouldered fellow had his back turned to Ron, and he was cradling something in his arms. Whoever he was, he wasn't supposed to be there.

Ron drew his empty revolver with his bloody hand and challenged the figure. "Turn around nice and slow." He hoped his opponent wasn't the challenging type, for his bluff wouldn't stand up to scrutiny.

The large man did as he was asked, turning around to face

the dwarf. Once he was in plain sight, Ron saw what he was holding; it was the body of Raethanon. As the large man stepped closer, his features became more apparent, and a similarity to the dead shaman was quickly apparent.

"I have come for my father," the large man said, staring down at the dwarf. He didn't seem angry or hostile, merely mournful.

"I can't let you take him," Ron said, his hand shivering in pain as he continued to grip the worthless pistol.

"I was not asking," Raul said plainly. With a minor blip of light, the large man vanished with the body in hand.

Ron was left shaking his head again, feeling he had ultimately failed. The mad shaman had been stopped, and there was hope that his curse was over, yet his son now lived—a son who had been dead for decades. What that meant for Selwood, Nevada, and the entire American West was anyone's guess.

Ron tucked his revolver back in its holster and turned around as the door to the office flew open, and a young rancher rushed in. "Deputy Grimes," the young man called, spotting the dwarf. "It's the doc. Come quick!"

Following the young man across town to Doctor Wilson's practice, Ron dreaded what he knew he'd find. There was no escaping the obvious. Wilson had been caring for Fletcher Atwood, and must have been there at the time of his death.

The large house with decorative trim stood as a familiar sight, one Ron had wished to avoid for the near future. Stepping into the lobby, he saw the claw marks on the edge of the door leading into the operating room, a door that had been locked from the inside. The undead Fletcher must not have known how to operate the lock, and the unthinking cadaver had torn its way through. What awaited in the room beyond was depressing beyond measure.

"Doc Wilson's dead, turned to stone!" an observant cowpuncher said needlessly, as Ron saw for himself.

Ron's mood dropped down another notch toward despair, seeing the doctor had been the first victim of Fletcher's animated cadaver. Wilson had been the most competent doctor in town, and he would be sorely missed.

"Whatcha think we should do?" the young man who'd fetched Ron asked.

"Ask the Marshal," Ron said, unwilling to make more decisions. "And go get somebody who can patch these up!" he shouted, sticking his damaged hands up in the air.

The young rancher rushed out to find another doctor, as Ron slumped down on the waiting room couch, sinking further into a pit of depression.

So many people had died, and Ron could do nothing about it. Worse still was the absence of Sheriff Doliber and Joella. They'd rushed off on their quest to find Raethanon, and it seemed they might have found him. The bullets in the shaman's wrist and knee may have come from them, but that he had escaped to Selwood was a bad sign. Odds were, Doliber and Joella had gone down fighting. They'd weakened the shaman for the final conflict, but ultimately had died with him.

Ron expected he'd be wearing the sheriff's badge again, and he didn't like the prospect. He wanted to close his eyes and forget about all of his troubles, but the sprite water prevented him from taking a nap. All he could do is worry and mourn the day's losses, and pray nothing worse was coming.

* * *

The stagecoach from Yucca junction rolled into Selwood near dusk. The twenty mile ride was quick and painless, though after spending hours on the train beforehand, it ended up being a final cramp in the pants. The passengers were generally glad to get out and stretch their legs, especially when the transport was packed.

Mactus Sellius jumped down from the coach, and his feet hit the ground heavily. The overweight elf was not very graceful, though his muscles remained fit enough to keep ordinary movement from becoming laborious. He had enough wealth from various cattle interests to keep him from getting his hands dirty most of the time, so he was becoming fat and lazy in middle age.

Selwood was the last place he wanted to be, but the message he'd received from Marshal Rodgers had piqued his interest. The Marshal claimed to have information of vital importance about his late cousin's wife, Joella. If he were right, that information would assure he left this dusty town with a fourth wife to add to his collection.

To Mactus, Joella was an ultimate prize, the eldest heir to the chieftain of Clan Talus. By rights, her offspring would someday take the mantle of leadership, symbolic or otherwise. By blood, they would be revered, and Mactus would share equally in the blessings. It was worth fighting for—even worth killing for—but a freshly healed scar in Mactus' right shoulder foretold of what would happen if he dared take that most violent of routes to win Joella's hand. The midge had already shot him once in the attempt, and Mactus wasn't going to give him a second chance.

If all went well, and Rodgers was being straightforward, then violence wouldn't be necessary at all. He'd be able to walk away with Joella fair and square.

Rodgers had an office of sorts tucked in behind a dentist parlor on the east side of town. Mactus didn't relish the walk, and ignored the various townspeople as they went about their business. Things seemed normal enough in town, and nobody would ever guess that a bloody shootout against enchanted cadavers had been conducted earlier in the day. Business waited for no one, and life was too short in the West for a man to remain idle for very long.

The Marshal's Station was a cubbyhole, barely suitable for civilized dealings. The narrow room was gloomy and pretty Spartan in decor, with only a desk and a gun rack. The Marshal was sitting in the corner, lighting a pipe, as Mactus made his presence known.

"Ah, Mactus, you got my message," Rodgers said after getting his pipe smoldering. "You're late."

"I had a meeting in Sacramento, but came as fast as I could," Mactus said, walking over. "Tell me, is it true?"

"That I can prove Joella's marriage to the dwarf is a sham? Yes," Rodgers said, looking reluctant.

"That's perfect!" Mactus said happily, tapping the Marshal on the shoulder. "You've always been a square dealer, my friend."

"Yes, but as I said, you're late," Rodgers said, setting the pipe between his teeth. "Joella's gone."

"Gone?" Mactus asked. "Gone where?"

"Nobody's entirely sure," Rodgers said. "She left with

Sheriff Doliber on a manhunt earlier today. Rumor has it she's dead."

Mactus felt his dreams slipping away as he saw the serious expression on the Marshal's face. This couldn't be true! The heir to the Chieftain, dead? No, that couldn't happen, not now when *he* was so close to winning her!

"Rumors are worthless," Mactus said, refusing to believe. "I want proof."

"We'll have it, soon enough. I've called in a tracker from the Marshal's Service, somebody who'll be able to trace Doliber's trail and lead us to them both. Though, I wouldn't hold out too much hope, considering what we already know."

"Tell me," Mactus urged, grabbing the only other chair he could see in the office.

The Marshal nodded his head. "Fair enough."

"And afterward," Mactus added, "you can tell me what evidence you have, in case she turns up alive."

## Episode 12:
## Heart and Soul

Joella woke up in a soft bed. Her head was pounding, and her eyes felt as dry as the desert. Her whole body ached, and she wondered where she was and how she had gotten here. Memory was failing her, as she sought to remember.

Doliber had been dying. That was the last thing she knew, but there had been more. How much more, she couldn't tell. Had she done something, tried to save him? It was all a blur, and her head was throbbing too much for her to come up with the answer.

A door creaked, and the glow of lamplight floated into the room. Joella slid up in bed and rubbed her eyes, hoping they would clear. As the holder of the lamp approached, she recognized the familiar face. "Doreen?"

"Hello, cousin," Doreen said, looking tired. The bags under her eyes and the ruffling of her dark hair showed that she'd been woken from sleep.

Craning her neck, Joella saw stars out the window behind the bed, and realized it had to be quite late. "How long have I been here?" she asked.

"Since the medics brought you in," Doreen said.

"How did they find me?" Joella asked, knowing how far this place was from the desert. The Sellius farm on the outskirts of Ravenna-West was several hundred miles to the west, and she'd had little contact with her people in months. There was no way they could have known she was in trouble, or where to find her.

"You don't remember? *You* found *them*," Doreen said,

taking a seat on a stool by the bed. "You teleported into the center of town around noon. They say it was one serious burst of light, though that's what happens when you overtax your latent abilities. It was some stunt you pulled."

Joella tried to remember the action, but it continued to elude her. It made sense, though. All mystical forces were controlled by thought. Magic energy was channeled and focused through different regions of the brain, and there was only so much energy a person could pump through that organ. Each person's spell casting capacity was different, and to overexert yourself would inevitably lead to harm. The first and most common sign of excess strain was memory loss.

If a few seconds were all she couldn't remember, Joella felt fortunate, though only time would tell how extensive the damage was.

"What about Doliber?" Joella asked.

"Your sheriff is going to be fine," Doreen answered. "His injuries were serious, but easily treated. It's good that you got him here when you did."

Joella was relieved to hear the news. A warm sense of elation flowed over her as she thought about the valiant lawman and his daring moves. She'd been having a hard time putting him out of her mind before this incident—now she was positively enthralled. It was impossible for her to deny what was happening, though part of her was reluctant to admit it.

Doreen shook her head. "Oh, Jo, what are you getting yourself into now?"

Joella looked back at Doreen, wondering what she was talking about, until she recalled her cousin's inherent empathic abilities. The woman was reading her emotions, and maybe even her thoughts! "No, it's not what you think."

"The devil it's not," Doreen rebutted. She quickly calmed down and returned to a consoling tone. "Listen, Jo, I know you, and I can sense what you're feeling for that human. You can't hide it. Not from me."

Joella said nothing, but wore the discomfort on her face. This was all new to her, the feelings for Doliber, and it had been so long since she'd felt anything for a man, let alone a full-blooded human. She wouldn't be rushed into admitting anything, not even to herself.

"It's nothing I'm prepared to talk about," Joella answered.

"Okay," Doreen conceded with a reassuring smile. "Whatever the case, your secret's safe with me. Just watch out for those marriage-sisters of mine. You know how Hittie can be, and Yuba is just plain naive."

"Where are they?" Joella said, worried all of a sudden. "And what about Mactus, for that matter?"

"Everyone in the house is asleep, and Mactus..." Doreen started to giggle. "Mactus is in Selwood, looking for you."

"Oh," Joella said, not amused. "I suppose a certain Marshal sent for him."

"He didn't say who sent it, but he did receive a telegram, and left in a hurry. How ironic, that you are here while he is there?"

As funny as it seemed, Joella didn't feel like laughing. Not after all that had happened—all that could still happen. If Marshal Rodgers was following through on his threat, she would be facing a difficult decision in the near future, and there was no telling which choice she'd make.

If Mactus learned the truth, that her marriage to Ron was an unconsummated sham, then he'd have a legal right to claim her as his wife. No matter that Mactus already had three, Elvish tradition permitted polygamy, and limited the whims of women. Under Clan Law, she would be mandated to marry him, or be shunned as an outcast, displaced from her family and any Law-abiding elves, forever.

It had been bad enough when she'd just abhorred the thought of wedding Mactus. Now, she was developing genuine affections for another man. Could she truly live with someone she despised, as she pined for another? It might be a moot point, as she wasn't sure if her feelings were serious or if Doliber would ever consent to a courtship. Yet, if she accepted her fate according to Clan Law, she'd never find out, and that would haunt her for the rest of her life.

The affairs of the heart were her only concern. Never mind the mad shaman she and Doliber had been fighting. That all seemed irrelevant now.

Doreen grabbed the lamp and stood up, yawning as she got to her feet. "Well, it's late. Try to get some sleep, and we'll talk more in the morning."

"Right," Joella said, feeling wide awake.

"And watch your thoughts tomorrow. There's no need to give them any more excuses to entrap you."

Doreen walked out of the room, taking the lamp with her, though the light of a crescent moon still glimmered faintly through the window. As late as it was, Joella had no desire to sleep. Her mind was too active as she stared up at the stars, questioning fate and dreaming of what the future might hold.

* * *

The morning was bright and sunny, but Joella didn't feel like sunshine. After spending six hours in deep contemplation, she wished for clouds. Reflecting upon her hopes and aspirations had done little more than bring out the negative probabilities, leaving her in a pessimistic state of mind. The weather ought to reflect her mood, she thought. Such pleasant summer weather was not suitable for her gloomy circumstances.

It would have been only a minor irritant, but Joella allowed her disdain of the sun to grow abnormally. She could use that to deflect prying thoughts, and confound passive readings. If the voyeuristic busybodies tried to extract some nuggets of truth from her mind, they'd have a hard time of it.

There was activity throughout the house. By dawn, all three wives were busy, tending to children and cooking breakfast. The house smelled of sizzling meat as Joella made her way toward the kitchen, where Hittie was laboring over a hot stove. The amount of food she was preparing looked massive, far in excess of what the dozen children and three mothers might consume, though then Joella recalled the many ranch hands that worked here. They had their own eating room, away from the family, as the dozen laborers were kept separate from their employers at the Sellius farm. Not all elves had such an elitist attitude about their hired help, but Mactus was a stickler for the old-world customs, where workers and landowners didn't mingle at mealtime.

Covering the massive skillet filled with link sausages, Hittie turned around and smiled at Joella. She wiped the sweat from her brow and offered Joella a cup of root tea, and she wouldn't take no for an answer. After serving the beverage, Hittie turned back to her cooking, unable to engage in idle banter at the moment, although she was eager to engage in lengthy conversation.

Joella took her tea and continued through the house. Stopping at the doorway to the music room, she saw Yuba, the pale-haired wife with wide thighs and narrow shoulders. The second of Mactus' wives, she could always be found entertaining the children. Playing piano, reading stories; she was the nurturing type, although not terribly bright. She was still very much a child at heart, something far alien to Joella's jaded mindset. The naïveté of a sheltered housewife had to be so peaceful, though it was a sort of peace Joella would never know, even if she found the perfect mate. The complexities of the world had already educated her far too much. In that respect, she was more like her cousin, Doreen.

Moving on to the family dining room, Joella found Doreen sitting with a couple of the older children, going over school work before breakfast. From the sound of it, they were running through long division, something Joella had hated growing up. She remembered how she'd wished to be human at that age, since most human girls she'd known weren't learning such intellectual material. They got to play a lot more, and learn the satisfying ways of keeping house, but the women of Clan Talus were more than maids and homemakers. It was their job to educate the children, teach them to survive and thrive in the world when they grew up. They taught the boys to make their mark in society, and they taught the girls to teach the next generation, and so the pattern perpetuated itself.

Schooling had never been Joella's strong suit, as she'd always had a Tomboy streak. She'd felt so fortunate these last months, serving as a sheriff's deputy. For the first time in her life, she really felt as if she were where she belonged, doing something that mattered. Though, she also now appreciated the education she'd received in her youth, for it had taught her to be independent, and stand up for herself among men. Without that training, she'd never have had any choice but to be another wife.

"Morning, Jo," Doreen said as Joella sat down.

Joella smiled in acknowledgement, and sipped her tea. It

was a tad bitter for her taste, but it was soothing on the nerves.

The children turned away from their schoolwork and locked their attention onto the guest. The two girls were both dark haired with dimpled chins, looking like thin versions of their father in feminine form. Oddly enough, Mactus may have made an attractive lady if his chromosomes had been a little different.

"Why don't you tell Cousin Joella what we have planned for the day?" Doreen suggested as the girls continued to stare.

"We're going to Grayson's, to learn about powders," the taller of the two girls said. She didn't sound too enthusiastic, but her sibling smiled at the prospect.

"Yeah, we'll learn how the chemicals are imbued with magic to make them work. Maybe we'll even get a sample," the younger girl said.

"Don't get too excited, Dorcas," Doreen cautioned. "Alchemists don't make a living by giving their product away. But, if you're very attentive, I'm sure we can afford a cup of Sweet Blue."

Dorcas smiled and clasped her hands in glee.

"Ought to save your money, Dorc," her sister said. "Better to have a decent wedding dress picked out for Alec."

The smile dropped from Dorcas' face. "You're just jealous, Marla."

"Jealous that you're betrothed to that Alchemist's son? Hardly. I'll take my doctor any day."

"He's a dentist, Marla, not a doctor, and he's ten years older than you. At least my betrothed is the same age."

"That's enough," Doreen said sternly. "Is this how you behave in front of company?"

Both girls smiled at each other, and Doreen shook her head. It had all been a staged show for their guest.

Joella was only slightly amused by the little exchange, as she recalled the cynicism her cousins had often shared about their betrothals growing up. Most elf girls knew who they'd be marrying by the time they were five, and it often became a social game of whose future spouse would outdo the rest. Her own betrothed had turned out to be a half-breed outlaw, so her whole outlook on the arranged marriages was pretty soured.

"Mother says you're going to be our aunt soon," Marla said, shooting Joella a playful look.

"Which mother?" Joella asked.

"My mother," Marla scoffed. "Don't you know?"

Before Joella could be embarrassed by ignorance, Doreen interjected, "Marla is Hittie's oldest."

"Of course," Joella remarked, noticing the similarities in the eyes. They were both large and blue, with a little yellow flake near the left iris. How she had missed the unique variation was beyond her, but her mind had been distracted by the whole betrothal banter.

"So, is it true?" Dorcas asked, sounding enthusiastic again. "Are you going to marry dad?"

Joella looked down at her tea cup. "I don't think so."

"Cousin Joella is already married," Doreen added, trying to lessen Dorcas' disappointment.

"Yeah, to a filthy midge," Marla said, almost spitting the slur.

"Marla!" Doreen snapped.

"It's true, and everybody knows it was just to get out of marrying father!" Marla persisted.

Dorcas turned away from Joella and looked ready to cry, while Doreen dug her fingernails into Marla's arm.

"I will not have you talk to Cousin Joella that way," Doreen said.

Marla yanked her arm free and stood up. "She's not *my* cousin." With her head held high, she walked out in a snit.

Doreen sighed. "Twelve years old, and she acts like she's twenty."

"She acts like her father," Joella remarked, noticing the similarities. That pigheaded, elitist attitude was unmistakably a Sellius trait.

"Why do you hate dad?" Dorcas asked, sounding sad.

"I don't hate him," Joella said, trying to appease the girl. "I just don't want to marry him. We're very different people."

"So is mom, but she married him," Dorcas said, looking over at Doreen.

"Yes, I did," Doreen said, putting her arm around her

daughter. "But Cousin Joella is even more different than me. She needs to find her happiness elsewhere."

Dorcas leaned comfortably against her mother, and then gathered up the books on the table. She hurried off to store the texts before breakfast was served.

"She likes you," Doreen mentioned after Dorcas left.

"I didn't realize I'd made such an impression," Joella said, realizing how little time she'd spent with the Sellius children. She'd grown up with Doreen, but hardly seen her since. After getting married, they'd both gone their separate ways, despite their husbands being first cousins. While Doreen's spouse was a respected businessman, Joella's had been a half-human scoundrel, and nobody had mourned his death at the hands of a certain dwarven gunslinger.

"I think Dorcas just likes the idea of you. She's heard a lot of stories about the two of us growing up. The other wives are so different from either of us, so she wants another woman around she can relate to."

"What about your other kids? How are they coming along?" Joella asked.

"Jerome and Billy seem pretty bright, but they're too young to really tell. They'll likely end up like their father, which isn't such a bad thing. You really are too harsh on Mactus, you know."

Joella didn't respond to the accusation, and instead downed the rest of her tea. The whole conversation had left a bitter taste in her mouth, similar to the roots of the drink. She had her reasons for disliking Mactus, and they weren't what she led everyone to assume. All his wives thought she disapproved of Mactus as a man, but in all fairness she couldn't stand him because of her own domineering attitude. She and Mactus were very much alike in many ways, but she was loath to admit it, even to herself.

The quiet didn't last long, as Hittie arrived to set the table for breakfast. Doreen and Joella helped her with the place settings, and as they finished Yuba arrived with the pack of Sellius children, ten in all, who took their places as expected. The older children helped the younger ones to settle in, and once they were seated the food was served. The assortment of sausage, eggs, and freshly baked rolls made the rounds until everyone had their plates full.

Before anyone ate, a short prayer was said by Hittie, and she kept it quite short for the sake of the impatient kids.

Eating with the family didn't bother Joella, and it reminded her of the times she had visited her different cousins during her childhood. They'd all belonged to such large families, with multiple wives and multiple children like this, and by comparison her own home had been very small. Her father had chosen only a single wife, and that marriage had only given them two children in all their years together.

Looking around the table, Joella's thoughts drifted to the sister she hadn't seen in years. Sara was twelve years younger, so Joella felt more like an aunt than a sister to her, though she hadn't been home to see her in years. A lot of that had to do with her parents, and their very proper lifestyle. Since civilization had taken hold in the west, her folks had conveniently forgotten about the years of adversity they'd endured to establish their comfortable surroundings, and they now had no time for Joella's "foolishness," as they liked to call it. She wasn't prim and proper, though she didn't much approve of them, either, so the disrespect was mutual.

One of these days, she'd have to pay them a visit, but the longer it took the better.

After the pleasant meal, the children left to perform their chores or play games, while the wives stayed to clear the table of dishes. Joella insisted on carrying a few, even though a guest was normally absolved of such responsibility. She didn't feel right unless she was pulling her own weight, and it didn't take much effort to carry a few plates. Though Doreen objected, Hittie certainly appreciated the help.

After the dishes were washed, Doreen took Joella outside, where a carriage was rigged and waiting. It was about time they headed into town, to check on Sheriff Doliber. Dorcas and Marla accompanied them, for their important trip to the Alchemist's Parlor awaited.

The half hour ride into town was pleasant on a fine summer morning. The fields of grain were rich green and wildflowers were blooming by the edge of the road. The rhythmic clomping of the horses' hooves and the creaking and thumping of the carriage wheels blocked out most of the exterior sounds, but Joella could imagine the birds singing as they passed a few acres of pines. This was the land of her fondest memories, from a time before life got too complicated. What she wouldn't give to hike the wild hills and run through those hay fields again!

The fields and forests abruptly vanished, as the stone and wood buildings of Ravenna-West appeared out the carriage windows. The town was the pinnacle of elvish society in the American West, with all the amenities of its New England counterparts. Though hardly a built up malaise like Boston or New York, this small and orderly town had running water, working sewer and waste systems, and there were even a few enterprising businessmen talking about setting up a power plant to accommodate the new Edison bulbs! Electricity was the wave of the future, to rival the stalwart magics of past eras.

The hospital was the only brick building in town, sitting right beside the log walls of the Alchemist's parlor. It was a convenient stop for all four passengers of the Sellius' carriage, and as they got out Doreen ushered the children over to visit Mr. Grayson, so Joella could visit with her sheriff in private.

There was a nurse at the front desk as Joella entered, a young lady with round ears but a narrow face. There weren't any full-humans in Ravenna-West, so she knew the lady had to be at least part-elf. Pointed ears generally dominated, even in half-breeds, so it was doubtful the girl had more than a single elvish grandparent. While the mongrel's exterior was pretty enough, her attitude left much to be desired. She was strictly professional and never cracked a smile, even as she answered Joella's queries.

"Your sheriff's fine," the receptionist said. "Down the hall, on the left, third door."

Joella wasted no time going down the hall, and she felt the cold stare of the receptionist watching her every move. She couldn't get through the door fast enough for her liking.

The room where Doliber was sleeping was well lit by a mystic orb in the ceiling. It gave the feel of sunlight, even in the wholly enclosed space, and its cost was excessive. Many an amateur magician made his living recharging such devices, or creating them outright. No doubt, the expense would be tacked onto the bill, and the star pinned to the occupant's chest reassured the hospital staff that they'd get paid, one way or another.

The sheets were soft cotton, and so was the mattress from the feel of it. Joella pushed down on one corner and wondered how nice it would be to sleep on more than that corn husk-stuffed thing at the boarding house. A regular bed in a house of her own; the best of both lives she'd known. The comfort of her youth, coupled with the freedom of her present. That was something worth fighting for.

The stool beside the bed wasn't so comfortable, but she sat there and looked at the sheriff. He was lying on his back, situated with both arms across his chest, as if positioned for a funeral. The thought was a bad memory of what might have been, and she wanted to shake him awake to put an end to the mental imagery, but she refrained. He'd been through a great ordeal, and deserved his rest.

Joella sat there for another minute in silence before something happened.

"Are you going to stare at me all day?" Doliber asked abruptly. He turned to face her and gave a pleasant smile.

"Don't scare me like that," Joella said, slapping the edge of the bed.

Doliber let out a few chuckles, but remained fairly sedate. He was never one for large displays of emotions, though he obviously had them.

After the humorous moment passed, Joella asked, "How are you doing?"

"Very well, considering what happened," Doliber said. "I'm glad you were able to surpass your limitations."

"You're welcome," Joella said, knowing it was as close to a 'thank you' as she'd get. His genuine gratitude was worth far more than the phony platitudes of a superficial expression.

In the terse silence, Joella caught herself staring, and started to blush.

"What?" Doliber asked, further amused.

Fighting back the emotion, Joella coughed and recomposed herself. "No, nothing," she said, feeling ill prepared to reveal her innermost feelings at the moment. She was still coming to terms with them, herself, and felt it an inopportune time to blurt out a confession of love. The man was recovering from serious trauma, and had more important things on his mind.

"It's something," Doliber corrected, sliding up in bed. As the covers slid down to his waist, his healed abdomen was clearly exposed. The bullet hole was no more, but a smooth scar remained; a sign of highly-skilled elven medical mysticism. While Guild medlocks would remove all traces of an injury, elf medics often left such traces, as a reminder. Some of them claimed there was a medical rationale to leaving the skin ill-repaired, though the honest ones admitted it was pure tradition.

*It's always about tradition*, Joella realized. Everything her people did was bound by their past! Good or bad, it didn't matter—*as it was, so shall it be;* a familiar mantra from Sunday meeting.

"There is more to this than you're willing to admit, isn't there?" Doliber said calmly.

Joella looked at him sheepishly and replied, "Yes."

"Good," Doliber said. "Then you're ready."

"For what?" Joella asked.

"Tutoring," Doliber said.

Joella blinked, caught wholly off guard by the statement. "Tutoring?"

"Your teleportation powers have great potential, and there's no reason the range and scope of that ability can't be significantly expanded. Who knows? There may even be other latent powers you could uncover, as well."

"You're saying you want to tutor me?" Joella asked, feeling slighted.

"In part," Doliber said. "It would take a real commitment, but if you're willing I'll sponsor you."

"Wait—sponsor?" Joella asked, totally confused.

"To the Guild Academy," Doliber suggested. "You are under thirty, correct?"

"Twenty-eight. What does that have to do with anything?"

"Thirty is the cut-off for apprentice admissions," Doliber said.

Joella shook her head. "Just a minute. Who ever said anything about going to an Academy? And isn't the Guild an organization for *human* magicians?"

"There's an elvish chapter, such as it is," Doliber said. "But you'd receive much of your instruction from me, as part of my own training."

"Your training?"

"Yes," Doliber said, starting to laugh again.

"What?" Joella asked.

"You're repeating what I say," he replied.

Joella realized the humor in it, but didn't find it funny. Everything he said made her question his meaning, and every answer left her more confounded.

"I've had a lot of time to think in this bed, relatively speaking," Doliber said. "Our encounter with Raethanon proved something I've been reluctant to admit. I'm not good enough."

"That's ridiculous?   Good enough in what way?" Joella challenged.

"Magic proficiency.  You were there.  You saw it.  I failed. That shouldn't have happened, and it wouldn't happen to a true Master.  That's why I've decided to go back to the Academy, and take the Master's Examinations."

"Oh," Joella said, oblivious to what that entailed.

"As I said, you can come with me.   Part of the Master's Exams involves tutoring an apprentice; my *first* apprentice.  That could be you, if you're willing."

"Wait, how long are these examinations going to take?" Joella asked.

"Approximately a year," Doliber replied.   "Your own apprenticeship would last twice that, assuming you progress apace."

"What about Selwood?" Joella asked, standing up. "We have responsibilities..."

"I'll resign," Doliber said. "I'll have to if I wish to reach my full potential, but once I'm a full Master I'll be able to serve in a far greater capacity."

"Are you sure about that?" Joella asked.  "None of the other Guild Masters serve anything but the Guild.  You've said as much. They have rules against it."

"Things change," Doliber said with a knowing look in his

eye.

Joella stood there, staring at him for what seemed like hours, neither of them speaking a word. She'd come here, hoping to quell some of the confusion in her heart and soul, only to find herself further conflicted. How could he make such an abrupt decision, and abandon the people he was sworn to serve and protect? It didn't seem right to cut and run, even if he could come back stronger at a later date.

"This is wrong," Joella finally said, breaking from her quiet daze. "You can't just leave Selwood. What about Raethanon? He's still out there."

"No, he's not," Doliber assured her. "Haven't you read the paper?" He looked around his bed, searching for something. "I had it here an hour ago. Elvish neat-freaks."

"You're saying someone else stopped Raethanon?" Joella asked.

"Deputy Boron Grimes, assisted by Marshal Edward Lowell Rodgers. There was something about animated cadavers, too, though I have the feeling that was a case of journalistic sensationalism. The threat is over, and it was solved without me. Nye County will get on fine whether I'm there or not."

"No, I don't believe that," Joella said, raising her voice. "People need you. They depend on you!"

"The decision has been made," Doliber said, growing cold.

"Well, I won't be going with you," Joella pouted.

"Then you're fired," Doliber said.

"You can't fire me. You quit."

"I'm still sheriff at this moment, so I can," Doliber said. "So, there, you're no longer a deputy. Now there's no reason you have to remain in Selwood."

"Oh, there are plenty of reasons. For one, I'm married—sort of. And another thing, I can just get the new sheriff to reinstate me after you're gone."

"Don't do this," Doliber asked. "This isn't what I wanted."

"No, what you wanted was to drag me off to that Guild of yours, to become an elvish warlock."

"To become more than you are, so you can make a real difference," Doliber said passionately.

"We *are* making a difference, both of us, right there in Selwood," Joella reiterated. Calming down, she continued. "I see what this is all about. You lost. For the first time, your magic couldn't put you over the top, and you failed. Welcome to the real world, Doliber. That's what the rest of us have to deal with all the time, but we learn to overcome our limitations, not run away from them."

"I'm not running from anything," Doliber rebutted.

"That's exactly what you're doing," Joella said. "Going back to the Guild, it won't solve anything. There'll always be somebody stronger, somebody deadlier. No matter how prepared you think you are, you'll never be *good enough*."

Doliber lowered his eyes thoughtfully, and considered her words. It was a long while before he spoke again, and when he did his confidence was gone. "I don't know what you expect me to do."

"Please, stay," Joella pleaded.

"Why do you care so much?" Doliber asked.

The heat of the moment overwhelmed Joella, and instead of speaking she answered with action. Leaning in, she planted her lips against his, and refused to let go until he kissed her back. Once she felt the acceptance of his mouth, she pulled away and hurried out the door, leaving him to think about her response.

Closing the door, Joella sniffled and wiped tears as they began to form in her eyes. The intensity of the encounter had left her with a heavy heart, and she wondered if she'd made the right decision. Only time would tell.

## Episode 13:
# Winds of Change

Bettina Carter had her eyes shut tight as she stepped out of the cell. Her arms were shivering in anticipation, and her heart was beating out of her chest. The moment of truth was at hand, and she would now discover if the curse had truly been lifted, or she would remain a perpetual prisoner of the sheriff's jail.

Three steps and a deep breath later, Bettina opened her eyes to see the open hallway in front of her, and no transformation had occurred. She turned her arms over and stared at the regular pink skin. A teardrop splattered against her hand, as she wept with relief and sadness.

It felt good to be free, but part of her would never leave that cell. While she had sat there, a prisoner to evil magic, the life she'd had planned was taken from her. The love of her life was dead, and the peaceful little town she'd been so desperate to escape had been torn apart. How could she ever feel normal again?

"You're free to go, Miss Carter," Sheriff Doliber said, ushering her down the hall, toward the main office. They kept going, ignoring the cat calls and grumbles of the other prisoners until they were through the office and at the front door.

"It's already dark," Bettina said, seeing the faint glimmer of the flaming streetlights.

"Your brothers sent a carriage," Doliber said, helping her down the front steps toward the conspicuous vehicle.

It was little consolation that her family had bothered to send a transport. None of them had been bothered to see her during her great ordeal, and that apathy was the final straw. None of them gave a damn for her, and she wasn't going to sit through an awkward meal or pretend it was a glorious homecoming. She might stop by to see her mother in the morning, but for the night she had a different destination in mind. She would stay with Margaret Atwood, and help console her. They had both loved Fletcher, and it was dangerous to mourn alone.

Boarding the carriage, she ordered the driver to Atwood Manor, and waved farewell to the sheriff. She wouldn't miss him or any of his deputies. They were a most strange group, and their faces would only serve to remind her of her ordeal.

Some faces were best left forgotten.

Doliber shut the front door and walked to his desk, wondering if this truly were the end. He'd held this post for less than two years, and in that time he had done everything in his power to safeguard the people of this town, and thwarted many threats that any ordinary sheriff would have been incapable of tackling.

Magic was such an ever-present threat in the world, a holdover from ancient times that wasn't going away in the sight of science and technology. In fact, magic was becoming even more prevalent, and in the American climate of free-flowing information secrets once controlled by the Guild were now becoming common knowledge. Any amateur magician with the mental pathways to process the ethereal energy could be a serious force for good or evil, and somebody had to keep them all in check. Who better than a Guild-trained warlock?

Doliber had gone into this line of work thinking he was the answer. Now, he wasn't so sure.

Sitting down at the desk, Doliber grabbed a cigar from the box, but he didn't light it. The sweet taste of tobacco was growing sour, as he contemplated his own dependence on the substance. Smoking was another distraction that kept him from the greatness he desired. It made him weak.

Tossing the cigar back into the box, Doliber heard a scraping sound. Glancing toward the little alcove under the stairs, he saw a match spark to life, as a man lit a smoke. He stared at the glowing tip of the cigar as the smoker spoke.

"You figure she'll be okay?" Jesse James asked from his dark corner.

"I wouldn't venture a guess," Doliber said dejectedly. He slammed his fist on the desk and growled in frustration.

"It's not your fault," Jesse said. "You should let it go."

Doliber stood up and stormed toward the stairs. "When I seek your council, Shadow, you'll know it!" He clomped up the treads, feeling in need of a good night's sleep.

A door upstairs slammed, and Jesse shouted, "I'll just guard the prisoners, then?" When no answer came, he blew out a plume of smoke and smiled.

* * *

Marshal Rodgers was sitting at the counter of the Lucca Saloon, nursing a shot of Kentucky bourbon like it was the last of its kind. He didn't drink often, and when he did it became a savory ritual. Nobody paid him any mind, as the place was packed with the regular crowd. You'd never guess the town had lost some of its most prominent citizens only a day earlier, not from the raucous behavior of the hard drinking gamblers.

The shot was half gone when a conspicuous figure stormed into the saloon, weaving through the maze of tables to reach the solitary Marshal. The lawman didn't notice until it was too late. A fist impacted the back of his head, forcing him to spill the rest of his whiskey and almost choke on the drop that had been trickling down his throat.

"You son of a bitch!" Joella cursed as the Marshal turned around on his stool.

Rubbing the back of his head, the Marshal said, "I take it you've seen Mactus."

"Not yet," Joella said, slapping him across the face. "I talked to the High Minister in Ravenna-West this morning. He's already drawing up annulment papers for my marriage. You planned this all along, whether I cooperated or not!" She moved to slap him again, but the Marshal caught her wrist.

"All I did was send a telegraph, stating what I knew about your relationship with the dwarf. You sleep in separate rooms, you're never seen together except on the job, and there is little chance of you ever having spent the night together."

"All hearsay," Joella said, ripping her wrist from his grasp. "But it doesn't matter. The High Minister has made his judgment, and deemed it sufficient."

"Leaving you single again, unless your deceased husband's next of kin decides to claim you for his own."

"Mactus will never have me!" Joella challenged.

"That's your problem," the Marshal said, turning back to the bar. He waved toward the barkeeper to refill his shot glass.

Joella wanted to put a bullet in his back, and if she'd been more like her late husband Vincent, she would have. Too bad her moral compass was more finely tuned. The Marshal was a despicable human being, but he didn't warrant a death sentence.

All that Joella could do was leave, and consider her options in a more secluded location. Before she reached the door, the Marshal shouted over the din of the crowd.

"You know, it's not too late for you to sleep with that dwarf. That would shut down the annulment, for sure."

Joella cringed at the thought and kept on moving.

"Might want to do it someplace real public, too!" the Marshal shouted after she was outside.

Joella ran out into the darkened street and screamed. A few passers-by stared at her, but she didn't care, and the impassioned cry was short lived. She regained control of herself after a few moments and thought hard about where she would go from here. Her moment of truth was fast approaching, and her options were few. What she chose to do in the next hours would define the course of her life forever, and the wrong choice would assure that her life would be spent in misery.

Neither option seemed very pleasant. All she had left to answer was, *what could she live with?* Could she live to disown her family heritage—their rights and traditions—in the name of her own wants and desires? Could she stand to marry Mactus and be his fourth wife? Could she bring herself to consummate her marriage to a dwarf, even one as honorable and respectable as Ron Grimes? She would find the answer very soon.

The Bormans' boarding house was her destination. The place had been her home for these past few months, and she hoped it would provide her with at least one more night of rest before she dared to confront Mactus. Even with the anxiety racing through her veins, she could force herself to sleep. It was an uncanny talent she'd always had, and it came in handy whenever stress was on the rise. Fatigue only exacerbated emotions, and being well-rested could give her an edge. At least, she'd be thinking clearly when she made her ultimate decision.

Stepping into the entryway, Joella was ready to head upstairs, having no desire to eat dinner with the other boarders. However, the dining room was directly to the right of the entryway, and before she could escape she was spotted. One familiar yet unexpected voice turned her blood to ice in an instant.

"It's about time you showed up," Mactus called her.

Joella slowly turned to look upon the dining room, and there he was. The overweight elf with his dark sideburns and fine gray suit was sitting at the head of the table, taking a meal with the Bormans.

"Come, have a seat," Mactus said. It was more of an order than a request.

A few other boarders were at the dinner table, as usual, though many seats were empty this night. There was no way Joella could politely refuse, and under the circumstances it seemed imprudent to be rude. Fighting down a lump in her throat, she walked over and sat down at the far end of the table, keeping herself as distant from Mactus as possible.

Mrs. Borman got up and started to prepare a plate for Joella, as Mactus finished off his serving of mashed potatoes.

"What are you doing here," Joella asked, trying not to sound too offensive. It was difficult in her current state of mind.

Mactus looked amused by her question. "Do you need to ask?" he said after scraping his plate clean.

Joella didn't respond, unable to think of what to say. The lump in her throat was moving down to her stomach.

"Enough of this," Mactus said, sliding his plate away. "You've had your fun, playing this little game of yours, but it's over now. Time to grow up and settle down."

"With you?" Joella asked, shaking her head.

"Yes!" Mactus hit the table, incurring worried stares from the others at the table. He quickly curbed his frustration and set his palms against the table in a sign of passivity. "We are legally obliged to marry, and I will have you."

"Why?" Joella asked. "Why is it so important that you have me? I'll never love you, and you already have three wives who do."

"Love isn't everything," Mactus said. "As an elf, you should understand that. Our marriages are sometimes more about mutual respect and social standing than emotional entanglements."

"But I want more than that," Joella said. "I don't want to be some stepping stone for your ambition. I want to live my own life, with whomever I want."

"Well, I'm not stopping you," Mactus assured her. "I can't force you to obey Clan Law, but you know the consequences if you don't."

"I do," Joella admitted. Her voice felt hollow to her own ears as she realized what had to be done, and what she was about to lose forever. Connection to her family, to her people; she would be forever shunned, considered an outsider to any who continued to subscribe to the old ways.

As painful as it was, she knew she could live without that connection. She'd grown so distant from her own people in recent years, it didn't seem to matter that much. Yes, she would miss some things about it, and there would always be that longing to see a home that wasn't quite there anymore, but the alternative was to become a slave to that life. Better to be an outcast.

"You'd really turn your back on our people, just to spite me?" Mactus asked.

"Not to spite you, but to save myself from you," Joella corrected.

Mactus stood up and adjusted his collar. "So be it. If you want to renounce your heritage, that's your prerogative."

Joella felt a great weight lifting off her chest, realizing she'd made the right choice. Mactus would be out of her life forever.

"Of course," Mactus continued, "this means the Chieftain's line will continue through your sister now."

"So?" Joella asked, feeling the weight returning.

"So, I'll just have to marry her—when she's of age, of course. A little over three years to go, if I've not miscounted."

"You can't do that," Joella challenged.  "She's already betrothed to Harry Bergen's son."

"Oh, you haven't heard?" Mactus said. "The Bergens all died last winter; typhoid, no less.  That leaves Sara's hand up for grabs, and you know how tight your parents were with mine.  I have no doubt they'll welcome our marriage, if I only ask."

"You're mad," Joella said, utterly disgusted by the proposition.

Mactus walked over and stared down at her.  "Either way, I win.  My heirs will lead Clan Talus.  The only choice you have in the matter is whether they'll be your children, or your sister's."

It was a deplorable tactic, and it made Joella sick to think of her sister trapped by Mactus, but it didn't matter.  She'd come this far, and a stubborn selfishness did run in her family.  Even if it meant abandoning her little sister to this wicked man, she couldn't condemn herself.

Swallowing hard, Joella steeled her nerves and said, "I will never marry you."

Mactus flinched, as if she'd spit in his face.  Straightening up, he headed for the door, walking rigidly and quickly.  Reaching the door, he turned back and said, "You're a disgrace to the race!"

"I guess that makes two of us," Joella replied.

The door slammed shut, and all was silent at the table, as the handful of boarders recovered from the tense exchange.  The remaining food was getting cold, as nobody seemed eager to eat anymore.

Whatever little respect Joella might have had for Mactus was gone.  He'd played every card in his hand, and he'd only served to drive her away further.  After that deplorable stunt, threatening to marry Sara, Joella knew there was no way she could ever stand to be under the same roof with such a man.  She could only pray that he wasn't being sincere about her sister.  If not, she wasn't sure what she'd do to stop it.

"I'm so sorry about that, dear," elderly Mrs. Borman said as she began to clear the table.  "He seemed like such a charming fellow before you arrived."

"I'm sure," Joella said, knowing how polished Mactus could be when conducting business.

"For sure, we'd never have let him in here if we knew what he had in mind," she affirmed, her feeble husband nodding agreement.

"Thanks for the support," Joella said. "I guess I'll be staying for a while longer, if you'll still have me."

Mrs. Borman smiled reassuringly, and walked off with the dishes, letting Joella know where she'd be staying for the foreseeable future.

* * *

The evening was cool up on the Flat, even at the start of summer. The Silcox Ranch house was a glowing gem amidst the desolation, with magic orbs shining in every room. The rich green fields outside glistened in the moonlight as Ron Grimes trotted his horse toward the house, feeling awkward about the social call. The old man had asked to see him after the whole Raethanon fiasco had been settled, and by borrowing the translocator he was able to make the trip without delay.

Leaving his horse outside the corral in the back yard, Ron walked back to the front door and gave it a good knock with his left hand. A semi-competent parlor magician had managed to mend the cuts on that hand, but two fingers on his right remained broken. It seemed he would have to wait for them to heal the old fashioned way.

Ron didn't have to wait at the door, for a servant answered with expectant haste. The plucky Irish girl ushered him into the parlor, where Albert Silcox was sitting with a few business associates from Yucca Junction.

"Mr. Grimes, come in!" Silcox said, waving him over. The older man looked healthier than ever as he stood up to shake Ron's hand.

"Your ankle seems to be better," Ron remarked as he offered his left hand.

"And you seem to have a problem there," he said, grabbing Ron's right hand in a tight grip. There was a surge of pain at first that made Ron curse, but it quickly faded.

Pulling his hand away, Ron unwrapped the bandages and looked at the formerly broken fingers. Flexing them gently, he found they were perfect healed.

"I guess your magic's back," Ron remarked.

"As I said, knitting bones is simple," Silcox replied. "Please, have a seat."

Ron took the last empty chair in the room, a padded wingback sitting beside the stone fireplace. There were only coals on the cast iron grates; otherwise it would have been a bit hot for his liking.

"It's good of you to come so quickly," Silcox said. "I was surprised to get your telegram, saying you'd be arriving tonight. It was quite a distance to come on such short notice."

"I had some help with that," Ron said, feeling the translocator rubbing up against his thigh. He had it hanging beside his pistol, for it rode well there. The pretty crystalline rod would have been quite a showpiece, if he'd been the type to boast, but he was far too cautious and suspicious to reveal the device in mixed company.

"You see, boys, he's quite resourceful, this one," Silcox said to his assorted guests. Most of the men mumbled and nodded in agreement.

Ron didn't like being strung along or kept in the dark, so he cut right to the chase. "Exactly why did you bring me out here, Mr. Silcox? It wasn't just to heal my fingers, was it?"

"Oh, hardly. In fact, I invited you here to discuss your future," Silcox said. He made a hand gesture toward a nearby servant, and the girl hurried over to refresh his drink. "Care for some cognac?"

"No thanks, I'm on the job," Ron said, feeling the need to justify his refusal. He wasn't a brandy drinker, though knowing the powerful ranch magnate, it seemed imprudent to refuse based purely on personal preference alone.

"Very professional," Silcox replied, looking satisfied. "I appreciate sobriety, especially among public servants."

"Enough flattery, what do you want with me?" Ron asked.

"The no nonsense type; another fine trait for a lawman, don't you all think?" He glanced around at his guests and continued. "Mr. Grimes, I invited you here to meet some of your constituents. These friends of mine are some of Yucca Junction's most prominent citizens, and I figured I'd introduce you."

"A pleasure, really," Ron said, feeling awkward. "I'm afraid I'm not much for high society functions, though."

"Of course, you're the common man candidate, salt of the earth, one of the people," Silcox said, grinning and waving his fist.

"Candidate?" Ron asked, feeling confused. "What are you talking about?"

"You impressed me the other day, Mr. Grimes. The way you handled yourself with that unholy monster, the lengths you were willing to go in order to safeguard the people of this county; why, it's only logical that you continue as our sheriff."

"I'm flattered, but we've already got a great sheriff."

"I hear Doliber is planning to resign," Silcox mentioned, "and I'm not one to sit around and wait to see what shakes out. That's why I brought you here, to voice my public endorsement of your candidacy for the office of sheriff."

It wasn't a bad thing to have his ego stroked by this wealthy cattle baron, though Ron had to wonder if it was sincere. Was the man acting solely with the well being of the citizens in mind, or was there a less altruistic agenda afoot? When it came to elections, self interest always dominated the scene, whether it was a local selectman's seat or the White House.

Ron could only imagine what a wealthy rancher could do with a sheriff in his back pocket, though he refrained from making any allegations.

"Tell me, Mr. Grimes, will you step up if he steps down?" Silcox asked, putting him on the spot.

Ron didn't think long before he gave an answer. "If Doliber really does leave, then I'll consider it."

Silcox smiled and leaned back in his chair. "Not the most thrilling of declarations, but we'll take it." He raised his glass in a salute, and finished the last mouthful. Several of his colleagues did the same.

Ron didn't feel the urge to stick around for a stump speech, and politely excused himself. There were more pressing matters to handle in Selwood, and he felt the protection of the County Seat was more important than pandering to a few aristocrats. Before he could escape, Silcox got up from his chair and extended his hand again, ever the gracious host.

"You will be our sheriff someday, Mr. Grimes. Don't doubt it for a second."

"Maybe," Ron said, tipping his hat to the man, "but for now I'm content to be a deputy."

Without further comment, Ron headed for the door, wondering how he had impressed the man so much. Yes, his actions on the Flat had been competent, but without a little help from Joella they would have both been dead men.

What was it that allowed Albert Silcox to put such faith in the capabilities of a dwarf?

A northerly breeze was blowing in off the desert as Ron mounted his horse, ready for a quick trip back to Selwood. All it would take was the right thought and a twist of the translocator to take him all the way, though he felt like riding. The moon was bright in the sky, and the Flat was a pleasant sight when hidden by the gloom. He could imagine he was riding anywhere, even as he ventured back toward a little corner of the world that had become his home, and the people he called his friends.

# An Outlaw's Salvation:
**Jesse James Joins the Cast-**

One thing that really made *West of the Warlock* a success was the inclusion of real-world characters into the mix. In the middle of the story, we bumped into Wyatt Earp and Doc Holliday, who gave the story a more down-to-Earth feel. When writing a Western, it is important to incorporate little bits and pieces of authenticity, to make the story really come alive. That may seem like an oxymoron when you have elves and spell-casters thrown into the mix, but if anything the blend of fact with fiction is even more crucial.

Getting into the sequel, I knew I needed another kick like I had with the Earp Vendetta Ride. That's when Jesse James decided to make an entrance.

It was a wild idea to bring the famous outlaw into the magic-infested world of Selwood, Nevada, and to do it I knew I had to play around with reality even more than I had with the previous book. Jesse James was shot in April of 1882, and this story takes place in June. I could have copped out and made this alternate version of James have a different backstory, but I felt that that would diminish the impact of his appearance. Therefore, I had to conceive a way to quite literally bring him back from the dead.

The undead version of Jesse James, otherwise known as the "shadow-ganger" (a blending of "shadow," and "doppelganger"), allowed me to inject him into the story while maintaining the real-world lore of the famous outlaw. Additionally, we have the "moral imperative" implanted, where Jesse must atone for his sins, or suffer a living hell.  It makes him a reluctant hero, to say the least.

To be fair, I wasn't entirely sure of the extent Jesse James was going to play in the book.  My first inclination was to only include him in a single chapter, to supply a teleportation device for Doliber and Grimes to get back to Selwood.  However, as I began to explore this character, I found that he could be used to a far greater extent, and he was just too good to throw away.  So, I had Doliber drag him into the ranks, and the rest fell into place.

After reading The Curse of Selwood, you're no doubt wondering what else may lie in store for Jesse.  You can be assured that he'll be back in the third volume of this Fantasy Western series, and there may be even more in store for him after that. Time will tell.

**Cover to Cover:**
**Behind the Design Phase.**

Back when Hall Brothers Entertainment was preparing to release The Curse of Selwood, they commissioned Paul Milligan to design a cover, something that would equal or surpass what he had done for West of the Warlock. Before putting together a finished piece of artwork, he sketched out eight concept covers. Phillip and A.C. sent me the eight, and asked for my input, expressing their own feelings about which covers would work best.

For your viewing pleasure, the following two pages will display the eight sketches that were made, to give you an idea of what "might have been."

As you'll see, the second from the left on the top row was the template we settled on. All three of us agreed it was the logical choice. It was somewhat in homage to the first book in the series, and it helps to maintain the uniformity of the first "trilogy."

Of the other designs, the bottom left and bottom right corner designs were universally rejected. A.C. thought that the second from the right on the bottom could have potential if done right, and both Hall brothers expressed interest in the top second from the right, though it wasn't quite what we were looking for. That design had too much of a dark feeling to it, I believe.

Not much was said about the top left and right corners, either way.

I gave a lot of consideration to the bottom second from the left. The dark figure looming over the train jumped right out at me, and I might have selected it under different circumstances.

That covers just about everything regarding the covers. Enjoy this rare peek into the creation process!

# About The Author

Martin T. Ingham is the author of various Science Fiction & Fantasy works, including *West of the Warlock*, *The Guns of Mars*, and *The Rogue Investigations*. His work has appeared in numerous print anthologies and online venues. Influenced by the greats of speculative fiction (Heinlein, Asimov, Herbert, etc...), he utilizes wit and wisdom to create stories for today's readers with his own unique voice.

When he isn't writing, Martin likes to dabble in numismatics, horology, antique auto restoration, and he likes to play with guns. He currently resides in his hometown of Robbinston, Maine, with his wife, Jenna, and their four children, Sylvia, Wyatt, Kathryn, and Lois.

Learn more about Martin's works at his website:
http://www.martiningham.com

www.ingramcontent.com/pod-product-compliance
Lightning Source LLC
Chambersburg PA
CBHW031337170626
46807CB00002B/748